Magic in the Outback

Ally always thought her life might be a little backwards, but upside down? Dangling helplessly, still strapped in her seat, she thought there could never be anything worse than being in a plane crash. She was wrong.

Elyce M Peterson

ISBN: 1492204617
ISBN 13: 9781492204619

Library of Congress Control Number: 2013918894
CreateSpace Independent Publishing Platform
North Charleston, South Carolina

*To my family and friends for all their support.
And especially to my mom, who always believed in
me, even when I didn't believe in myself. And
finally to a Heavenly Father above for giving
me the gift of this book.*

Table of Contents
❋❋

CHAPTER ONE	-	A NEW DAY	1
CHAPTER TWO	-	TRAVEL TIME	13
CHAPTER THREE	-	FAVOR	23
CHAPTER FOUR	-	THE MEETING	33
CHAPTER FIVE	-	ULURU	43
CHAPTER SIX	-	INTUITION	59
CHAPTER SEVEN	-	ENDURANCE	65
CHAPTER EIGHT	-	COMFORT	73
CHAPTER NINE	-	DARCI'S RESOLVE	81
CHAPTER TEN	-	FRIEND	89
CHAPTER ELEVEN	-	REPENTANT	97
CHAPTER TWELVE	-	CHANGES	105
CHAPTER THIRTEEN	-	TEMPTING	111
CHAPTER FOURTEEN	-	MUTUAL CAUSE	121
CHAPTER FIFTEEN	-	MUD AND RIVER	129
CHAPTER SIXTEEN	-	FLATTERED	139
CHAPTER SEVENTEEN	-	SHELTERED	149
CHAPTER EIGHTEEN	-	THE DANCE	161
CHAPTER NINETEEN	-	DARCI'S RESTLESSNESS	171
CHAPTER TWENTY	-	FRENZY	177
CHAPTER TWENTY-ONE	-	DARCI'S DISTRACTION	183
CHAPTER TWENTY-TWO	-	REVEALED	191
CHAPTER TWENTY-THREE	-	CONFESSION	201

CHAPTER TWENTY-FOUR - SURVIVED   209

CHAPTER TWENTY-FIVE - A NEW BEGINING   215

EPILOGUE   221

1
A New Day
※◈※

The sun which blossoms into a new day,
A day of trial and chance,
To meet each day with a smile
And to begin the night with a sigh,
Knowing tomorrow the sun will rise again.

My personal motto, like a valiant warrior's call to arms. I've repeated these words so often to myself that they're forever etched into my brain. Solid like a dedicatory prayer carved in granite. These words usually gave me some kind of comfort, some solace in this crazy world, but not today. Today they seemed to drift into other thoughts that my mind didn't want to let go of.

A loud angry blast from a horn woke me from my mindless daze. I quickly jerked the car back to the center of my lane.

"Hey, watch it lady, what do you think you're doing?" the guy in the car next to me yelled as he passed by.

I glanced over just in time to see him flash the typical highway salute. This jolt finally made everything start to connect to my brain again. I was instantly aware of the music in the background, then the mindless chatter of the advertisements.

The steady stream of cars slowly crawled in the same direction, most of them wanting the same thing—to get home. As I slowly moved along I just kept thinking. I wanted to roll my window down and ask the person in the next car, "Hey, have you ever had one of those days when you wonder to yourself, 'What's happened to my life, all my goals, my dreams? When did I stop living and just start existing?' Well I've had one of those years."

I casually glanced over to the car next to me. A nicely dressed woman was talking to herself, and as she moved I noticed a small flash of blue in her right ear.

"Oh, a Bluetooth," I thought.

She caught my eye and I grinned at her awkwardly. I could see a confused and annoyed look come across her face as though I was intruding on her conversation. She quickly turned and sped up so we weren't directly next to each other.

I adjusted myself, fighting off the stupor that comes with such a long drive. I turned up the radio and tried to get into the music, but there was no getting around my thoughts.

The day started like any other. I woke up startled, grabbed my alarm clock, and checked the time. Normally I gave myself an extra twenty minutes, but when I finally focused on the numbers on the clock, I shot out of bed as if the shock from the lack of time was pure electricity. I rushed to the bathroom, washed my face, brushed my teeth, and started to fix my hair.

I didn't always feel so lucky to have my hair. Growing up I found that my dark, thick, wiry hair was more of a curse placed on me to give me torture. But now it was nice to be able to just wet, scrunch, and go, allowing my curls, even though a bit wet to hang loosely around my much too round face, to dry on their own.

As I looked in the mirror, continuing my morning ritual, I examined my eyes. I always felt that if I had one positive feature, it was my eyes. Sky-blue outlined with black lashes—I didn't even have to wear mascara. But this morning it was like my eyes were trying to tell me something, something that I couldn't understand. I stared deeply into the mirror, trying to make sense of it. Then, giving up, I pulled my cheeks down with the tips of my fingers and then pushed them back up.

"Yep, I'm still me." I said to myself looking back. "No time!" I yelped suddenly as I looked at my watch.

I threw on the closest clean thing I had in my closet. My standard black pants and my "crap-I'm -late," shirt. It's the perfect blend of unnatural fibers that allows the person who hates to iron or who seemed to be always running late to get dressed and out the door with ease.

I work for an insurance company at a small desk in the corner. So I never really feel like I have to primp. Not that I would anyway.

After working a few hours I ate lunch with my friends. Well, not so much my friends as co-workers, in our break room.

Okay, I eat alone at a corner table, watching everyone, listening to their laughter, wanting to get in on the joke, but staying right where I always sit—alone. Listening and observing. That's what I call it. It's really being too withdrawn to get involved.

In the afternoon I had a great conversation with my boss.

Mr. Bryant is the type that has a soft teddy bear—like feel about him, even though he's big like a mountain. He genuinely likes people and tries his best to give everyone a chance. But you don't want to get on his bad side.

When I heard his door open I didn't notice him walking toward me; I usually tried to just keep my head in my work. But that wasn't going too well lately. His deep, low voice startled me as I heard my name.

"Ally, can you please come into my office?"

Those words always make a person shudder, even if it's good news.

I put my pen down and nervously walked over to his office just a few yards away. I could feel what seemed like a million eyes on me, everyone watching as if I was going to see the executioner. I walked in and turned just in time to see him close the door behind me.

My day ended with what had to be one of the most remarkable events of all: I actually spoke to the hottie in the office.

I was standing in the elevator when a hand reached in just in time to reopen the closing doors. It was Andrew. All of the women's and some of the men's mouths would start to salivate whenever he was in the room, mine included. He was just too good for words. Everyone made bets that he had to have been a model of some sort, sometime in his life.

He quickly stepped in, and I subconsciously moved to the corner of the small space as if by doing so I could disappear or make more room between us. He leaned casually on the bar at the back, turned, and smiled.

"Hi."

His lips curved up on the ends and his perfect white teeth almost glistened. I never thought anyone could be so charming with just one syllable. I looked into his chocolate eyes that were such a beautiful contrast to his soft blond hair. And the only thing that came out was a soft muffled, "Aaw."

My one chance and my self-defeating behavior got the best of me. I quickly looked down, feeling the burn of the embarrassment on my face. The door opened and I darted out as quickly as I could, not wanting to look back. My day was finally over.

My thoughts of the day were swiftly passing by when I suddenly realized that I was pulling up to the front of my house. A typical red-brick suburban rental, which seemed to be put together with scotch tape and glue, where I live together with my two younger sisters and mom as roommates.

Gina, the middle, with her sun-streaked hair, emerald eyes, and great figure, always seemed so confident and outgoing and ready to take on the world. And even with a little of a diva undertone, she has always been more career driven then myself.

Megan, the no-nonsense, down-to-earth, sassy, blue-eyed redhead, always seemed to have the ability to take the simplest things and create something great and wonderful. It sometimes made me a little jealous, her being the youngest.

Since my sisters were just finishing college and my mom's health wasn't great, and with the rollercoaster the economy was on, it just made sense for us to stick together.

As I pulled up I noticed a familiar white minivan parked along the curb, a bumper sticker that read "My child's an honor student" proudly placed on the back window. There was only one person who might be visiting: Darci.

Darci had to be my very best friend in the world despite the fact that she was my first and favorite cousin and we were five years apart. Growing up she was the big sister I didn't have. She always watched out for me and took me under her wing when I needed a little guidance, making sure she was there when I needed her.

She wasn't much taller than me, but she had such an outgoing, vibrant personality that she more than shadowed me. Her hair was always fixed perfectly with the blond highlights twisted in and out of her soft curls, her lips always brightly colored and ready to give a smile at any given moment. Her eyes, a mixture of green and brown with just a touch of gold flecks, seemed tired from years of dealing with the mistake she calls her ex-husband.

I loved when Darci could come over or when we would talk on the phone for hours. Time always passed so quickly when we were together. Although lately we hadn't had the same kind of connection, and today I really needed a listening ear.

I sat in the car for just a few minutes gathering my thoughts.

"What was I going to say? What would they say?"

I pulled the key out of the ignition, grabbed my purse, and reached over to the passenger seat and grabbed a box filled with all the trinkets and personal items that

I had collected while I worked at my job for the last three years. I got out and closed the car door with my hip and anxiously walked up the drive to the door.

The front door shut behind me and before I could put the box down in the entryway, a chorus of three sweet voices squealed happily.

"*Ally!*"

Darci's three vivacious children came bounding up with so much excitement that they almost knocked me over.

There was Ryan, the studious nine-year-old. Dark straight hair like his dad's with little wire glasses that always seemed to slide down the bridge of his button nose, he was average height for his age, but you could already see that he was going to have the build of an athlete, even though his thoughts were never on sports.

Next was seven-year-old Miles. He had an abundant amount of energy. It was always hard for him to stay still for any amount of time. Miles was already growing faster then his brother. Even though he was two years younger, he matched his brother in height, although his build was still pretty slight, which matched his feathery light hair and features.

Then there was Amy, the sweetest three-year-old anyone could ever meet. Her soft ringlets framed her sweet rosy face, while her wide inquisitive eyes were always questioning everything around her. She amazingly seemed to have an intelligence of a child much older than herself. At times she even intimidated adults.

I put my box down and wrapped my arms around them in one big hug, kissing Amy's cheek, and then trying to do the same with the boys.

"What are you guys doing here?" I asked as I finished giving my last hug.

"I had a late meeting," Darci answered with her usual cheerful voice as she came out from the kitchen. "so I asked your mom if she could pick the kids up from school."

"Oh, I see," I responded, trying not to draw attention to myself. She put one arm around me and gave me a quick sisterly embrace.

"Okay gang, go and get into the car. I'll be right there."

As the kids all raced each other out to the car, Darci chuckled, then turned to say her good-byes.

"Well, I guess I better g…Hey, are you okay?"

She changed her train of thought mid-sentence when she looked at me, carefully examining my face.

"Yeah, I'm fine," I lied, trying to hold back the tears from one of the worst days I'd had in a very long time, but I was never very good at hiding my feelings.

"You seem upset. What's going on?"

"Nothing, I just had a bad day, that's all. Everyone has one of those days every once in a while."

I didn't know who I was trying to convince, her or me. I stood there, not really looking at her, waiting for the awkward moment to pass, my box of office stuff sitting beside me on the ground.

"Ally," Darci's voice broke into my thoughts. "You forget who you're talking to. I know when something is up. I know you better than you know yourself." A soft snicker came out with her last words. "Now what's going on?"

I looked up at her, her eyes focused on me, waiting for some kind of response. Not knowing why I hesitated, I twisted my body uncomfortably and picked at my thumbnail with my index finger, acting as if I had done something wrong and didn't want to confess it.

I took a deep breath and decided that if I was going to get over this unsettling feeling that had crept into my mind, she would be the best person to confide in.

I'd do it; I could tell her why I was down, why I had a box full of stuff. Maybe she could help me make sense of this whole day, my whole life.

"Well," I started, "do you ever feel like you...."

Just then Miles came crashing through the door.

"Mom, Mom, we need to go! We're going to be late for karate."

He grabbed her arm and started pulling on it with such force; if he were any bigger he might have pulled it right off her body.

"Come on," he continued.

Exasperated with all the tugging, she looked at her watch. Her eyes got big and the sound of rush came out.

"I'm sorry, Ally, we've got to go. Can we finish this later?"

I murmured a soft "yeah" as I nodded dejectedly and thought, "Why do I even bother?"

I really couldn't feel too angry at her though; she had her own life and her kids. She had to take care of them. I'm an adult; I should be able to solve my problems without the help of someone else. But today I just needed someone to listen.

I was still standing in the entryway after Darci shut the door when my mom's voice rang from the kitchen.

"Ally, is that you?"

My mom, Dorothy, is an older version of myself, but with fiery red hair and a talent that would put even the queen of crafts to shame. She has never been a large woman but the love and compassion for those around her outweighed everything in all measurements.

I grabbed my box from off the floor and carried it into the kitchen with me. I took a deep breath because I knew what was coming next. It's not that I didn't want to talk with my mom about what happened today; I just knew that as soon as I opened up to her, I was also opening up the tears that were soon to follow. She just had a way of getting all the emotions out even if I didn't want to share them. At least with Darci I could be miserable and still stuff my emotions. I guess that's why I wanted to talk with Darci so much. I wasn't ready to bare everything at the moment.

As I walked into the kitchen she looked up from the pan that she had dinner cooking in and broke into her loving smile I'd seen so many times through my growing years.

"How was your day?" she asked.

I set my box, reminder of my day, down on the table. The loud thud it made caught her attention immediately.

"What's that?"

"Well, I had a great day. I lost my job."

"What?!" I could hear the surprise in her voice as she almost knocked the pan onto the floor. "What happened?"

"I don't know. Mr. Bryant called me into his office and said that things weren't working out. I was making too many mistakes and they just didn't have time to waste fixing them."

He actually had said so much more, but at that moment I couldn't remember it all. I didn't want to. He was right.

"I'm sorry, honey," she said as she turned down the stove and gave me a big hug.

My mom has always known the exact time to come over and give me the right amount of comfort at the precise time that the tears would start rolling down my face. If she knew she had this gift she kept it secret, but it was one of the best and exasperating talents she had.

And there they were, the drops of moisture that I knew would come. All that had happened on this one day came out in floods of tears. I felt as if I had shrunk from the adult woman that I was back down to the little girl that depended so vastly on her mother's love. My sobs were filled with emotions that were so intense that there had to be more to what was going on in my life than what the day had brought; a day of trial and chance. Maybe this trial was telling me I needed to take a chance. A chance on something, but what?

After what seemed like hours of crying on my mom's shoulder, I regained my composure, grabbed my box, and went to my room. I dropped the box just inside the door and flopped down, exhausted, onto my unmade bed. I laid there looking around my room as though everything was spinning out of control, yet everything seemed so clear and distinct.

The rustic country comforter lay mangled at the bottom of my bed, the pile of unwashed laundry waiting in the corner, and the pictures of all the people I loved placed as evenly as possible on my light pine dresser: my mom, my sisters, Darci, and Darci with her kids.

There was the one picture of Darci and me that I enjoyed more than any other. It always made me smile when I looked at it. It made me think of some good times, and even though the picture itself wasn't perfect, the day it was taken was.

As I laid there watching all the colors of my room swirl around me, the contrast of black and white startled me. Luck had taken his place. My cat climbed up onto my chest and had started demanding my attention. Automatically I began to stroke his sleek black fur. My fingers could feel each vertebra as I moved down his narrow back. His nose nudged against my face as if his fur could wipe away whatever was bothering me. All it could do was wipe the tears.

"I lost my job, I'm out of work, now what?" I said to him as I closed my eyes.

I lay still, stroking my Luck while everything around me grew more and more faint. Scenes in my head quickly becoming part of the past, my body slowly allowed each muscle to contract and relax as weightlessness filled every part of me.

When I opened my eyes it was bright and sunny. I hadn't meant to, but I had fallen asleep and slept through the whole night. Still in my clothes from the day before, my body just gave in to all the emotions that rushed through me.

I grabbed my clock from my nightstand. "12:05," I thought as I read the time. "Well, I guess you can wake up whenever you want when you don't have anything driving you to get up."

I looked at the time again. "No wonder I'm hungry." I was so emotionally drained that I didn't even eat dinner.

I pulled myself up and sat there with my feet hanging off the side of my bed. Luck still sat next to me. Even though I was still tired, enthusiasm surged through me. The night's sleep had made things clear. I knew what I had to do, what my next move was. I wasn't working so there wouldn't be anything holding me back. My enthusiasm went straight to adrenalin as my plan quickly started to form in my head.

My mom was still in her pajamas as she sat at the table finishing her juice and toast, swallowing the last of her many meds. None of us were ever early risers. I sat down across from her, my eyes wide with excitement.

"Good morning, or should I say afternoon," she said, wondering what my mood was going to be like. "How are you feeling?"

"Great!" the words flew out of my mouth full of life and excitement.

"Okay, you're quite chipper this morning, what's going on?"

"Not much, I just know what I'm going to do now. I have a plan."

She looked at me cautiously, studying my mood. I could see her head tilting just slightly and her arms automatically crossing in front of her. This was usually the routine when we told her something that she didn't believe or something she thought was not in our best interest.

"Okay, what's your plan?"

"I feel like I just need to do something. Something different or drastic in my life. I've decided that I just need to get away."

"We're having a family reunion soon. That would be a great time for you to get away."

I knew she wanted to help, but she didn't quite understand where I was going with this plan. I really didn't know fully where I was going with it either. I just knew that when I said I needed to get away, I meant far away.

"No, I need to get away now, just me. I just need to get away from my life."

She stiffened as if my words were scraping on something unpleasant.

"What are you talking about?" I could hear a slight twinge of hurt in her words.

"Well, don't take this the wrong way. I'm not saying I want to get away from you or the girls. There is just a piece of my life that I think has gotten lost and I need to find it."

Still confused: "I guess I don't understand."

"I've been saving money for awhile now, so I have a nice little stash set aside. I thought I could use it to get away."

"Where were you thinking of going?"

Before I could even really think exactly what I was saying it came out with power and conviction, as though the place itself had a secret power over me.

"Australia."

"Australia? Why do you want to go to Australia?" she said nonchalantly.

She grabbed her plate and glass as she got up from the table. Her manner was suddenly relaxed and casual as though the words I just spoke drifted by without any weight to them at all.

An abrupt annoyance came over me. "Does she think I'm kidding?" I wondered silently. I had to give her a response quick so she knew that I was serious about my decision, even if it wasn't the exact reason.

"Well, when I was over there I didn't get to see the sights much. I missed a lot."

Six years earlier I had gone to Australia as a missionary for my church. It was one of the greatest experiences in my life. The beauty of the country and the kindness of the people always brought back such great memories. One of the hardest things I had to do was leave this experience behind me and bound forward into a life that I wasn't sure I was ready for. I just didn't know why. In so many ways I always felt like I left a part of myself there, and I felt like it was time to reunite those two parts of my life.

"Are you sure you want to go to Australia? You know how you are about flying," she remarked.

"I'll be fine. I'm not as bad as I used to be." A bit of personal denial came through my words.

I have never been a great flier. I am always the one that would rather drive to a destination if we can avoid flying. But I would fly if I had to.

This irrational way of thinking had been with me since I went on a trip as a young girl with my dad. We had been flying when I woke up from a dream knowing that we were falling from the sky. My dad assured me that all we were doing was descending to our destination. And of course he was right. But ever since then I always get a bit skittish about flying. Okay, scared out of my mind is a better description.

My mom wasn't even finished questioning me about my sudden decision to go halfway around the world. It did seem a bit out of character.

"Okay, help me understand this. I know you're upset, but why would you take your savings and blow it on an expensive trip to Australia, when you should be using it for your bills and personal needs until you get working again?" she asked, with anger starting to overcome her patience.

"I know, it doesn't make sense to me, either. I just know that it's something that I have to do. Don't worry; I have enough for this month's bills as well as my trip."

I knew this was true. I didn't realize until last year how much I had actually saved. And I had plenty.

My mom and I went back and forth for quite a while. She would ask me questions and I would give my answers the best I could. And I would give my reasoning and she would give her rebuttal to each of my comments. But when it came down to it, I had made up my mind and nothing was going to get in my way. For whatever reason, I felt so strongly about this trip. I knew I had to go. It was as though something strong and powerful was pulling me toward some kind of chance.

2

Travel Time

❊❂❊

I looked out the window next to me, the terminal getting farther and farther away. I turned forward and took a deep breath. I could feel the anxiety coursing through my body, every nerve end twitching as my heart beat hard and fast as though it would pound right though me. The flight instructions came on our small screen in front of us as we rolled down the runway and paused. Then the words that I always dread hearing but know are inevitable.

"Flight attendants, prepare for takeoff," The captain's voice rang out through the cabin.

"Here we go," I thought as my stomach turned nervously.

The plane roared down the runway faster and faster, picking up speed as it moved effortlessly. The power of its thrust slightly held me back against my seat. I looked out the window again as the wheels lightly lifted from the ground, like a graceful bird taking off. I could see the airport becoming smaller and the rows of shops and homes starting to look like pieces of a Monopoly game. As much as I hated to fly, this was always the one thing that fascinated me. I loved to look down and see the quilted patterns of God's beautiful earth.

I made it through the first leg of my travels and was just getting use to flying when the flight attendant came by for our lunch order.

"Lunch?"

I wasn't really in the mood to eat; there was too much anxiety filling me up. But I was still a little hungry.

"I guess I'll have the turkey sandwich."

"And you, Ma'am?" The flight attendant asked the lady next to me.

"I'll also have the turkey sandwich."

She was a simple woman with long, dark hair pulled over her shoulder opposite me. Her smooth milk-chocolate skin accented her wide smile with such brilliance, it was almost too hard to look at. She had a very friendly disposition and her style of clothing made me think that she probably was from some kind of Polynesian culture. Everyone I had ever met from the South Pacific always seemed to ooze hospitality as well as kindness.

Our flight seemed to take forever. I tried to sleep but the seats were too small and close for comfort. I would closed my eyes and lay my head to the side next to the small window and try to drift off, but then the plane would jerk and my eyes would shoot wide open. At one point I almost drifted off when I felt a sudden weightlessness against my body. I sat up quickly, adrenalin flowing rapidly through me as if I had taken a straight shot of pure caffeine.

I heard one of the other passengers ask about what had happened. Her voice squeaked and I could hear a slight quiver in her words. She sounded as concerned as I felt. The second voice, a deep, low masculine tone, calmly explained.

"Sometimes planes hit an air pocket, which makes the plane suddenly drop. It's not that big a deal."

"It's not that big of a deal?" I grumbled to myself, so low that the women sitting next to me wouldn't hear.

Just then the flight attendant passed by and the first voice inquired if this was the case. She kindly agreed, but made no point on dwelling on it, then asked if she could get them anything.

They both answered, "No, thank you."

After she left, the second voice, who seemed to know what he was talking about, made another comment that made the bumps stand up on my arms.

"We probably only dropped a thousand feet."

"A thousand feet!" I gasped quietly. That was it; there was no way I was going to be able to fall asleep now.

After the drop it was pretty smooth, though I still had a hard time sleeping. A few more hours had passed and we started to descend. It was our first layover on our journey. There were two all together: first in Tahiti and then Fiji. It was nice to get off the plane, even if it was just for a short time.

I walked off the plane and into the terminal. The air was moist, even being inside, and there was a sweet smell of something floral that seemed to swirl around every open space. A man was singing and a women was greeting everyone with what I guessed was a traditional Polynesian type of dance. It felt like I was in one of those old movies where you get off the plane and you're met with the locals doing the hula and putting a lai around your neck.

"So where was mine?" I thought, a bit disappointed. "I guess they just do that in the movies."

I walked around the gift shops, bought a few souvenirs for my mom and sisters, and then just sat and waited to get back on the plane. The time difference was really starting to take its toll. My eyes started getting heavier and I had to keep forcing them open as I waited.

I sat down in my same seat as before and fastened my seat belt immediately. My Polynesian neighbor was no longer sitting next to me. A large, older, balding, pale man with glasses had taken her place, and next to him sat a woman, not at all as large as he was. She had a refinement about her along with being very maternal. They both were very nice looking and were very well dressed. By the looks of them you would have thought they were on their way to a business meeting. He was in a dark blue suit and tie and she in a neatly tailored dress.

As they sat down next to me they both acknowledged me kindly.

"Hello, how are you doing today?" The gentleman said, a calm and peaceful tone in his voice.

As I turned toward him, something square and shiny on his lapel caught my eye, but I was too tired to take much more notice of it than that.

"I'm fine, how are you?" I replied politely.

"Oh, you're American, that's wonderful. My wife and I are from Ohio."

"That's great," I said, trying to sound cheerful.

"We've been here in Tahiti for quite a while, and we're taking a tour of the South Pacific before we go home."

I smiled and nodded as I tried to listen intently to his comments about their long and exciting journey, but my eyes and thoughts got heavier and heavier. I didn't mean to and didn't even realize when it happened, but somewhere in the conversation I had fallen asleep.

My mind drifted in and out of some kind of conscious state. I remember the flight attendant asking what we would like to drink.

"Soda," I mumbled so softly that it might have just been in my head.

I remembered hearing something about landing and the shuffle of people leaving. This must have been our next layover. If it was our final stop, surely someone would have woken me.

I felt surprisingly refreshed when I opened my eyes.

"How long had I been asleep?" I wondered as I looked at my watch.

I pulled my fingers through my tangled hair as I tried to make some sense of things. I looked over next to me and I had a new neighbor: a rugged outdoorsy-looking man in his forties or late thirties, all decked out in khaki and a plain and simple shirt. His light, sandy-blond hair seemed to be pressed against his head as though he'd been wearing a hat for quite some time. He was intently watching the movie on the small screen in front of him. It didn't look like anything I had seen or even cared to watch, so I just turned to stare out into the empty boundless space of the pale sky.

As my mind wandered, the flight attendant came by to ask what we wanted to eat, then shortly thereafter brought our meal. I ate it so vigorously that the man next to me couldn't help but smile.

"I love to see a sheila that can eat," he said with a slight chuckle. "G-day, my name's Tom. I woulda introduced myself earlier but you were snoozin' away."

I could feel my face start to flush, but I was very hungry. Did I sleep so long I skipped a meal? But to eat so enthusiastically was a bit much. It must have been nerves. Embarrassed, I turned and looked up into his smiling hazel eyes.

"Hi," I said, swallowing my latest bite. "Sorry about that. I guess I'm really hungry."

"No worries," he replied, finishing his dish.

As I was finishing up my meal, the plane jerked and my heart quickly followed suit. Then the plane jerked again. The light above our heads flashed as the "Fasten your seat belts" sign came on. Mine was already as tight as it could go. I picked up the small square napkin that I received with my meal and started twisting and turning it through my clutched hand and rolling it around tightening, its shape closer and closer.

The two flight attendants moved slowly down one isle and up the other, collecting trash as they went. I didn't even notice when they came past us. I was just concentrating on my breathing to get me through the heavy turbulence we had entered. I held onto my napkin so tight that it had formed a solid little ball in my palm.

"Excuse me, ma'am, are you okay?" the flight attendant asked.

She obviously noticed my tenseness.

"I'm fine," I lied.

"Is there anything I could get you?"

I could tell that she sensed my uneasiness and probably felt sorry for me, and it was her job to help me feel comfortable.

"Yes, can I get a water and…," I looked down at the mangled napkin that looked more like a small golf ball, "another napkin?" I smiled sheepishly and handed her the ball.

She looked at my napkin and smiled. "Sure."

One big sigh escaped my lips louder then I had meant and caught Tom's attention.

"Nervous?" he asked.

"Just a bit."

"Oh, don't worry, I fly all the time and I haven't crashed yet. Besides if we did go down, you would only have about a minute to think about it. Then it's all over."

"Thank you, that just makes all my worries go away," I said sarcastically.

"You know, statistics say…"

I cut him off before he could go on. "Excuse me, Tom, right?" He nodded. "I don't mean to be rude and I know you're just trying to make me feel better about this whole thing, but you're not."

I took another deep breath and exhaled long and slow. Tom looked over at me, his eyes examining me carefully.

"I'm sorry, I didn't mean to offend you."

"You didn't; I'm just really nervous," I said, inhaling again.

"What you need is a good stiff drink to calm you down."

He started to reach for the call button. I quickly reached up and pulled his hand away.

"No, thank you. I don't drink."

His eyes narrowed and one eyebrow lifted suspiciously at me as if I were holding a secret from him.

"You don't drink?" he asked. "You mean you don't drink the hard stuff but surely you have a beer or a glass of wine once in awhile?

"No, nothing."

"Well, bugger, I've never heard that one before. Why not?"

I could hear the choked laughter behind his words.

"It's hard to explain. It's a mixture of religious and personal beliefs. It's something I choose not to do."

I couldn't tell if my explanation amused him or earned his respect. He just stared at me, scrutinizing everything I had just said. I figured the best thing for me to do was change the subject.

"I'm Alison by the way, but I go by Ally."

"Well, Ally, It's really nice to meet you." Tom reached over his body and put his hand out. I looked at him, placed my hand in his, and with one motion shook his hand.

Time seemed to pass so quickly after meeting Tom. We got so immersed in our conversation, I only noticed the bumps and shakes once in awhile when they got really bad. I would pause for a moment, grabbing my armrest until it passed, then continue with the conversation.

We talked about our jobs, our families, the fact that we were both single and loved to travel—even though I hated to fly. I found out that he had a fish, and I had a cat, that would probably eat his fish. We just went on and on. He would ask questions and I would automatically tell stories. He even made me laugh so hard at one point that a loud snort came out unexpectedly. Anyone walking past would have thought we had known each other for years, or at least longer than the few hours we actually did. I was surprised when the captain announced that we would be landing soon. I knew we didn't have much time left.

"So, I guess I just got to a point that I just had to get away," finishing a thought I was telling Tom.

"Ally, I get that, but what I don't get is if you're so afraid of flying, why did you choose to come clear across the world to get away? You could have found plenty of places to go in the states," he asked curiously.

Before I had a chance to respond, a voice came over the intercom and filled the cabin once again.

"Attention, ladies and gentlemen, we are beginning our final approach into Sydney. Please put your trays and seats into their upright position. And please turn off all electronic devices. On behalf of the crew and myself, we would like to thank you for flying with us, and we hope you will fly with us again. And if you are visiting, we hope you enjoy your stay here in Sydney."

"Wow, we're here already," Tom said and chuckled. "Ally, I don't know what your plans are while you're here, but if you need anything, give me a ring. I own a small travel agency here in town and I can help you with any travel needs. Here's my card."

He passed me a sleek white card with red and black writing on it, and some kind of gold design. I looked at it briefly and put it in my bag.

"Thanks."

The plane abruptly touched the ground and it felt as if we were going to skid right off the runway. As we taxied into the terminal, Tom and I had a bit more conversation while we waited to grab our carry-on bags. Then we shuffled into the path of passengers and made our way out.

"Well, I guess I better get my bags and head on to customs," I sighed as we finally made it out of the terminal.

"Yeah, the baggage claim is just around the corner there, and customs is straightway from there," Tom explained.

"Well, Tom, it was really nice meeting you and I really enjoyed our conversation. It made the trip a lot more bearable. Thank you."

"It was nice meeting you too, Ally," he responded politely.

"Well, I better go. Thanks again."

I gave Tom a soft smile and shook his hand good-bye. As I turned and walked away, a touch of melancholy came over me. As many times as I had flown and had talked to the person next to me, I knew the ending result. You have your brief time with this person, and then they're gone. They go live their life and you live yours. And you never see them again. And I knew this was the same. We had definitely had a rapport, but it was over and it was time to move on.

I found my bag quickly as it moved around the carousel, and with a big huff I pulled it to my side. I rolled it over to the customs gate and gave the heavyset man my passport. He looked at it carefully and then looked at me. He might have been trying to decide if it was me. The picture was about six years old and I was about twenty pounds heavier now. But I still seemed to keep that youthful look. I thought about renewing it but it was still good, so why worry about that? He looked at me again, then took his stamp and crushed it hard onto the page and gave it back to me.

As I ambled through the airport, there was a kaleidoscope of cultures and languages. People of all sizes, shapes, colors, and ages all intermixed with one another. Everyone was hurrying to get to their next destination. It was such a stunning display, I just watched and took it all in as I made my way outside.

When a taxi pulled up in front I jumped in and gave him the name of my hotel. I couldn't help staring out the window, watching the shops and the homes pass as my thoughts raced back to the first time I drove down these roads from the same airport, six years earlier as a missionary. Life had changed a lot since then. Now here I was again. What would this place have in store for me this time?

My heart raced with excitement as I thought about the fact that I was taking a bold step into a new direction of my life.

The taxi pulled up to my hotel and the driver and I both got out at the same time. He got my bags and I paid him for his services.

The hotel was just your typical hotel: clean and tailored, the matching couch and chairs in a muted rust-colored fabric with multi-colored strips on the cushion. The paintings on the walls reminded me of something you might see in the deserts back home but without the kangaroos running across them. It all seemed so familiar even though I was thousands of miles away from home.

A young woman was standing at the front desk helping a gentleman check in, typing on her computer.

"Here ya go, Mr. Sanson. I hope you have a great stay with us," She said smiling as she handed him his key.

She was a very nice-looking woman with strawberry-blond hair and light olive-toned eyes. Her voice was soft and sweet as she acquainted herself with each guest she spoke to.

"Next." I walked up to the counter. "Welcome to Circular Quay Inn."

"Hi, you should have reservations for Ally Pierson." I said a little hesitantly. You never know if something is going to go wrong.

As I waited for her to type in my name, I stood there looking around again at the interior of the lobby.

"Yes, Ms. Pierson, Let me just get your key," she said, interrupting my observation.

While she got my key I noticed a rack of brochures in bright colors detailing the many things to do while visiting.

"I could use this one. And that looks fun," I murmured to myself as I started picking out the different activities that I might enjoy.

"Here ya go, Ms. Pierson, room 1112. I hope you enjoy your stay here in Sydney." Her soft voice echoed the same words she had said just a moment earlier.

My pace to the elevator was quick and eager. I pushed number eleven and I could feel my pulse race with excitement. As I walked into my home for the next two weeks. I couldn't help but feel overwhelmed with emotion. I was here, I was clear across the world from my family, my friends—the few I had. Miles away from my life as I knew it, no worries, no complications. Everything in the last weeks, well the last year, had brought me to this point. My time to live was here. I threw my bags on the bed and rushed over to the window. As I threw open the curtain I took in a deep breath, slowly letting it out and gazed at the sights that lay before me. Sydney was such a beautiful scene as the sun melted into a hazy, tawny sky.

I fell back and bounced slightly on the bed. I grabbed the brochures that I picked out and thought about going through them—I was too excited to wait any longer. But as I started to mull over each one, the same heaviness my eyes had felt earlier was back. I rolled over to my side and pushed my way up to the pillow.

"I'm just going to close my eyes for a few minutes," I said to myself as I yawned.

Exhaustion and jet lag had taken over. I lay there resting, and as my mind slowly settled, a smile of satisfaction crossed my lips and I fell carelessly asleep.

3
Favor
✳✳✳

I twisted my wrist to see the time and tried to focus my eyes on the small numbers circling the simple face.

"What time is it?" The numbers stared back at me. "Two o'clock; is that a.m. or p.m.?" I looked over at my open drapes and noticed the light shining through. "*P.m.!*"

I had slept through the night and most of the day. At first I was frustrated that the trip had worn me out so much more than I had thought. Then all at once I didn't worry so much about the time and the thrill of just being in this foreign land kicked me into gear. I couldn't wait, and since I had already wasted half a day, I thought the most logical thing to do would be to see the nearby spots first and get them out of the way. I rushed to the bathroom to start my regular routine.

"Shoot," I moaned. "I was supposed to call home and let Mom know I got in okay."

This was a customary thing we did. Growing up it became a general rule that we would let everyone know where we were. Just in case something were to happen, someone would have an idea of our activities. And even though we were all grown, we liked to give our mom some piece of mind.

I looked at my watch again and started figuring out the time difference in my head.

"Okay, if it's 2:00 p.m. here, and we are about thirteen hours ahead, that would make it about," I was counting on my fingers, "1:00 a.m. yesterday. I better wait to give them a call."

I thought about it for two seconds then chuckled at the idea of the time difference.

"They're probably still up," I decided.

There were three short rings; then the familiar voice on the other end.

"You've reached the Pierson's. We're unable to get to the phone right now, but if you leave your name and number, we'll get back to you soon," my sister's voice chimed.

Beep.

"Hello, hello, it's me. Sorry it's so late, but answer the phone," I yelled, trying to make sure they would hear me if they were asleep. "Helllloooo," calling out again, my voice a little too annoying. "Well, you're probably sleeping. I just wanted to let you know I got here fine. I'll call you later."

I was just about to give up when I heard a groggy voice on the other end.

"Hello."

"Hi Mom, sorry for calling so late, I just wanted to make sure you knew I got in okay."

"When did you get there?" she mumbled.

"Last night, but I crashed as soon as I got to my room and didn't wake up until now."

"What time is it there now?" she asked.

"It's a little after two p.m."

"Oh, that's nice."

I could tell that she wasn't very coherent and she may not even remember the call in the morning. I thought it might be better if I spoke with someone who would remember.

"Mom, are the girls there? Can I talk to one of them?"

"Yeah, hang on. I think they're watching a movie."

I could hear the creak of the bed and the exertion in her breath as she got up.

"Gina, Megan," her voice echoed down the hall.

A faint sound of laughter and music became louder as she entered the living room. I could here the familiar dialogue from their favorite movie, then nothing but the sound of my mom's voice.

"Ally is on the phone, will one of you talk to her?" There was a slight rustle in my ear as my mom passed the phone.

"Hello," Gina's voice came through.

"Hey, I just wanted to talk to someone else, mainly because I didn't think mom would remember I called."

"Oh, okay, so how was your flight?" she asked.

"It wasn't bad, a little bumpy, but I survived."

I couldn't help but be curious about the movie I heard in the background. I wanted to know if my suspicions were right.

"Are you watching what I think you're watching?" I chuckled.

"I don't know what you're talking about," she responded, a light lilt in her voice.

"Goofball." We both laughed.

Then Gina's voice turned slightly serious. "Hey, yesterday Darci came over and was kind of upset that you didn't tell her you were leaving."

"Didn't you tell her it was a spur-of-the-moment thing?"

"Yeah, but she still seemed upset."

"I'll give her a call later and talk to her. Well, I better go. This is going to cost a fortune."

We both said our good-byes and hung up. I did need to call Darci, and I planned on it, but what would I say? *Sorry that I didn't call. Sometimes I feel like I'm losing my mind and I had to get out of Dodge.* I would call her, I just didn't know when. I couldn't right now; it was too late. It was okay to call home, there were no kids around to wake up, and I figured someone would be up watching movies.

After I got dressed I sat down to organize my day. I wanted to get the most out of the time I had left. I pulled out a map and charted the best course I could go. First to The Rocks, the old prison barracks that had been transformed into shops for the typical tourist. Then it was a short walk over to the Opera House, then a ferry ride around the harbor.

I grabbed the brochures once again, looking to see what else I could do when the words *"Experience the magic in the outback"* in bold, black writing caught my eye. I opened it up and began to examine the information inside.

"A three-day trip," I read. "Come join us for a walkabout. Spend two starry nights camping in the shadow of one of the wonders of the world, Uluru (Ayers Rock). Then join us as we mingle with the locals of Alice Springs."

The words sounded so intoxicating. To see Ayers Rock, to actually go on a walkabout. Well, a planned walkabout. But did I have enough? I looked down at the price.

"Five hundred dollars!".

It was a bit out of my price range, but this was what I was here for, to get out of my comfort zone and live life. I couldn't pass up this opportunity; I could squeeze that out for a three-day trip.

I found the number on the back page and dialed—excited about the possibilities, but when the sound of a busy tone rang through the receiver, I couldn't help but feel a bit of disappointment. After trying and retrying the number three or four times, my disappointment was turning into discouragement.

"Maybe I'm not supposed to go," I tried to convince myself. "It's too much money, anyway."

I looked down at the reddish-brown formation on the front and sighed.

"After all, it's just a rock."

But as I continued to stare at the picture, an overwhelming sense of determination came over me. This was my chance, my chance to do something so not me. But there was more to it. I felt so strongly that I was meant to go. Like my pull to come to Australia, I felt the same familiar pull to see Ayers Rock.

I decided if I couldn't make my reservations over the phone, I would find the travel agency and make it in person. I grabbed my bag and the map and took off for the day.

From where my hotel was located, it was just a short stroll to the bus stop. I didn't mind taking the bus as some people do; it's cheap and it gets you where you need to go. I always like to watch as each person gets on and off the bus, wondering what their story might be. I wanted to know what made them happy or why they were so sad, and if their story was similar to mine.

After mulling over all those questions on the bus, a street sign caught my eye. I realized that I had missed my stop and I needed to get off. I pushed the button on the pole next to me.

"I'm sorry, but a need to get off," I called to the bus driver.

His eyes glared at me while his mouth puckered and he murmured quietly under his breath. The bus came to a sudden stop and everyone jerked forward. Those standing practically fell onto each other.

"Thank you," I said as I walked off the bus.

The driver huffed as he closed the door behind me and I caught the last phrase of his irritated murmur: "Stupid American."

I turned to glare at him but the bus was already headed down the road.

My first stop was The Rocks. I remembered coming here six years earlier, and it seemed as though nothing had changed. They still had all the little shops, each one a different motif.

There was the traditional Australia gift shop for the typical tourist, with all the Sydney and Australian logo merchandise, stuffed koalas and kangaroos, and mugs with the Opera House on the front. T-shirts had sayings like "Do you love Australia? I Didgeri-Doo" written in black and brown on a white background with an Aboriginal flare to it.

There were the clothing shops that sported everything from local to high end designers; floral shops with rows of all assortments of colors and fragrant aromas that would make any girl beam with delight; bake shops with a sweet bouquet of their own that you could taste as you walked past; store after store I could spend forever in.

As I made my way through the first half of the shops, I realized that it was getting late and I still wanted to find the travel agency. I found a little café and sat down so I could pull out my map and the brochure. I matched the address to the map. I couldn't believe it—it was only four or five blocks away. And I couldn't help the big smile that came over my face.

"I am so, supposed to go on this trip," I said to myself, excited that things appeared to be going my way after all. I put everything back into my bag and flung it over one shoulder.

It took me longer then I had thought it would to get to my destination. Were Australian blocks bigger than ours, or did I just mess up on the distance? I had to of walked twice as far than I thought I would. Finally I saw it sitting between a fruit shop and a bank. *Down Under Travel and Tours.*

It was smaller then most of the travel agencies back home. As I walked in the tinkle of a small bell rang above me. Posters of Ayers Rock and different landmarks of Australia adorned the walls. Next to them hung different types of Aboriginal artwork. A fan in the corner was blowing at full speed, and a curtain tied to one side separated the front of the office from what seemed like a small back apartment. It didn't really look like the most reputable place.

"Be right there," I heard voice from the back call out.

I stood in the middle of the small office, trying to decide if I should stay or just go. Just then the voice from the back walked through the half-tied curtain. My eyes widened as I reconized the sandy-haired man. His hair was still flat against his head as though he just took his hat off and wearing a simple white knit shirt and the same khaki pants as before.

"Tom?" I asked, stunned.

"Hey, well what do you know, it's the American." His lips formed into a wide grin. "So, you decided to use my services after all, aye?"

I had forgotten about the card he gave me when we left the airport. It was still in my bag.

"This is your agency?" I asked, trying not to show my embarrassment.

"Sure is, been here bout fifteen years. I have the best tours in the territory. It's on my card."

"I have to tell you, Tom, I didn't come here because I remembered your card. I picked up this brochure," I pulled the pamphlet from my bag, "and saw the ad for a three-day tour of Ayers Rock and thought that would be great to do. I didn't even notice it was your agency."

Truth was, I didn't pay too much attention that he owned an agency. When he told me about it I was pretty hung over with all the jet lag.

"Which tour?" he asked. I handed him the colorful folded piece of paper. "Right. That is a great trip." I smiled with great enthusiasm. "But unfortunately we're not having any tours right now. It's the raining season and we don't get a lot of tourists this time of year," He said, apologetic as he handed the pamphlet back to me.

"Oh, I see," I sighed.

I couldn't hold back the disappointment in my voice. I automatically let my shoulders slump and my eyes shifted downward, concentrating on the pamphlet I was holding. I was really looking forward to having an adventure and getting out of my comfort zone by doing something different. I thought for sure that some kind of universal cosmic force was pulling me in that direction. I could feel it in me.

"Well," I finally said, "maybe next time. I better go; thanks anyway," I grimaced, and turned to leave.

"Wait, I'm sorry about the trip. Let me make it up to you. How bout dinner?" he offered.

"No, that's okay, it's not like it's your fault."

"I know, but it would make me feel better." He looked at me with a touch of pleading in his eyes.

"All right," I said, giving in to his generosity. I *was* getting hungry. "But nothing fancy."

"Right."

I should have known that he really wasn't big on the elegant and chic. He took me to a small local pub. It was quite noisy from everyone watching the game on the small television above the bar. The pool tables at the opposite end as well as the dartboard were both overflowing with patrons waiting for their turn. Tom ordered himself a large pint of beer and fish and chips. I ordered a diet soda and chicken and chips.

"So, have you been enjoying your stay so far?" Tom asked as he stuffed a handful of fries in his mouth.

"Yeah, I've only been here a day, but it's been good." I said, stuffing my own mouth.

"Then why do you seem upset?"

"I'm not upset."

His question caught me off guard. I thought I was being very pleasant and happy. Did he see something in me that I didn't even see myself? This made me a bit uncomfortable.

"Why do I seem upset?"

"Your eyes look a bit dim."

"My eyes look dim?" I thought.

As if he could hear my mind, he responded very naturally, "You have very expressive eyes. They practically tell your whole story."

"Wow," I thought again.

Well, if they told my whole story, he must be bored silly. I was disappointed though about the trip and maybe that was coming through. Since he probably already knew my thoughts—my eyes obviously giving it away—I felt I might as well fill in the blanks.

"You're right, I guess. I'm a little down about not being able to see Ayers Rock. I wasn't really planning it in my trip, but since I decided to go I was really looking forward to it. So there it is. You caught me."

I finished with reluctance and continued eating my meal.

He sat there looking at me, motionless, his eyes focused. Then, as if a light bulb turned on over his head, his lips curved into a pleasant, crooked smile.

"I have an idea." There was something kind of sly in his comment. "I have this mate that has a small plane who might be able to take you. Do you want me to give him a ring?"

My brain was trying to be the good guy and not be selfish and put Tom out, but my heart was screaming, "Yes of course call him I may never get another chance!"

"No, that's okay, I don't want to be a bother."

My eyes must have given me away again or he heard it in my voice. He grabbed his cell phone out of his pocket and pushed just one button.

My heart started to pick up its pace as I waited.

"Hullo, mate, how you been?" He stopped to listen.

I tried to hear what the voice on the other end might be saying but the pub was too loud. All I could do is wait for whatever outcome Tom had planned.

"That's good," he continued. "Oh, really? That's hard to believe." He began to laugh at something that must have been extremely funny.

I started to feel uneasy, wondering why I was just sitting there. Obviously I could have been doing something else.

"Well, let me get to why I called. Do you remember that favor you owe me?" He paused. "Do you still own that little plane of yours?" Again he paused. "Well, there's this Sheila who needs a ride to the Rock. That's right. Can you help?"

This pause seemed so much longer than the others. As I watched Tom, I saw his face turn from cheerful to determined. He got up and sauntered away from the table. It was obvious that he was having a heated conversation with the person on the other end. Suddenly his mood changed and he turned and gave me a thumbs-up. He came and sat back down, his phone pressed against his chest.

"He said he can take you tomorrow for a short trip, let ya walk around a bit, then have you back the next day, for seven hundred dollars." He shook his head as he spoke—there was no need.

"Seven hundred dollars for just a day trip, plus a room for the night? I'm sorry, but that's too much. I was willing to pay that for a whole weekend but not for just a few hours. Thanks, anyway."

I finished the last fry and grabbed my bag for my credit card. Tom had been a great help, but it was time to give up and go back to the hotel.

"Hold on," Tom said as he laid his hand on my arm. "How much do you want to spend?"

He asked with that sly sound to his voice again.

"I don't know," I said, shrugging. "I thought is would only be around two or three hundred dollars? The highest I could go for the flight is three fifty."

He smiled and got up from the table again. I watched anxiously as the conversation obviously was going back and forth from Tom to the mysterious person on the other end.

"What is he saying?" I wondered aloud.

I waited for what seemed like forever. Finally Tom turned towards me, winked, and gave me a gratifying smile as if he were the one waiting for some good news. His swagger was even more pronounced as he came back over to the table and practically plopped himself down in his chair, obviously pleased with himself for being able to maneuver things to go in his favor.

"Okay, then, three fifty it is. He'll meet you at nine a.m. at Wind Croft Airfield." He said, grinning.

I nodded agreeably. "Now, how do I get there?" I asked, still amazed that he was able to convince this other individual to go along with his plan.

"I'll give you directions. Do you have a pen?"

I grabbed my bag and rummaged through it. I always like to make sure I had whatever someone might ask for. Pens, paper, band-aid, headache pills, whatever the need, if I didn't have it one time, I would add it to my growing collection.

"Here." I handed him a very normal ballpoint pen that I had taken from the nightstand in my hotel room.

He scribbled a messy little map on the back of a cocktail napkin, then a name and address under it, and handed it to me. I looked at the map and wrinkled my forehead, trying to decipher it. I concluded that I would just look it up on my map when I got back to my room.

"Thanks," I said and grinned.

"Well, I better take you back to your hotel. You've got a big day tomorrow." he offered as he grabbed his receipt and mine from my hands.

"Hey, I got it."

"Don't be daft, Ally, what kind of bloke do you take me for? I'll shout."

"Fine," I grumbled, "thank you." I turned red as the words came out.

The drive back to my hotel was quiet; the sound of the radio playing soothing contemporary rock filled the space around us. I was already getting tired again, as the jet lag was still hanging on. As I watched the buildings pass by, I thought of the strange silent conversation that took place and how Tom was able to convince the other party to take me to my desired destination. This kind of picked at a nerve but I didn't know why. Curiosity finally got to me, and I broke the rhythm of our silence.

"Tom,"

"Yeh?"

"What did you say on the phone tonight to get your friend to take me tomorrow? And for a lot less then he was asking for?" I felt like I was interrogating him.

"Not much, I just told him a bit about you." He paused and his lips formed into a smirk. "About your… personality."

Personality. I didn't know what that kind of interpretation meant here in Australia, but back in the states when a man described your "personality," it wasn't good. By the time he had finished his comment he was pulling in front of my hotel.

"Don't worry, it'll be right." he said reassuringly.

"Okay, well, thanks for everything, for dinner and especially tomorrow."

"You're welcome."

I got out of the car and started walking to the door. Just as I was about to walk in, Tom yelled out his window.

"Ally!" I turned to acknowledge him. "I hope you enjoy your trip." He had that same sly sound in his voice, as if there were something in his words that I should grasp. I just smiled and waved back.

When I got back to the room exhausted again, I quickly got ready for bed but decided I needed to prepare for my excursion before going to sleep. I snatched my bag off the table where I had tossed it when I came in, and started filling it with things I thought I might need. My camera was a definite, mini first-aid kit, and a few snacks in case I got hungry before I got back. I put each item in one by one, probably getting a little overzealous with what I needed—it was getting pretty heavy. I looked at my bulging bag, considering what I could possibly leave behind.

"Oh, well," I thought, "better safe than sorry."

I zipped it close and set it next to me. Next I pulled the folded napkin with Tom's scribble of a map out of the front pocket of my bag, then grabbed my map of the city and laid it flat on the bed. I studied the scribble again, still confused, finally giving up on his drawing. I looked at the address that he managed to write legible enough to read. The words were dark and heavy, and pressed firmly into the fibers.

Jackson McQuewen
Wind Croft Airfield
1229 Wind Croft, Sydney
Hangar 27

4
The Meeting

I woke up tired, still fighting the jet lag, but I was excited about doing something new and different, something completely out of character for me. The rush pulled me to my feet easily. I grabbed my towel and went to take a shower. The water was hot and soft as it enveloped my whole body, waking me up completely. When I got out steam was still lingering around me, and I had to wipe the residue off the mirror a few times. Then I saw it: fear. Fear was starting to penetrate through the bubble of enthusiasm I felt for this trip. And the words that I say to myself so often came back.

"What am I doing?" I shook my head, trying to dislodge the question. "Get a grip," I thought, "you know you want to do this."

I dried my hair as much as I could with a towel and repeated my usual wet, scrunch, and go routine. Then I put on what I thought would be the best attire for me—jeans and a T-shirt. I was always more myself in jeans than anything else, especially a skirt or a dress.

I looked at my watch to see how much time I had and realized that time was slipping past faster then I had thought. I slipped my socks and Keds on, not even bothering to untie them, grabbed my backpack from where I had left it after I packed, grabbed my sweatshirt in case it got cold, and I flew out the door.

It probably took the taxi about twenty minutes to get me to the small airport. Deep down I was hoping it would last longer. The fear that I felt earlier was back and it brought anxiety and doubt with it.

We stopped just outside the chain-link fence. I could see the small runway past a line of simple large metal sheds with oversized doors. Some were open with different sized aircrafts in them, some closed. I paid the driver and stepped onto the concrete, flung my bag over my shoulder, and took a deep breath.

"Things are about to change," I thought to myself. "My life as I know it is never going to be the same."

The taxi drove off and left me to find my way. I walked through the gate and started looking for the right hangar. One by one I could see the big numbers on top of each huge door. One, three, five, seven on one side, two, four, six, eight on the other side.

"Well, at least they're going in sequence," I said out loud.

I walked along for about another ten minutes before I found the right hangar. A beautiful sleek, white plane with blue stripes down the sides was sitting just outside, the engine roaring ready for my arrival. Its glossy shine looked as though it had just had a wash. Probably customary when going on any type of trip. Its long narrow body appeared as though it could hold quite a few passengers, like a smaller version of a 747.

"This must be the plane that they use for their tours." My mind reveled at the idea that this trip wasn't going to be quite as terrifying as I had thought. "But didn't I hear Tom say his friend had a small plane? What is his definition of small? Did he arrange different transportation?" All these questions swirled in my head, making me a bit dizzy. Then I realized I didn't care.

"This is great. I'll have to do something nice for Tom when I get back," I mused with a smiled.

As I started walking towards my air taxi, looking for the pilot or anyone in charge, the plane started to roll away. I started to pick up my pace, trying to get closer. I knew I was a bit late, but they couldn't even wait a few minutes?

"Wait!" I yelled as my walk turned to a run.

With each step I made the plane seemed to move faster and further away from me until it was gone. Exasperated, I let my bag slide off my shoulder and fall to the ground.

"Now what?" I huffed.

I placed my hands on my waist, irritated, and looked around, one direction then the other, trying to decide what to do. My taxi was gone, the plane was gone, and the only logical thing I could do was call another taxi and head back to the hotel. I pulled out my cell phone then realized that I didn't have the number. I didn't think I would need it.

I started walking back to the front gate, hoping to see an office, phone booth, or just someone with access to a phone book. As I strolled back to where I started, I noticed one of the hangar doors open and the nose of a much smaller plane, white with faded brown stripes, peeking out the front. I looked up at the big number above the door and it hit me: Hangar twenty-seven.

The beautiful shiny plane wasn't my ride; it had just been sitting there, waiting to taxi out to the runway. My ride was the little white-and-brown nose peeking out the door, as if it were saying, "Ha, ha, it's me!" A flood of panic came rushing back as I contemplated the outcome of flying in something that seemed so unstable. But I was determined to stick to my plan.

As I approached the hangar door, a pair of greasy jeans and a dirty T-shirt were bent over the front of the craft, his head so far into what he was doing I couldn't see it. The muscles in his arms were madly flexing as grunts and brash cursing in a low, gruff, Scottish brogue flowed out from inside the metal casing.

"Um, um," I cleared my throat. "Excuse me." He didn't acknowledge me; he just kept working.

"Excuse me." I raised my voice a little.

Still nothing. This was starting to annoy me.

"*Excuse me!*" My voice rang out shrill and hard.

"Aye," he finally said, acknowledging my presence.

"Are you Jackson McQuewen?"

"Tha's me, bu' everyone calls me Jack." His smooth accent flowed out easily, bouncing off the metal hood of the plane.

As he spoke he stood upright, wiping his hands on a greasy towel. He had to be at least a foot taller than me. When he turned around, for just a brief moment I stopped breathing. His sapphire eyes took me off guard, brilliantly blue in color encircled by dark, long lashes. He was gorgeous. His dark, ruffled hair helped the color of his eyes stand out even more. And even though he had at least a couple of days worth of whiskers on his face, his skin looked smooth and flawless. I shook my head slightly, breathing again, hoping he wouldn't notice my distraction.

"I'm Ally Pierson. Tom called you last night about taking me to Ayers Rock."

Embarrassed, I tried not to look directly at him. But as I glanced down away from his amazing face, I couldn't help but notice the dirty T-shirt that clung slightly against the apparent muscles that lay underneath, which made things even worse. I could feel the heat on my face from the flush I knew was coming. Thankfully Jack didn't seem to notice my obviously pink cheeks when I looked back up at him.

He studied my face for a few moments. Then I watched as his eyes moved down to my feet and back to my face again, confused he raised one eyebrow.

"Ya can't be the same girl," he finally said, shaking his head.

His look went from confusion to disappointment, or maybe it was disgust. It made me feel uncomfortable, self-conscious, and hideous. I felt like an ugly piece of furniture that no one would ever want. It only took about two seconds for me to figure out why he was acting this way.

"Tom," I thought as my heart sank and the realization came to me.

He must have told Jack that I was something I wasn't. Maybe a beautiful, long-legged model type with long flowing hair. Then to have a short, stubby, frizzy top show up, no wonder he was confused.

"Personality," I scoffed under my breath.

How could he do that to me? How could he do that to him? It wasn't slyness I heard in his voice; it was amusement, his end of a good practical joke.

I stood there, sorting through all my thoughts. Jack was apparently disgusted with the whole idea of taking me. Tom had obviously used me to get a good laugh and I was stuck with a choice, to leave embarrassed and hurt or to take advantage of the situation that presented itself.

I still wanted to go see Ayers Rock and Jack had committed to take me. Even though it was for all the wrong reasons, there was my answer. This was a business arrangement and he had to take me.

I deliberately stood up straight mustering up all the confidence I could find and looked him directly in his eyes, trying not to let them distract me.

"Well, unless you talked to Tom more than once last night, I'm her. Sorry to disappoint you." My voice was a bit sour. "So, are you still going to take me or what?"

He stared at me for a second, examining my attitude. Then he casually reached to the side and picked up a small box that was sitting on a metal cart next to the plane. He shook it hard until a long, round object came out. He placed it between his lips, then pulled out a shiny silver lighter and flipped the cover open, covered the end with his other hand, and lit the cigarette. He took one deep drag and exhaled right in my face.

"D'ya have the money?"

I coughed slightly and fanned the smoke away. All the attraction that I had felt just moments earlier seemed to vanish with every puff of smoke in my direction.

"Yes," I responded.

"Then I'll take ya. Bu' i's goin ta cost ya five hundred, not three fifty," he said, taking another hit of the cigarette.

"What?" I yelped in disbelief.

"I fergot abou' tax."

I looked at him, my forehead furrowed. Asking for extra was probably his way of getting out of taking me. Or getting back at me for being different than he thought. But it wasn't my fault. I was just a pawn in Tom's joke just as much as he was. Realistically, though, I couldn't afford what he wanted. Not for just a few hours.

"You know what, that's more than I wanted to spend, and I only brought so much with me. Thanks anyway."

I turned to leave.

"Wait," he said abruptly. "How much do ye have with ya?"

I thought I could hear something light in his words, something that sounded a little like desperation. Then things started falling into place—falling to my advantage. He needed this job; he needed my money, however little it was.

"I have just enough to pay you, a room for the night and get something to eat." I couldn't help the slightly smug smile coming across my face.

"Well, d'ya have a credi' card? I could put part of i' on tha' and ya can pay the other part in cash," he replied with a smug grin of his own as he inhaled another drag.

"Seriously, that's too much. I'm just going to forget it." I started to walk away.

"Okay, look, there is a tax, bu' I'll only charge ya an extra fifty dollars. Can ya live with tha'?"

"I don't think so."

"Twen'y five."

I examined his face closely and he looked pretty sincere. Maybe he was as tired of the games as much as I was.

"Fine," I said.

I reached out my hand to shake his, and he threw the remains of his cigarette on the ground and flattened it with the sole of his shoe before grabbing my hand a bit too firmly. We both flinched as we felt a shock from the static electricity, then he jerked my hand hard, like I was a male business partner finalizing a business transaction.

"I need ya ta fill ou' a few papers before we leave. And I need a shower," he said as he put his tools away.

We walked down the row of hangar doors until we came to a building that was more like an old warehouse. There was a front section with a few different desks in it, and some chairs sitting on the opposite side. On the walls were charts and maps of different locations. A big box that blew out cool air was sitting high in a corner with red ribbons blowing out from the bottom. On the other side of the room was another door leading to another part of the building I couldn't see.

He sat me down at the first desk, and after rummaging through a large metal filing cabinet, he handed me two very long pieces of paper. I took a pen out my bag and started filling out what looked like some kind of insurance paperwork. I even saw a question about "in case of death." That didn't help my anxiety at all.

"I'll be righ' back," he bellowed as he left. "Hi, Max."

A short, balding man was sitting at another desk on the phone conducting, some kind of business of his own. He waved casually as Jack passed him and disappeared through the far door. Then he turned and gave me a nod of acknowledgment. I responded politely with a smile and a nod of my own.

Just about the time I had finished the paperwork Jack emerged from the other room. He had changed into a pair of clean jeans and a dark-blue cotton knit shirt, which made his blue eyes even more irresistible. He had shaved off all the whiskers from earlier and his face was just as smooth and flawless as I had imagined. And his hair was no longer ruffled but perfectly styled. I could start to feel a slight irregular beat to my heart. Then he pulled out another cigarette and it was normal again.

"Done?" he asked as he snatched the papers from my hands.

"Yeah." I answered, surprised by his abruptness.

"Le's go," he said, then casually turned to the bald man who was still on the phone. "Bye, Max."

As I climbed into the small plane next to him, I didn't want to give Jack the satisfaction of seeing my anxiety, but the truth was I was a ball of nerves, like yarn unraveling quicker than I could bundle it up. I took a deep breath and fastened my seat belt, and put on the headset that Jack handed me. The engine sputtered a few times before it finally turned over. This wasn't a good sign. How many times had I heard the same sound coming from an old car we owned, giving its last mile to get us to school or work or the store, then never starting again? This made me very nervous.

"I'm okay, I'm okay," I repeated to myself. "This is going to be fun." I closed my eyes and forced a smile.

"I' takes a bi' ta get her goin', bu' once she does, i's smooth sailing the whole way," he yelled over the roar of the engine. I just grinned.

It took us a few minutes to taxi out to the runway, then a few more to wait our turn. Jack, meanwhile, pushed buttons and flipped switches as he talked on his head-set to the tower while we made our way into position.

"Okay, tower, this is six-zero-seven tango. We're ready for takeoff." Jacks voice flowed loud and confident.

We slowly started down the runway, picking up speed as we went, with a little bump here and there, going faster and faster. I thought my heart stopped for just a moment when he quickly pulled back on the control stick and we were airborne. I automatically closed my eyes quickly and held my breath.

"Please keep us safe. Please bless that everything will be all right. Please bless that we won't die," I prayed earnestly.

I opened my eyes and slowly let out the air I was holding so carefully in my lungs. I looked over at Jack who had a slight half-smile across his face.

"Ye've never been on a small plane before, have ya?" Jack asked with a bit of amusement to his tone.

"No," I replied.

"Then why are ya doin' this?" he asked curiously.

"It's a long story."

I looked away, not wanting to meet his gaze.

"I have nowhere ta go."

I didn't respond; I just kept looking out the window, trying to stay calm.

"So Elsie, you're American, righ'? Whit brings ya ta Australia?"

"It's Ally," I said, irritated.

"Sorry, Ally. So whit brought ya?"

He was attempting to be civil, so I decided that I would at least be polite and civil back.

"Well, I was here about six years ago as a missionary for my church, and I thought since I didn't get to see everything I wanted to, I would take the chance now."

I looked over just in time to see Jack roll his eyes. I could tell that he wasn't a religious person, and anyone who was ranked low on his scale of qualities that made good company. But that's a big part of who I am. I wasn't going to hide that fact from a man who, after tomorrow, I would never see again. I would just keep it low-key.

"So, I thought I would tour a little."

"Bu' why now?" he asked as though he was trying to solve a riddle.

"It was just a good time for me," I lied.

"Hum."

"What?"

I was starting to get frustrated. What was he searching for?

"Nothin', i's jus' in'eresting." He paused for a moment then continued. "How long have ya been planning this?" he asked curiously.

"Why?"

His questioning was making me nervous. What did it matter to him when I planned my trip, or why I was here?

"Why are you asking so many questions?" I growled.

"I'm just tryin' ta understand yer motivation."

"My motivation?"

"Usually when someone takes a holiday ou' of the blue and i's so fur from home, tha' usually means they're either hidin' or runnin' from something."

"I'm not hiding from anything," I murmured.

He looked at me with suspicion, his eyes questioning every word that I said.

"Look, let's just say that right now it was a good time in my life to get away, and leave it at that okay."

"Okay." he agreed.

My words came out hard and firm. I didn't know why. It wasn't that I was trying to hide anything. But I didn't even really know myself what the pull was that brought me here. And how could I even try to explain it? Especially to a total stranger, and one that I could tell didn't even like me. That pretty much ended the conversation.

After flying for quite awhile without crashing, and a short landing to refuel, I started to relax. At least I tried to look relaxed. I had come prepared though. I had brought a couple of tissues to have something to hold on to and pulverize besides my own fleshy arm or thigh or any part of my body I could grab onto.

While I constantly concentrated on keeping my upper body calm and motionless, my nerves were leaking out of other body parts. My leg started to bounce vigorously out of control. I didn't even notice until Jack reached over and placed his hand firmly on my knee—a bit of irritation in his touch. I looked down at his hand and without any thought I brushed his hand away. I could feel embarrassment come over me as my heated, flushed face gave me away.

It seemed like forever that we had been flying, only having had our one conversation. I didn't mind; he was my pilot and I was his passenger—purely a business relationship.

We suddenly broke through a cover of wispy, white clouds and there it was: the huge majestic formation, Ayers Rock, glowing a bright amber hue against the blue sky.

"It's beautiful," I marveled.

"I's a rock." Jack's voice contradicted my own.

"I know, but look at it. I had no idea that it would be this amazing."

"I's a rock," he said, annoyed.

I turned and scowled at him. "Can't you just appreciate God's beautiful workmanship?"

Jack scrunched his face as though he smelt something rancid. "I's a rock." He was even more annoyed than before.

"Okay, it's a rock." I said, aggravated. "I'm just saying it's beautiful."

"I've never understood whit the big deal was. I's a big mound of sandstone in the middle of nowhere." His comment was a bit glacial.

I gave up. I just shook my head and stared out the window, watching as we got closer and closer. I pulled out my camera and took pictures as the view went from amazing to incredible. And just about the time I didn't think we could get any closer without flying directly into it, Jack turned and we flew around and up over the top.

I couldn't help a girlish giggle of excitement and a smile that was one of the biggest I've had in a long time. I looked over at Jack, hoping to share my enthusiasm, but his face seemed so severe. So I just enjoyed the view on my own.

"See down there?"

He pointed to a small runway connected to a small airport, the volume of his voice reaching louder than the sound of the engine.

"Tha's where we're landin'."

"Down there," I repeated.

I was amazed by how the small airport was so close to our destination. It didn't seem normal to have an airport out in the middle of nowhere.

The corners of Jack's mouth curled up as I felt the plane descending at a pretty quick rate. My heart started to pound furiously as we started our descent. I clung to my seat and my prayers of safety rang through my head again.

5
Uluru

The plane landed smoothly, but my nerves weren't as restrained. It took me a few moments to recover.

"Well,' were here," he said as casually as if he had just dropped me off at my hotel.

We taxied in from the small runway and pulled next to other small aircrafts like his, but they all looked like they were in so much better condition. There were some that had two seats like his, some four seats. There was one, a little bit away, that looked like the same bright, shiny plane that I had mistaken for my flight back in Sydney. As we walked by I realized it was the same one. I chuckled to myself as I passed Jack, who was holding the door open to the terminal.

"Whit's so funny?" he asked.

"Nothing, personal joke."

It was much cooler in the terminal than outside I almost had to put my sweatshirt on to stop the slight shiver that rolled through my body. Even though it was fall, outside was still a little too hot and sticky.

I tossed my bag over my shoulder. "Now what?" I asked anxiously.

"I think there's a shu"le tha' will take us ta the hotel, jus' ou' front." His voice was indifferent as he pointed to the front entrance.

The next morning I woke, got dress and excitedly went down to the lobby ready to go and waited for Jack. When Jack stepped out of the elevator it didn't look like he would be going with me.

"Aren't you coming?"

"Why should I? There's nothin' tha' I want ta see." His eyes narrowed as he watched my reaction.

"So, what are you going to do while I'm gone?"

"I'll jus' stick aroun' here. I think there's a pub or somethin'."

He stood there holding his leather coat while his eyes searched for any kind of escape from my presence.

"Okay." I looked at him in dismay, than turned to leave. "Oh, Jack…, I don't think you'll be going to any pub here."

I turned back and nodded toward a vacant spot in the corner of the hotel. The empty space was covered in plastic and caution cones were spaced around just outside the perimeter. The sign that was taped to the plastic read, "Remodeling will reopen in December."

"Urrr," he groaned, "I guess I don't have a choice. Le's go."

I could see in Jack's face that he wasn't happy with the idea, but I was glad he was going with me. Even though he was just my pilot, it was nice to have someone with me. It didn't seem quite as foreign and remote.

I sat down in the seat four rows from the front and scooted over so Jack could sit down. I shouldn't have been surprised when he sat in the row in front of me and stretched out his long legs, taking up both seats, but I was. I was used to people I traveled with to sit next to me and keep me company. Then again, I usually just traveled with my family. I brushed off the annoyed feeling that came over me and just enjoyed the ride. This way of travel was always so much better.

It was about a quarter after eleven when we finally reached the Uluru-Kata Tjuta National Park cultural centre. I was amazed that there was so much to see. I had looked up Ayers Rock, or Uluru as the locals called it, online before, but just for information about this massive sandstone formation, nothing about touring around it. When I saw the cultural centre and everything it had to offer, my mouth practically hit the ground. Jack's face was still blank and indifferent when he exited the shuttle.

"Well, it looks like you can sit in a pub here and wait for me," I pointed to the bar just inside a small restaurant, "or you can come with me," I offered.

"No, thank ya, I'm goin' ta sit in here and take i' easy. Ya go ahead."

He walked over to a big cushy chair that was right inside the bar and plopped himself down, kicked his feet up, and signaled a waitress. I started to walk away, but then a thought trickled through my mind. I watched him carefully.

"You're not going to drink, are you?" The very idea made me nervous.

"I may have a pint or two. I's been a very long mornin', and I need ta git a li"le blootered." His lips curled smugly at the corners.

"Do you think that's a good idea since we have to fly back in just a few hours?"

"I'll be fine. I'm Sco"ish, remember?" He said a little arrogantly.

Just then the waitress came over and took his order. It made me nervous thinking of Jack drinking when we would be leaving so soon, but there was no way to stop him. Even if I wanted to, there was no way of winning this battle. If he got too drunk I would just have to take another flight, even if I had to use all my money.

To my great relief I heard him order a soda as I walked away and I began to relax as I realized that he was responsible and professional. Then I couldn't help a slight smile as I thought of the exchange of words between us, because I kind of liked how, in some strange way, he was teasing me.

I bought my guidebook and walking map around Uluru, and was about to follow a group outside when I heard my name, or what should have been my name, being called from Jack as he sat contentedly in his cushy chair.

"Hey Elsie…"

Jack was sitting there, his feet still propped up on the chair next to him, and a tall glass of soda in his hand.

"Don't be ta long, I said I'd brin' ya fer a few hours, bu' I need ta git back. I have a late, late date tonigh'."

He took a big gulp of his drink and laid his head back onto the back of the chair. His eyes were closed and his smile was almost wicked.

I walked around, looking at the different exhibits and artifacts of the aboriginal culture, taking my time. A group of tourists were sitting just outside the building in a half-moon circle on what looked like logs cut in half with smaller logs for legs, whispering back and forth as if they were waiting for some type of instruction.

A man wearing khaki shorts and shirt, much like Tom had been wearing, but with a park logo on it, came and sat down at the front of the circle. His wiry dark-and-white hair shot out from underneath his cowboy-like hat. His skin was dark and leathery with deep-lined wrinkles, aged from too much sun and so much wisdom.

"Palya."

He greeted everyone as he smiled; then he sat down. His smile was so big and bright it made the lines form natural long dimples on either side of his mouth.

"That is *hello* in the Anangu language. The language of my people."

He raised his hand like a choir director would to start his choir off into a song and everyone in unison sang, "*Palya!*"

"Now, this also means *good–by*, so don't say it twice or people may leave you."

The crowd chucked at his attempted humor.

"My name is Warrigal, but you can call me Fred, and I am your guide to the knowledge of the Dreamtime."

His words seemed true but scripted. This all sounded very interesting so I decided to join the group and sat down as he continued, his voice low and majestic.

"This is our story, our beginning, told to many generations," he began.

"It was the first day of time. The sun rose from the land, and the land was. Its brightness and warmth brought forth the spiritual Ancestors. The Ancestors, with the sun, crossed the land and sang the land and all creation into existence. Some Ancestors sang the plants to life and watched over them. Some, the animal, and every creature. You sometimes can hear them speak to them in the wind as their songs pass by your ears. You can almost hear them calling out their names. Others sang even the seasons, with the wind and rain and heat, to existence.

"The Ancestors decided that they should leave particles of life itself to govern the land. These were called Guruwari. They provide a link back to our Ancestors even today.

"Once the Ancestors covered the earth, they tired and returned to their beginning to sleep. And here is where they sleep until they are needed. And so ended the Dreamtime, but not the story.

"It is said that Uluru is the place were the Ancestors placed the records of the Dreamtime, and it sleeps with the Ancestors still."

As I listened intently I could see others leaning in to catch every word. I noticed I was doing the same, making sure I heard everything. I shifted slightly in my seat, and then continued to listen to the story.

"Years and years later, two spirit tribes had a plan to honor the Ancestors in ceremony and celebration, but the furthest tribe was distracted by lizard women who came to them, so they didn't show themselves at the celebration. The host tribe was offended with their disrespect to the Ancestors and a great war between the two tribes broke out. Many spirits were lost. The land mourned and formed Uluru as a mark of its grief for those who were lost, a constant reminder that there should be peace.

"After the battle, the spirits that were left counseled together and swore an oath that they would watch over the land together in harmony."

"One spirit, the most peaceful, brave, and respected, spoke up and promised that as the others would watch over the land, the plants, the animals, and the seasons, he would watch over man. For man... ," he paused and winked at a woman in the front row as if a second thought came to his mind, "and woman are our spirit brothers and sisters. And they all agreed.

"This is why our land is sacred, and why the Ancestors have asked the Elders and the Elders have asked us to ask you that as you visit Uluru and our land, you respect it. Please do not climb Uluru. Do not go into restricted areas that are marked. There are some places that are very sacred to this people.

"I would like to thank you for your time with me. To hear our stories and our history, again my name is Fred I will be here if you have any questions and would be happy to answer them. Palya." He got up and waved.

Everyone answered in one chorus, "Palya."

I couldn't help myself; I was so into the story I was almost entranced by it and I had to join the chorus.

Everyone got up at their own pace and went their different ways. Some thanked our storyteller as they passed him, some stopped to ask him questions about his story, and other questions about the culture. I could see the start of a path past the visitors who were talking to Fred. I picked up my guidebook and map and looked up my starting point. Liru Walk; that's where I needed to go.

I didn't notice the different visitors spaced here and there, coming and going as I started down the trail, each of them talking to one another. I was just enjoying the walk, looking for different plant and animal species, when I almost ran right into a group of tourists that were stopped in the middle of the trail. Their guide was explaining the difference between two types of plants.

"I'm sorry," my head rose from looking down at my book, "I wasn't paying attention."

"That's okay," the guide said.

As I passed them I thought I heard a few snickers and comments. But one comment caught my attention.

"I'd hate to be out here by myself."

The words were simple enough, but they had so much weight to them. I looked back at the group as I continued down the path and it hit me—two by two or three or more, some in groups. Every person that passed me was with someone, and I was alone. In one tiny moment the weight of all that was wrong with me seemed to pull me downward, as though gravity had a hold on me and wasn't going to let go. I was alone. It wasn't that I didn't have someone by my side walking next to me. Inside I felt completely and utterly alone. Something was going on and I didn't know what and I couldn't explain it. Whatever it was, I was alone to face it. I froze where I was.

"*What am I doing here?!*" the words were screaming in my head.

Panic started to leak into my mind and I started to hyperventilate. Why was I so panicky all of the sudden? This had been a great trip so far! Just then, as if from nowhere, a small aboriginal woman with short, curly, gray hair, a floral shirt, and red knee-length shorts passed by during my little episode, and even though I didn't understand her words, I understood her kindness. I figured that she saw that I seemed out of breath from the hike, even if it was really due to my hyperventilation.

She murmured a few words to me that I didn't understand, walked me over to a large rock, and sat me down. I smiled at her graciously and she smiled back. She pulled out a bottle of water that she had in her bag and offered me a drink. I didn't really think I needed it, but I didn't want to offend her, so I took it.

She tenderly stroked my hair as she spoke again what seemed like directions on how to get back or where to go, pointing to me, then to the trail, then to me again. Didn't she know the trail all goes to the same place?

Still not understanding her, all I could do was smile. She placed her soft, wrinkled hand on the side of my face and spoke again, wistfully pointing outward to the nothingness in front of me and smiled. I gave her back her water and she gave me another reassuring smile; then she walked away; leaving me to myself. I watched her walk to the bend in the trail, where she turned and waved. I waved back, and with one last sweet smile, she went around the bend and was gone.

"What a sweet woman," I thought.

I was so preoccupied with the woman's care that all my panic had disappeared. I was able to think clearly again. I sat on the rock, looking out into the never-ending desert, just thinking about my life. Why was I so unhappy? I thought back to my last day at work, the day that was the last straw on my camel's back. I suddenly remembered the whole conversation I had with Mr. Bryant.

"Ally, can you come into my office?"

I walked in and turned in time to see the door shutting behind me. I sat down in the chair directly across from the chair he sat in at his desk. He was quiet as he sat down and looked at me. Then he began.

48

"Ally, you know I like you. You've been a great asset to this company," I nodded slightly, "but I've noticed a change in you lately. You've been coming in late, your production level has gone down, and you're making major mistakes on your work. Is there something going on? I would really like to help if I could."

"No sir, not that I'm aware of. I've just had some things on my mind."

"Is it something serious with your family?" he asked with concern in his voice. "How's your mom's health doing?"

"She's fine."

"Look, Ally, I'm trying to help you out here. I'm a pretty good judge of character, and I know you're not the type to slack off like this. But I need a good reason why this is happening; medical, family, anything, or I'm going to have to let you go. We just can't afford to waste time correcting your mistakes."

"I'm sorry, Mr. Bryant, I don't know what to tell you." My voice sounded empty and hollow.

He looked down at his desk and sighed, "Then I'm sorry, Ally, I'm going to have to let you go." He grimaced as he said the words.

I got up from my chair and headed toward the door.

"Ally?"

His voice stopped me and I turned to look at him.

"I do think you're a good worker and a good person. When you get things figured out, come back and see me and I'll see what I can do."

I just nodded. All I wanted to do was get out of his office, out of the building before the feelings of repulsion and failure overcame me and the tears started.

The memory of that day brought everything back, the same sense of being a failure. But I wasn't lying to him; I truly didn't know why I was the way I was. That's why I was here, to figure out who I am. I needed to find that lost part of me, that part that made me happy, truly happy again.

I crossed my arms in front of me, trying to hold myself together, when I realized the weather was starting to cool off. The wind was picking up and sand was blowing into my face. Automatically I covered my eyes to shield them from the wind, and without even realizing it, my emotions overcame me. Tears streamed down each cheek.

I sat there trying to regain my composure when I thought I heard my name being called. It was faint and the wind was whipping past me so I brushed it off. I could hear the sound of the aboriginal performers as they sang and played their instruments for the tourists. I figured it was probably time for me to keep going. I looked at my watch to see how much time I had left, and to my surprise it was so much later than I had thought.

"Crap." I winced as I thought of Jack. "He's going to be so mad."

"Ally!"

This time I was sure I heard my name and the anger behind it. Jack was bounding up the trail toward me. His lips were in a straight line, his jaw clenched.

"D'ya know whit time i' is? I told ya not ta take too long! We need ta git back."

"I'm sorry, I lost track of the time."

"Whit were ye doin'?" he asked.

"Just thinking."

"Thinkin'?" Anger still filled his voice. "The place is closing. I had ta come ou' here lookin' fer ya, and you're just ou' here thinkin'. Le's go." He turned and started walking away. "Hopefully we don't miss the last shu"le," he grumbled under his breath.

"I said I was sorry, what else do you want me to say? And it can't be closing, they are still having performances."

Anger was now starting to enter my voice. He was taking things way out of proportion. I started walking behind him, trying to keep up with his long strides.

"Whit are ya talkin' abou'? The only performance they had was the storyteller."

"I heard the singing," I said, confused.

"I don't know whit ya heard, bu' there was no singin' or music anything while we've been here."

I slowed my pace, trying to make sense of what he was saying and what I heard. Lost in my thoughts, I suddenly remembered I had to get gifts for my family.

"Oh, I just need to stop by the gift shop before we leave."

He stopped dead in his tracks. "Wit?" he glared at me through narrow eyes.

"I just need to stop by the gift shop. I want to take home some souvenirs." My words came out a little shaky.

"Ya had plen'y of time ta do that earlier. If ya wouldn' have spent all yer time thinkin' ya could have go"en all the souvenirs ya wanted. If ya think I'm goin' ta was'e anymore time waitin' fer ya, ya have another thin' comin'. I don't care if ya are payin' me. I told ya I had a deadline ta make."

"Deadline." I grumbled under my breath.

"Now, le's go."

He started rushing back up the trail again, not even waiting for me to take one step. I was angry myself. He was being so unreasonable. I just needed a few seconds to get a couple of things. After all, when was I ever going to make it back?

"Fine," I huffed, "if I can't purchase a souvenir, I'll take a natural one." I bent down, searching, and picked up a bunch of different sizes of rocks from the ground.

"Whit are ya doin'?"

His voice was suddenly behind me. I jumped and turned to face him.

"I thought since I can't get to the gift shop I would take a few rocks from here home with me."

"Ye're not gittin' on my plane with those."

"Why?" I asked, confused.

"You're not suppose ta take anythin' from here."

"It's a rock," I said, slightly smirking, echoing his words from earlier.

"The legends say tha' if ya take a piece of the land i' can bring ya bad luck. Didn't ya read the guidebook?"

I cocked my head slightly and looked up at him, amazed that he was so superstitious.

"It's a rock."

"I don't care, yer not gittin' on my plane with those."

"Okay, okay."

I turned my hand, palm down, and watched as each rock fell and hit the ground.

Bareley making the last shuttle, we got back to the airport in what seemed quicker time than when we left and hurried over to the plane. Once again the engine sputtered and coughed as it tried to start. My nerves were already tightening from the anxiety.

"Maybe we should wait 'til morning and have someone look at it," I suggested.

"She's fine, i' jus' takes a few times," Jack sneered, annoyed by my suggestion.

Just then a drop hit the front window, then a few more.

"Great," Jack moaned, still trying to get the engine to turn over. "come on, girl, ya can do i'. Come on."

Still nothing. As his fingers started to tune white from twisting the key so hard, I thought for sure it would break off in the ignition.

"Urrrrr."

Exasperated, Jack hit the control stick as a few very descriptive words spilled out of his mouth. His reactions to his dead plane made me nervous, he was so angry. Just then a downpour of a million drops of water fell from the sky. Jack chuckled slightly under his breath. By his chuckle I knew he'd given up the fight and that we weren't flying anywhere tonight. I sighed quietly, relieved that we weren't going to try and outrun the storm.

"Well, le's go."

Jack once again sounded annoyed with me. It wasn't my fault the plane didn't start or it started to rain. It was really starting to get on my nerves.

"Where?" I asked.

"Back ta the hotel."

Outside the rain was falling so hard that it formed a sheer gray curtain everywhere you looked. I pulled out my umbrella from my overly prepared backpack and opened it. I offered cover to Jack but he declined. He was soaked in a matter of seconds.

I couldn't help noticing how the downpour made his relatively loose shirt cling so deliberately against his whole torso, outlining every aspect of his perfect frame. His hair turned to dark curls as the water dripped down his cheek and off his amazing long lashes, which seemed to enhance the blue of his eyes more than ever.

I wished that my eyes were just as stunning. Maybe if my eyes were that beautiful someone wouldn't be able to stop staring at me like I suddenly realized I was doing to him. I turned quickly before he could notice and see my facial color turn bright red.

We finally hailed a taxi; well, a taxi wannabe. Jack instructed the driver where to take us so casually, it made me curious. He obviously had been here before, but how many times? He seemed to know exactly where to go. That would explain the lack of interest with the scenery.

"You've been here before?" I asked, hoping for answers.

"Yeah, jus' a time or two… I'm such an idiot, what time is i'?" he asked suddenly.

"5:05," I answered, looking at my watch.

He didn't say anything else. He reached in his pocket and pulled out his cell phone and started looking for a number frantically.

"Hey, luv," his tone was trying to sound cool and confident.

"Hey."

With one word a female voice oozed out of the small receiver, smooth and sultry. I couldn't help but sit there a little nauseated listening—she was amazingly loud.

"I've been thinking of you and can't wait 'til tonight. I have everything ready."

"Did he just call a nine-hundred number?" I wondered, cringing at the thought.

"I hate ta tell ya this luv, bu' I'm goin' ta have ta cancel our date tonigh'."

"Why?"

The female's voice suddenly turned hard and shrill. Jack's face cringed as though he knew what was next.

"I know, luv, I'm stuck here a' the Rock and I can't git back 'til tomorrow."

His smooth talk seemed to sooth her attitude and she responded in that calm and sultry voice again.

"I'll miss you tonight. Don't be bad," she oozed again.

"Believe me, tha' won't happen." He paused.

Even though I was looking out the window I might as well have been looking straight at him. I could tell his pause was a glare toward me.

"I'll explain tomorrow."

Her light chuckle flowed out the phone like an amusing ring.

"All right, babe, see you tomorrow."

"Bye, luv."

Jack hung up the phone and placed it back into his pocket. I was relieved that the syrupy exchange was finally over. It made me uncomfortable listening to such a intimate exchange.

When I finally got to my room I was exhausted. It had been a very long two days with the flight and my walk around Uluru, not to mention all the emotional ups and downs throughout the whole day. It was hard to believe it was only a little after six. I flopped onto my bed, my eyes already closed. I was already falling asleep when I heard a knock at my door. I groaned as I pushed myself off the bed and answered the door. Jack was standing there already changed, his hair practically dried. He stood there in the doorway looking very uncomfortable.

"I was wondering if ye wanted ta git somethin' ta eat?" He didn't smile but his face wasn't in the scowl that I'd seen most the day.

Surprised, by his invitation, I wasn't quite sure what to say.

"Um, sure."

I didn't realize until then that I hadn't eaten all day. I guess too much was going on to think about food, which for me was unusual, but now that the idea was in my head I was starting to get hungry.

I woke up the next morning feeling so emotionally and physically depleted I could hardly get out of bed. My mind was whirling around the sleepless night I had after a pretty quiet dinner.

I had thought that Jack and I might get a chance to get to know each other better over dinner, but he was determined to keep our relationship purely business, only engaging in polite small talk about the weather, while lighting up one cigarette after another and downing pints of beer in the same fashion. He was right though; they didn't seem to have any effect on him.

After our uneventful meal, I was stunned, when before I even had my money out to pay my potion of the check; Jack took it and paid for the whole dinner. Afterwards we quietly walked back to our rooms. Jack passed his and continued to mine.

"Well," he paused, as if he wasn't sure what to say next."Thanks fer the company."

"You're welcome, I was hungry anyway" I smiled, and couldn't help wondering. "Is he actually being nice to me?"

He looked at me awkwardly and than patted my shoulder. "Sleep well."

As I watched him walked back to his room, I wasn't quite sure what to make of his actions, but thrilled his attitude had shifted. Then he stopped and turned.

"I want ta git off early in the mornin', le's not have a repeat of today, okay."

I sighed, opened the door, and went inside.

When I finally got to bed and tried to sleep my dreams kept me up and were now bothering me. I couldn't remember everything that went on in them they changed so often. I would constantly wake, startled, catching my breath, and as soon as I would wake up the images would disappear from my mind. Then, just when I would start falling into that deep restful sleep again, I would suddenly wake up, my heart racing, and then my thoughts would be clear once more. All night this went on until the phone rang with my wake-up call.

I met Jack downstairs in the lobby. He seemed refreshed and excited to get going. I on the other hand, dragged and just wanted to go back to bed. It seemed our attitudes had strangely switched.

We caught another taxi back to the small airport and I wondered if the small plane was even going to start up again. My mind settled on this thought as I leaned on the window and closed my eyes. I put my sunglasses on, trying to block out any of the bright morning sunlight that seem to stream right across my face. It didn't seem to take long before I felt my head starting to slip downward against the window. I automatically popped my head up and self-consciously looked over at Jack, wondering if he saw as I wiped a thin line of saliva that had trickled out from the corner of my mouth inconspicuously with my fingertips just as we pulled up to the airport.

We walked through the small terminal over to where Jack had to sign something to leave. I looked around at the new visitors coming and a few people leaving and suddenly saw a familiar face, even though I had only seen her once. The little gray-haired women who was so kind to me on the trail. She was wearing another bright floral shirt but with bright-blue shorts this time. I wanted to go over and say hi but I didn't want Jack to get upset; he was in such a good mood I didn't want to ruin it. Besides; what could I actually say? She couldn't understand me anyway. I had to just settle for a friendly wave and smile.

While I waited for Jack to finish I kept glancing over, hoping to catch her eye so I could deliver my friendly greeting. Jack was finished and we were just about to head out the door when she looked over. I was so excited that I was able to give her a small gesture of my gratitude from yesterday that my smile was so wide my cheeks hurt. She smiled back and I waved; she nodded in acknowledgment.

"Whit are ye doin'?" Jack asked.

I turned and looked up at him, my eyes still smiling.

"Waving at this sweet lady that helped me out yesterday when I was on the trail. She thought I needed a drink of water."

I didn't want to get into the whole story about hyperventilating and everything.

"Whit lady?" he looked around, trying to see her.

"The older aboriginal woman in the floral shirt and blue shorts." I turned back around so I could point her out to him but she had left. "Well, she was over there," I murmured.

He looked at me cynically, raising his eyebrows, a slight condescending smirk across lips. Then he turned and walked out to the plane.

The plane started up with no problem. It didn't sputter, it didn't cough, it didn't even roar. It just purred. I almost thought that we were in the wrong plane. Jack was almost beside himself that he didn't have to replace anything.

"See, I knew she'd be alrigh'. Ye jus' needed a break, didn't ya?" He almost seemed childish the way he patted and spoke to his plane as if he was speaking to a pet.

We took off with no problem, smooth and easy, much easier then before. I looked back at Uluru as we flew past, its radiant ginger red glowing in the sun, and marveled once again at its beauty.

"Just a rock." I scoffed at Jack's words from yesterday.

I leaned to the side and rested my head on the window and put my sunglasses on. My eyes were getting heavy again.

I yawned. "Man, I don't know why I'm so tired, I must still be going though jet lag or something," I said yawning again.

"Go ta sleep then," Jack suggested. "There's no worries."

It was probably Jack's subtle way of getting out of having to keep up any kind of conversation.

"I'm fine," I yawned once again.

I tried to keep my eyes open but they just got too heavy. My mind started swirling around all my different thoughts, my family, losing my job, my trip here, and the practical joke that Tom had played on Jack. I thought about the trail and the little gray-haired woman.

"What did she say to me?" I wondered.

Then there were the dreams that I couldn't remember. Why did they keep waking me up?

I was almost completely gone in my own lethargic state of mind when I felt a jerk in the plane. My eyes popped open and I grabbed onto the cushion beneath me as adrenalin rushed through my body, wakening me as though I had been asleep for hours. I looked over at Jack, who was still calm and relaxed: to him this was nothing.

"Relax, I's jus' an air pocket, nothin' ta git excited abou'," he tried to assure me.

Then the small plane jerked again but harder and lights on the instrument panel started to flash.

"Whit the…, whit's goin on here?"

Jack's voice changed from casual to concern. The fears that I had felt so many times in the last few days were nothing compared to this. My heart beating fast and hard, it took every part of me to keep breathing as I grabbed Jack's arm. He turned to me when he felt my grasp and tried to give me an encouraging smile, but there was a lack of confidence that wasn't there before. Even when the plane had a hard time starting, he always seemed self-assured and cocky; now he was worried.

"Jack, what's wrong? What's happening?"

He just kept hitting and pushing buttons on the instrument panel.

"Come on…," Frustration in his words.

"Jack, what's going on? This isn't funny."

"D'ye see me laughin'? Of course this isn't funny." He glared at me angrily.

It wasn't a very bright thing for me to say; I could understand the tone. It's just when I get nervous or scared I don't think straight.

"Mayday, mayday, this is six-zero-seven tango callin' fer assistance. We're abou' an hour and a half ou'side of Connellan Airport and have lost engine power. Mayday, come in… anyone, mayday."

Jack ripped his headset off his head, looked downward in front of him, then out his side window.

"Ye're religious, righ'? If I were ya I'd start prayin'. We're goin' ta have ta make an emergency landing" Jack's urgent tone cut into my panic like a hot knife.

"What?" I screeched.

"See down there?" he said, pointing out the side.

"Yeah."

"Tha's where we're goin' ta land."

"There!"

I started to hyperventilate and then held my breath as the plane quickly descended, swaying side to side toward the ground. I squeezed my eyes shut as the plane quickly drew closer to what was beneath us.

"Please get us down safely, please don't let us die, please keep us safe."

I kept repeating my prayer over and over out loud. I didn't care what Jack thought. All I cared about was asking for safety.

The plane seemed to bounce a few times touching down here and there as it skimmed barely above the ground. We finally hit hard, still moving forward, when there was a loud crack and a bang that seemed to hit the underneath of the plane. Jack continued pulling back hard on the brake, trying to put enough force behind it to stop us from moving. The sound of twisted metal scraping against the hard, rocky terrain reverberated in my ears. Then the plane abruptly dipped forward and I could feel the front of the plane plow into the ground. I braced myself, my arms stretched out in front of me. Then suddenly I felt weightless and disoriented, moving in strange directions, then nothing.

6

Intuition
❋❋

Bright blue numbers glowed 8:05 p.m. on the DVD player as we all sat around Aunt Dorothy's living room watching Ryan's and Miles's favorite movie. I glanced up at a picture of Ally, annoyed.

"How could she go to Australia without even telling me she was leaving?" I grumbled quietly.

Suddenly the low in the action of the movie was broken by a loud crash in the kitchen. I turned just in time to see the glass shards of a soapy floral plate stream across the kitchen floor. Dorothy was still, her body rigid and stiff as if she'd turned to stone. Her face was pale, her eyes wide, staring blankly out the window.

Terror flowed through me as I thought, "Oh no, she's having a heart attack."

We have all been very watchful over Dorothy the past year since she had her heart surgery, never taking any chances.

"Aunt Dorothy?" I called anxiously.

I laid Amy, who had fallen asleep on my lap during the first of the DVDs we were watching, on the couch next to me and rushed into the kitchen.

"Aunt Dorothy, are you okay?"

There was no response. I tugged at her arm to get any reaction. "Hey."

Then she whispered, trying to get her words out. "I have this terrible feeling that something has happened to Ally."

"What?" I was confused, trying to figure out what she meant.

She didn't respond; she just grabbed the phone off the holder and started dialing, constantly looking at a number on the corkboard next to the phone. I could see the stress in her eyes, which wasn't good for her heart, so I needed to keep her calm.

"I'm sure everything is fine. You don't need to get upset."

But she wasn't paying any attention to me. I could hear a polite voice coming from the other end of the phone.

"Yes, I'd like Ally Pierson's room, please?" I could hear the phone ring through the receiver—over and over.

Dorothy's face was strained as she hung up the phone.

"Well?" I asked, already knowing the answer.

"There was no answer." Concern and worry entangled in each word she spoke.

"She probably just went out for the day and is having fun."

I was trying to seem casual and relaxed. I knew Ally; she would take every opportunity she had to see what she could. She'd get busy doing something and lose all track of time.

Dorothy was still trying to get a grasp on the uneasy feeling she had as she slumped down into a chair at the table, not paying any attention to the glass that was still stretched across the kitchen floor. I grabbed the broom and dustpan that was lazily resting against the wall next to the washer and started sweeping up the glass fragments.

After a long pause Dorothy blurted, "No," answering my remark moments earlier, "something is wrong. I can't explain it, I just know it. Maybe it's mother intuition."

She sat there concentrating. "Maybe I can get her on her cell phone."

She grabbed the phone off the holder again and frantically pushed the buttons. Her fingers were so shaky that she could barley even dial.

"I don't think you can reach her on her cell while she is overseas," I said, trying hard not sound pessimistic.

I knew the reality of cell phones, how unpredictable they were, and I didn't want Dorothy more upset then she already was. But I also knew my aunt; it didn't matter what I said, she would still try.

"When Troy was over in Japan on business he called us a few times on his cell phone" she reasoned.

"I think he had a much better phone with a better package deal that allowed him to call overseas," I explained in return, trying to be understanding. "Ally's phone has a hard time connecting across town."

After a minute or so—frustrated and anxious—Dorothy put the phone down on the table harder than she had meant to. The noise caught the attention of Ryan and Miles. Still engrossed with the movie, they looked up for just for a second, then continued watching.

She sat back down at the table, her hands folded in front of her, and then she thoughtfully rested them under her chin. It seemed as though tears were about to fill her eyes, but she just sat there, motionless. It seemed as though she didn't know what to feel or how to react since there wasn't a sure sign that there was anything wrong.

I sat next to her, my arms around her frail shoulders.

"You know Ally; she'll probably call you as soon as she gets back. She'll want to tell you everything," I said, trying to comfort her.

Ally likes to keep in touch with Dorothy, especially now that Dorothy's health wasn't at its best.

"Just hope she doesn't get confused with the time change. Remember when she was in Australia before? She accidently called you at four a.m."

I chuckled at the memory. Dorothy also smiled, the tension easing from her soft face.

"Well, she did get the time off just a little when she called yesterday. She called around one o'clock in the morning. Scared me to death. I hate when there's a call that late or that early."

"Wait," I said, my voice surprised. "She called you yesterday?"

I was starting to feel that annoyance again.

"First she took off on this spur-of-the-moment trip without saying one word to me, and now this. Is she that upset at me?"

"I think the reason she called us and she didn't call you, *yet*," She emphasized *yet*, "is the time difference and she didn't want to wake the kids."

I looked over at the boys as they quietly watched their movie.

I sighed slightly. "The last time I saw her I could tell she was upset. I saw the box filled with her desk things and I could guess what had happened. But before I had a chance to get anything out of her I had to take the boys to karate. Then when I came over the other day to talk, she was already gone."

I felt a nagging tug at my stomach as I thought of how Ally needed to talk to someone that day and I didn't have time, and I couldn't help but wonder if my actions might have influenced her decision.

"I should have called her the next day," I muttered regretfully.

We both sat there at the table quietly, while the sound of the kids DVD boomed in the background. I thought it would be as good a time as any to find out some of the questions that started rolling around in my head.

"I have a question." The words seemed direct and persistent. Dorothy just nodded. "Why did Ally go on this trip?"

"I honestly don't have the faintest idea. When she got fired the other day she said she just had to get away from everything; be by herself to figure things out."

"But clear to Australia?" My voice became a bit cynical as I shook my head in disbelief.

"How did she pay for it?" I asked curiously.

"Well, she had some money saved up and she used that."

Dorothy seemed to be more herself again, going back to the sink, the soapy water now cold and sudless. She turned the hot water on to warm up what was in the sink and finish what she started.

"I love Ally," I continued, "but that's just so irresponsible. She should've used that money for her bills. After all, she's unemployed now. What is she going to do when she gets home? I can't believe she could be so irresponsible."

The irritation I felt crept through my body, touching each nerve with anger creeping up beside it. The more I thought about it the more it bothered me. Dorothy broke the flow of the irritation that seemed to be infiltrating into my whole being.

"I tried to talk her out of it and told her it didn't make sense to waste her money when she didn't have any income coming in. She just kept saying she had to get away and find herself again. We went back and forth for hours. But you know Ally, once she makes up her mind…."

"There's no changing it." Finishing Dorothy's thought.

I sat there thinking about Ally's abrupt decision to go on her trip. What did she mean, find herself again? Was there something I was missing? She seemed fine to me. Whenever we get together all we do is laugh and joke. It couldn't all be some kind of a ruse for my benefit. Those snorts of laughter were real.

"Why does it still aggravate me?" I thought. "Is it because she left on such a stupid whim?"

Then, as if someone shouted in my head, a sharp realization came to me. It wasn't that she left; it was that she left without confiding in me. She told me everything,

everything but this. It made me uneasy and empty. My eyes started to sting as I found myself suddenly staring at the table, concentrating on the light design of the wood.

"Mom?"

Miles broke my concentration. I didn't even notice that he had walked over and was standing by my side. I jumped when he tapped me on my shoulder.

"The movie is over."

"Okay, I'll be there in just a second," I finally responded as I rubbed his arm lightly. "Well, I better go and get the kids to bed."

I got up and headed toward the living room, taking a moment to turn to Dorothy. "Are we still on for tomorrow?"

"Of course!" She smiled. "What time?"

"I'm not sure. I'll call in the morning. Come on, boys."

Both boys chimed in at the same time, high-pitched and whiny. "We wanted to watch another movie."

"You can watch another movie tomorrow. Now let's go!" My tone was firm with authority.

I bent over Amy and jostled her just a bit to get her to sit up.

"Come on, sweetie, let's go home."

I picked her up and lifted her to my chest. Her body felt limp while her legs and arms fastened around me and she rested her head on my shoulder, closing her eyes again.

We all walked out to the van and the boys took their designated spots as the seat belts clicked in harmony. I put Amy in her car seat and fastened her in as well and then turned to give Dorothy a hug good-bye.

"All right, we're all set. Have a good night. Don't worry, she's fine." I managed to squeeze out a bit of optimism in my words.

I hugged her again and got in the van. The boys were quiet, already starting to fall asleep. I slowly started backing up. By the time I got to the end of the driveway and straightened up, Dorothy was already at the door waving good-bye. And even though it was dark I could still make out the worry and concern as it crept back into her face. The idea of leaving her alone made me uneasy. If I didn't know that Gina and Megan were going to be home soon I might have stayed. I waved to her one last time and headed down the poorly lit street.

The drive home seemed to be a long one, a lot longer than usual. As I drove I thought of Ally and her sudden decision to take a trip clear across the world.

"Ally, what are you doing?" I mumbled.

I couldn't figure it out. Out of all the places to go, why there? What was there that she couldn't get here? I knew she had been there before, but she never really said anything about ever really wanting to go back. She liked to travel, but she didn't like to fly or do much on her own. This seemed totally out of character for her.

I pulled into our driveway and woke Ryan and Miles up, then pulled Amy out from her car seat as she wrapped herself around me again. I helped maneuver the boys safely into the house and to their room, then laid Amy on her bed and managed to get her pajamas on. Her forehead felt cool to the touch as I bent down and gently kissed her while she yawned then automatically rolled to her side.

The boys, only halfway in their beds and half-changed, were already fast asleep. I rearranged the body parts that were hanging off the sides of the almost too-small beds and pulled the covers over their shoulders, and gave them a kiss on the forehead as well. I went back into the living room and practically collapsed on the couch.

My mind was racing with the conversation with Dorothy. I couldn't get the image of Ally out of my thoughts. An unsettling feeling of guilt kept coming back. If I had just put the boys karate class off a few extra moments, if I would have remembered to call her later that night or even the very next day, would that have helped? Would whatever was bothering her have been resolved? Or would she have gone anyway?

I sighed and looked at the clock. The image of Ally touring around Sydney made me grin a little, even though I still thought she was rash to leave like she did. I pulled my legs onto the couch and stretched my body the whole length of it. I smiled again as I stared out the window on the other side of the room as the image of Ally returned.

"I wonder what she's doing right now."

7

Endurance
※※

The sound of screeching twisted metal continued to echo in my throbbing head.

"Am I dead?" I wondered.

I slowly opened my eyes and looked around me. Everything was so distorted; I shook my head trying to make out what was going on and what was happening. When my mind cleared I realized that everything was upside down—the bushes, the landscape. The ground was the sky and the sky the ground. Then it hit me, I was the one upside down. During its rough landing the small plane had somehow managed to somersault itself until it was resting on its top. Once I comprehended that I was okay, I instantly thought about Jack. He was just as quiet as I was. Then I heard a soft moan. I looked over and he was moving.

"He's alive." A sigh of relief came out silently.

"Are ya okay?" Jack asked.

His voice sounded calm but concerned.

"Yeah, I'm fine, just banged up a bit, but I'll live. You?"

"I'm okay."

In one easy motion Jack unlocked his seat belt and rolled out of the plane. It was like watching acrobats from some kind of circus. He was so smooth and fluid, it looked easy. I just had to follow his lead and I would be out in a flash. But when I tried to undo my seat belt it wouldn't unlatch. I tried a few times but nothing. It was getting very frustrating; I didn't want to have to ask Jack for his help; I was use to getting out of things on my own. I didn't need a man to help me. After a couple of minutes I didn't have a choice. I was getting a little dizzy with all the blood rushing to my head.

"Jack," I called, "can you help me?"

"Can't git ou'?" he said, opening my door, his tone a bit smug and a little condescending.

"No, I wanted to get your opinion on how my hair looks in this position."

My hair was hanging straight down, curls shooting everywhere, but I wasn't going to let him get away with his attitude.

"Of course I need help."

He raised one eyebrow and slightly glared at me, so I thought I better change my approach if I was going to get his help. He could just leave me there all day if he wanted to.

"The stupid seat belt won't unlatch." My tone now was soft and humble.

He played with the latch for a few minutes and then all of the sudden I was free. I tumbled out of my seat and right into Jack's arms as we both fell to the ground. It took us just a few seconds to recover, then Jack stood up quickly, brushed himself off, and extended his hand. I grabbed it automatically. Suddenly he pulled me up so briskly that he overcompensated and I practically flew onto my feet and right into his chest, my free hand softening the impact. I paused for a moment to regain my footing.

"Thank you."

I looked up into his eyes, mesmerized, my hand still resting on his chest.

"Uh, ye're welcome."

His voice sounded uncomfortable as he stepped back and I realized that I was still touching him. Embarrassed, I moved my hand quickly and stepped back too. As my arm dropped to my side I felt a small twinge of pain, and a small stream of blood was starting to dry from my forearm to hand.

"So now what?" I asked nonchalantly, trying to act as if I didn't just stand there caressing some man's chest.

Jack pulled out his cell phone and tried to get any kind of connection.

"No reception," he murmured.

He slapped his phone shut and shoved it back into his pocket and pulled out his cigarettes. I heard him grumble something under his breath as he lit up, so low I couldn't quite make it out.

He looked around and inhaled a deep breath of smoke. His eyes narrowed on the distance around us. I could see in his face that he was trying to figure out where we were. To me everything looked the same. How could he tell?

"I guess we start walkin'."

"Walking, are you serious?" I almost chuckled at the thought.

Jack's expression turned serious. "I figure we're only abou' a one or two days' walk ta the nearest town. We'll have ta sleep ou' here fer a couple of nigh's, bu' i' won't kill us."

His serious expression started to change to a more impish grin. "Ya did want ta go campin' under the stars if I recall."

"Not like this," I said, slightly horrified. "Wait a minute, how did you know about that?"

"Tom."

"Oh, right."

That did make sense; I had told Tom about how I wanted to go on the three-day campout. I had forgotten that he had probably mentioned this to Jack when he made the deal with him. Or should I say when he planned his joke.

"Why can't we just stay here?" I could hear that I was sounding a bit whiney, so I tried to give a good reason for my question. "Somebody should start looking for us, shouldn't they? The airport knows your flight plan, so when you don't show up they'll know something went wrong and they'll probably send out a search party for us, right?"

"Aye...," He looked away from me, trying to avoid my gaze. "They will start lookin' for us, bu' they may not know exactly where ta look."

My voice started to sound anxious. "What are you talking about?"

"Ye see, sometimes ya may have ta alter yer course a bit because wind, the weather, differen' things. I's not always jus' a straight line from here ta there. And ye're only on the radar while ye're near an airport." He paused, then continued. "So le's say, yer instruments aren't the bes' and give ya some trouble, maybe the wrong readings. Ya might git off course jus' a wee bit."

"*What?*" I shrieked.

Jack shrugged his shoulders casually as if this kind of thing happened all the time. I couldn't help the rage that started to build inside me. I started to rub my forehead, trying to control my reaction. I wanted to go off on him.

"So let me see if I understand you correctly. You're telling me that we may not be found because your instruments may not be the best? And you flew clear to Ayers Rock knowing that your instruments were bad? Knowing we could get lost, knowing we could crash and we could die? And you still flew?"

With every word I spoke my voice went up an octave and became more shrill. I felt as though I was starting to lose it and I began feeling a little dizzy again.

"I didn' think we'd die, just maybe crash," he joked as I glared at him. "Besides, I needed the money."

"Let me guess, to get your plane fixed?!" The tone in my voice was hard and sarcastic.

"Look, I fly this rou'e all the time I could da i' blindfolded."

"Apparently you do."

"As I was saying, I have never had any kind of problem before. This was somethin' else, not the instruments."

"But you don't know where we are?"

"I have an idea, bu' ye're right. I don't know exactly were we are. Bu' I da know which direction we should go."

I didn't know what else to say; what was done was done. We were out in the middle of nowhere and I couldn't do anything about it. I crossed my arms and leaned up against the plane, holding in what anger I still had bottled up. I felt a little childish like I was throwing a temper tantrum, but I didn't care; I was too upset. But it wasn't just angry I was feeling. There were so many different emotions that were floating to the surface. I was scared and homesickness kicked in, and I was a little nervous about being out in the middle of nowhere with a complete stranger. At least I knew nothing would happen with that idea. He already showed his total lack of interest in that category.

Jack appraised me for just a moment, then said with the same firm voice. "Well, like I said, we're probably only abou' two, maybe three days from the closes' town. I's probably quicker than a search par'y will find us. We should head ou'."

I stayed leaning on the tail end of the upside-down plane, not wanting to give into Jack's reasoning. I just wanted to stay were I felt safe. But how safe was it really? Anywhere out here seemed dangerous. He made such a good argument though it made me feel a little better. I was almost hopeful that we would be okay.

It was odd how the fear I once had to get on and even see this small plane seemed to be all but forgotten, and now it was the only thing that made me feel safe. I didn't want to face the fear of leaving it behind. Reluctantly I peeled myself away from the security of the plane and started to follow Jack.

"Wait," I said suddenly.

I realized my backpack was still stored behind the seat I had sat in. I anxiously rushed over and grabbed it. I must have jolted Jack's memory, because he was right behind me grabbing his leather jacket that he had stuffed back in the same small space.

I placed my bag on the tail end of the plane and started rummaging through it, looking for the small first-aid kit that I packed.

"Being overly prepared pays off," I thought.

I pulled out the umbrella that I used the night before and my wallet and set them next to my bag. Then I pulled out the sunscreen, squirted a dab in my palm, and applied a thin layer all over my face. I looked at Jack, his head slightly cocked to the side, his eyes scrutinizing my every move.

"What? I don't want to burn."

Jack just shook his head.

I reached into the bag and started pulling out one thing after another. I didn't realize when I packed that I had brought so much stuff. Finally, after almost everything was out of my bag, I found my little white box stuffed with the very bare essentials for your typical minor emergencies. I pulled out a band-aid and ripped it out of its wrapper and secured it tightly to my skin, and then handed one to Jack. During our conversation I had noticed that he had received his own cut. He had a nice gash on his forehead. The blood had trickled down the side of his face like thick red sweat along his hairline.

"You have a cut right…." I said, pointing to the gash on his head.

"Thanks."

He took the band-aid from me and placed it over his cut, then curiously watched me as I started to put all my stuff back into my pack. Suddenly he reached over and snatched a small leather-bound book. The book was blue leather with an elongated front that had a snap to keep it closed. *Allison Pierson* was embossed in silver lettering on the cover.

"Whit's this?" he said with a scowl.

"My scriptures; you know, the Bible." I didn't think he would have ever read it, but the probability of him at least hearing the word *bible* was pretty good.

"Great." His voice was sarcastic as he rolled his eyes. "Jus' don't be preaching ta me the whole time. I'm not a religious person and I'm not in the mood."

"I won't.," He glared at me, then handed me back my scriptures. "Not the whole time," I chuckled under my breath.

I didn't think he heard me, but he stiffened up for just a moment, then relaxed. I somehow got everything back into my pack and zipped it up. I flung it over one shoulder and then slipped it over the other.

"Okay, I'm ready. Let's go."

Jack looked at me, his face confused by my sudden enthusiasm. I was a pretty good liar when I wanted to be. I wasn't so much trying to lie to Jack as to myself. If I could keep up this front it would help me get through this whole ordeal.

"Just stay positive and happy and you'll make it," I thought as I continued to smile at Jack who was still assessing my sudden mood change.

He gave me a wary look, his eyebrows plunging toward his nose. His mouth pulled up on one side. He shook his head again, yielding to my attitude, grabbed his coat, and started out into the never-ending boundaries of nothingness.

I didn't know how long we'd been walking, maybe two or three hours. The sun had already passed over the top of us and with each hour, every step, the heat beat down, draining the energy completely out of me as drops of perspiration beaded down the center of my back.

Jack and I, even though it was just us, didn't have much to say to each other. We just walked along in silence. This was really starting to grate on my nerves. Suddenly a familiar song rang in my head. I'd grown up singing the old melody with my sisters as we went to different family functions. I could feel the corners of my sun-dried lips form into a faint smile as I reflected on the memory. I started singing softly to myself, hoping if anything it would break the quiet tension around us.

The melody was a happy tune and it made me feel good inside. The song was working: it was giving me that extra little oomph I needed to keep me going and it kept my mind off of the unnerving situation I was in. The better I felt the louder I got.

"You are my sunshine, my only sun…"

"Ally, d'ye mind? Can ya stop singing?" Jack interrupting the second chorus of the song.

"Hmmm hmm hmm hum hum hum."

"*Ally!*" Jack snapped.

He stopped and glared at me, his anger catching me off guard, but my plan worked—sort of. I stood there motionless, waiting. He turned abruptly and started walking again. I was about to fall in behind him when I realized how drained I felt. It was as though every ounce of me became a noodle.

"Jack," I called as he continued walking.

"Jack," I spoke louder, trying to get his attention.

"*Jack*!" I yelled, finally stopping him.

"Whit."

"Stop, I've got to rest a few minute." I was trembling a little while I took off my backpack.

"Of course ya do," Jack murmured under his breath.

I thought I heard Jack's snide comment when he walked back to me. His teeth grinding as I found a boulder-size rock and sat down. I hoisted my backpack up onto my lap and pulled out a bottle of water. I opened it and let the water run pass my lips. It was warm—almost too warm—which made it taste a little stale, but it was wet. It still helped quenched the cotton that seemed to build up in my mouth.

Jack had his own thirst to quench. He pulled out his cigarettes and lit one up. As I handed him the water bottle a gust a smoke filtered out of his mouth and into my face. I coughed as I waved the smoke away from me.

"Does he do that on purpose?" I wondered as he took his drink.

I didn't know how long we would be out in the middle of nowhere so I thought it would be better to not drink all the water. I wiped off the end after getting it back from Jack, closed it, and started to put it back in my bag.

"So how much stuff do ya have in that thing?" he asked, blowing another puff of smoke at me.

"You saw part of it."

"Yeh, bu' what else do ya have in there?"

I set the bag next to me and started pulling out everything that I managed to stuff into a regular sized backpack.

"You saw my umbrella, sunscreen, glasses, and wallet. Of course my first-aid kit."

One by one everything came out of my bag.

"I also have another bottle of water, a granola bar, an apple, beef jerky, my scriptures, travel toilet paper for …well…you know, and a change of clothes. I think that's it." I looked at my stash, a bit pleased with myself that I could stuff so much into such a small space.

Jack looked at all my things, assessing what I had and what I really needed. He reached down and picked up my scriptures again.

"Ya know, ya probably wouldn't git so tired if yer bag wasn't so heavy." His eyes seemed to be fixed on the small book. "Maybe ya should leave a few things here?"

I could see it in his eyes. He didn't want anything that had to do with religion near him. I knew what his comment implied. I grabbed the book out of his hands and put it back in my pack.

"I'm not leaving anything here," I said firmly.

Jack blew another puff of smoke in my direction.

"Do you mind?" I snapped "I don't want to get lung cancer on this trip. Can you please blow your smoke somewhere else, away from me?"

"Fine," he sneered.

I could tell by his tone that I had offended him, but I didn't care; his smoke was making me sick.

Jack threw down his cigarette and crushed it into the ground with his foot.

"Le's git moving. We still have a long walk in front of us."

I quickly finished putting everything else in the bag, zipped it, and once again put it over my shoulders.

As we started walking again the sun was starting to fall a little quicker on the side of noon heading toward dusk. In front of us was nothing but dirt and bush, every scene the same.

"Jack, I know you don't know exactly where we are. But you do know where we're going, right?" I asked, concerned.

"Yeh."

"Where?"

"Straight'."

8
Comfort
※❈※

The warm fire flickered a hypnotic dance as I stared blankly in my own quiet trance, giving my eyes a rest from reading. Jack had walked over to the side somewhere to smoke his cigarette. He was trying to oblige my earlier request about the smoke.

I glanced over at him. I could see him wrapping his arms around himself, trying to keep warm. It made me feel a little guilty that he was cold because of how I felt.

"Jack, you don't have to stay way over there. Come sit by the fire." I tried to sound as pleasing as I could even though I knew he'd bring the smoke with him.

He sat down on the ground, his head propped up on a rock.

"Whit are ya doin'?"

"What does it look like I'm doing? It's called reading." Sarcasm oozed through my lips.

"I know yer readin'. Whit are ya readin'?"

I could see the slight moment in his jaw as his teeth clenched and his jaw locked when he made the connection that I only had one book with me.

"John 14:27," I said, not hesitating with my answer.

"I don't know why ya was'e yer time with all tha'."

"Well, I don't think it's a waste of time. It gives me comfort. And right now I need all the comfort I can get."

"Why's tha'?" he said smugly.

"Let's see, I almost died in a plane crash. Now I'm out in the middle of who know where with a total stranger. For all I know you could be a psycho killer."

"Believe me, love, if I were a psycho killer I would have killed ya back at the Rock."

He glanced over at me, the corners of his mouth turning into a crooked little grin.

"Ha, ha, funny," I replied.

I couldn't help but grin just a little myself, hoping he wouldn't catch it in the dim light of the fire. It was a little funny.

"Can I ask you a question?" I said.

I tried not to sound too invasive but I wanted to get to know Jack a little more. after all, we were going to be spending a lot of time together and I couldn't stand all the quiet.

"Whit?"

"Do you not have any religious belief at all?"

"No." His tone was mocking.

"Okay, then what helps you get though things?"

"A few pints, a good drag," as he inhaled his cigarette. "A nigh' with a leggy blond with two nice…"

"I get the picture," I interrupted.

"I was goin' ta say eyes." He smiled the same wicked smile he had sitting outside the bar at the Rock.

"Yeah, right," I mumbled under my breath. "So you don't have any belief of a higher being, in God or anything? You know even the aborigines believe in something greater than themselves. When we were at Ayers Rock I listened to the story of their history. They call it their Dreamtime. They believe the earth itself is a higher spiritual thing. See, most people believe in something."

"Not me. I don't believe in anything." Jack's answer was short and abrupt. He turned his head away from me and stared into the darkness. I could feel the tension that I had caused by my question.

"Why did I bring up religion?" I grumbled quietly. "That was stupid."

I knew he wasn't that type of guy and deep down I knew what would happen. There was just some kind of pull to get to know him more, to look deeper into who he was.

He was quiet for a long time. I decided to not press the question any further. Then all of the sudden he decided to break the silence.

"I used ta believe in God," he sounded distant and dejected, "when I was young."

He shifted his body uncomfortably as he looked at me. He sat up staring past me as though he were somewhere else, then continued.

"After my daw left, my maw and I would go ta church every week. Then when I was abou' twelve she passed away and I had ta live with my daw again. He was a real son of a…"

He paused to edit himself when he saw me shift uncomfortably at his choice of words. He took another hit of his cigarette and went on.

"He could care less abou' me. All he cared abou' was his drinking and gambling and maybe givin' me a good smack every once in awhile. I used ta pray that things would change and git be"er, bu' things jus got worse. So I stopped prayin' and moved ou' as soon as I could. I joined the army and haven't thought of God since."

When he finished I sat there, still not sure what to say, I started to understand why he was the way he was. I felt a slight twinge in my heart when I thought about what he must have gone through. And I wanted to help in some way, to make the thoughts of that old pain fade into a distant memory again.

"I'm sorry," was all I could say at that moment. I had to get my thoughts right.

"Well, that was another lifetime," Jack said as he returned to the present.

He inhaled another hit of his cigarette. He laid his head back onto the small rock he was using as a pillow and stretched out his feet, almost touching the fire. Then he put his arm not occupied with holding the cigarette under his head.

"You know, people always think that God can just make everything right," I said hesitantly, "but he gave everyone free will and a chance to learn through trial and error. Your mom was probably such a good woman that she didn't have to go through anymore trials."

"And I suppose I did?" He scowled at me.

"All I'm saying is that we all have the choice to do the right thing. Unfortunately, sometimes people make the wrong choice and others get caught in the bad choices they make."

I looked at him, yearning for some kind of resolve, hoping that what I said might help just a little, if any.

"Do ya really believe all tha' rubbish?" he growled.

"Yes, I do." I looked at him more thoughtfully.

Jack's eyes narrowed in on me as he inhaled a long breath of smoke and exhaled a cloud over him.

"I told ya I didn't want ya preachin' ta me. I'm going ta bed."

He crushed the small butt angrily into the dirt next to him and rolled over, facing away from me. As he rolled to his side he rolled over the small box of cigarettes and his lighter that he had in his pocket. He pulled them out, irritated, and set them to the side. I sat there watching his frame stiffen. I knew it wasn't from the cold even though the chill was starting to seep through my sweatshirt. I had touched a nerve.

"Tomorrow is not going to be pleasant," I thought as I listened to his low cursing as he tried to block me out and go to sleep.

I sat there again, watching the fire's flicker grow smaller until it was too dim to read. I put my scriptures back in my bag for the night. The flame's last flicker slowly came and went until there was nothing but a warm red glow coming from the black coals of the leftover wood. I sat there still, listening to the sounds around me.

Jack had fallen asleep quickly despite his mood; a gruff gurgled snore was evidence of that. Besides Jack, the surroundings were so hushed that every little sound seemed to be amplified. I couldn't place the sounds, where and what they were. Each rustle of a bush, a distant snap of a twig, made me jump. I pulled my sweatshirt snug around me, wrapping my arms around my chest.

Another crack of a twig and my heart stared to race. Panic replaced the calm from earlier when Jack was up. I struggled to keep my eyes opened. The heaviness was returning once again, but my fear was keeping me up. My nervous bounce came back as I continued to fight the urge to close my eyes. I couldn't stay sitting straight anymore so I rolled over to my side and used my arm as a pillow. I lay there watching the red glow going in and out of focus.

I don't know what time it was when my exhaustion beat out the fear and my eyes and body gave into that exhaustion.

Twisting and turning from a nightmare of a dream, I woke up with a start. My eyes popped wide open and I sat straight up, trying to catch my breath—Jack was still sleeping soundly. I rested my elbow on my knee and leaned my head into my hand, thinking about what scared me so badly that it would wake me so suddenly. My mind replayed just certain parts of my dream as I tried to gather my thoughts.

I was a child again, alone, a male figure hidden behind the dark shadows. I was running, always running. Then the strange image of Jack standing still and motionless, and my child self running again, but I couldn't tell if I was running from Jack or to him. That's when I woke up. Was my dream a warning? Was he dangerous, or was it something else?

My mind just kept racing and I couldn't concentrate. I lay back down and closed my eyes and took in a deep breath, trying to put my dream to the back of my mind.

I could see the bright sunlight shine though my closed lids as it was rising to another day, so bright that I automatically covered my eyes. The breeze was cool against my skin but warmer than it had been earlier. Everything seemed fresh and new. The sounds around me even took on a whole new feel.

I heard Jack's soft gruff voice say something to me, but he said it so soft that I couldn't understand it. I opened my eyes to ask him what he had said and was surprised that the sun wasn't quite as bright as I had imagined. There was just the soft, hazy, pink glow as it slowly peaked up over the land. I rubbed my eyes and shook my head just a little.

"That's strange," I whispered softly.

Then I remembered Jack had said something to me. I looked over at him, excepting him to be awake and watching my odd reaction to the sunless morning, but he was still motionless except for the movement of his chest. And the only sound he made was his gurgled snore surrounded by his rough breathing.

"It must have been the wind," I thought. "Sometimes when the wind goes through trees and bushes it will sound like talking. It's just another trick my mind played on me," I reasoned.

I thought about going back to sleep just a bit longer, but as I stretched I realized that I had a greater need at the moment than sleep. I reached to my side and snatched my bag, pulling just a few things out until I grabbed my desired item—the small roll of travel toilet paper. I got up quietly, not wanting to wake Jack. I'd be back before he even knew I was gone, and I tiptoed off to find a quiet spot all to myself.

I was headed back to our small camp only a few yards away when I heard Jack yelling my name.

"*Ally!*"

I could hear both the panic and irritation in his voice. When I came into view of him I could see both expressions on his face, panic outweighing the irritation.

"Is he really that concerned?" I thought, reveling in the moment, and then I answered him. "What are you yelling for? I'm right here."

He saw me walking up and his expression looked relieved. It quickly turned to anger.

"Where were ya?" He was practically snapping my head off.

"I had to use….um…" I paused, embarrassed, "the little girl's room." My face started to blush at the idea that I had to explain this.

"Ya can't jus' go walkin' off like tha'. Whit if somethin' happened ta ya? I'm still responsible fer ya until we git back." he griped.

His voice was hard but I could hear a sincere quality in his words. He was honestly concerned, even though he didn't want me to know it. He covered it up quickly with a few colorful words under his breath.

"Okay, I'm sorry, don't be mad. Next time I'll let you know where I am." I tried to sound compliant and trustworthy. But my voice had just a little lift to it and he thought I was trying to be sarcastic. He glared at me.

"We need ta git goin', Grab yer stuff," he grumbled.

Jack grabbed his jacket sharply from the ground where he had used it for his pillow when it had warmed up enough for him to take it off. He started off before I even had a chance to think. I grabbed my bag, stuffing my toilet paper back in the main compartment, and raced after him, stumbling just a little as I went.

When I finally caught up, Jack was some yards away. I was able to slow my pace a bit as well as my breathing. I put my backpack over both shoulders again and my steps became more rhythmic with Jack's. I glanced behind me out of habit, wondering if I had left anything behind. There was nothing there; I had everything with me. As I turned back around something caught my eye.

The sun must have hit a rock in just the right angle. It shot off a reflective beam of sunlight, which reminded me of a flash from a camera. It was gone with my next step. I turned back and realized I was starting to trail behind. I had to pick up my pace in order to keep up with Jack's long strides.

After a short time I could tell Jack's annoyance had died down; his pace became more casual. But we still weren't carrying on any type of conversation. I let my mind wonder, trying to distract myself from the uncomfortable silence.

"I wonder what's going on back home," I thought. "Or even back in Sydney. Do they even know we're missing? Someone, I'm sure, should be looking for us by now."

My mind conjured up images of our scheduled flight not coming in and a sense of panic surrounding the airport, news anchors on every channel reporting on our missing plane. Speculations flying about everywhere. Did they get caught in a storm? Was there foul play? And the true answer, was there something wrong with the plane? Anyone who knew Jack would think of this last thing.

I imagined a nicely dressed man sitting in front of a camera describing the scene. "In local news a small aircraft has been reported missing when it didn't show up at its destination yesterday. Reports say that there were two passengers: a young American woman who now wonders what the heck she was thinking, and a local pilot who often thinks way too highly of himself."

Then my mind flashed to an image of Tom sitting in a cushy chair tucked back behind his travel agency. Watching his TV, smiling at the joke he played on Jack—and me—then his smile slowly disappearing as he listened to the story and realized who they were talking about. Would he regret the joke he played? I replayed his reaction over and over again in my mind. His look always seemed so tortured. Even though I felt his joke was cruel I knew deep down that he never meant any harm to come to either of us.

The next segment of news played in my distracted mind.

"Search teams are at this time looking for the missing aircraft in hopes of survivors.

Their names will not be released until the families have been contacted."

As my imagination played out my scenario, realization over came me: "The families—my family." I gasped.

Did they know? What would they be thinking? Did they think I was dead or did they have the hope that I would survive? I started panicking and stopped suddenly, bent over, placing my hands on my hips and trying to catch my breath. I was hyperventilating again. Jack's steady stride slowed when he realized I was lagging behind, and then stopped altogether to see where I was.

"Now whit?" he said, surly.

As he walked closer to me I was sure he could see the expression on my face. Fear and anxiety was never a good look for me.

"Whit's wrong?" His voice was a little more concerned.

"I've been so worried about myself this whole time that I didn't even consider what my family is going through. This is going to kill my mom," I said.

"Now ye're exaggerating."

"Am I?" I sneered as I looked up at him. It was my turn to be upset. "You don't understand, my mom has a bad heart. This could actually kill her." The thought made me cringe.

I decided to take control of my emotions and controlled my breathing. I stood up straight. I looked out into the wide-open nothingness and closed my eyes, inhaled deeply, letting out a gust of air. I looked over at Jack who was examining me curiously as he watched my unexpected change.

"How many days did you say it would take?" I asked.

"Two or three."

"Then let's get going." My tone more fervent.

I got my composure back and tightened the straps on my bag. I was determined more than ever to get to civilization. Jack just shook his head and started to lead the way. I took a deep breath and followed right behind him.

9

Darci's Resolve

My white taxi with my three kids in tow pulled into Dorothy's driveway. The kids were laughing and screaming with excitement as they always do when we have plans to go to the mall and then a movie.

The whole way the boys were trying to convince me to see the latest action film with some superhero soldier and of course guns and bombs going off through the whole thing. I felt that the latest family-friendly film was the much better choice.

"No, were not seeing that one," I said for the hundredth time to Miles.

"But why?" he complained loudly.

"We are going to see something that everyone would enjoy. It's not a good show for Amy and I don't think Aunt Dorothy wants to go see someone get blown up."

He crossed his arms and slouched back into his seat with a loud huff.

All three kids ran up and into the house as soon as they got out of the van, not even bothering to knock. I followed right behind them. Gina and Megan already had their arms around them before I even got inside the door.

"Are you guys ready to go?" I asked.

"Just about! I just need to put some makeup on," Gina answered.

Gina is the type that has to make sure she looks her best every time she goes out. She's always been pretty, but she likes to put in that extra effort.

Megan, who was all ready to go, sat on the couch reading to Amy. Her beauty was close to how her personality was: fresh and bright, casually fashionable with a bit of a youthful flare, probably because she was the youngest. They were all beautiful in their own way.

Even Ally had a natural beauty about her. I looked over at the family picture on the wall and sighed. She never really was much into makeup, her skin too smooth and clear to worry about covering it up with all that, but when she really put it on—watch out. Her skin looks like porcelain, and her gray-blue eyes next to her dark curls is absolutely mesmerizing. Once someone really looks in them, they're hard to resist. I have to admit I get a little jealous sometimes that they all have such natural beauty. It's kind of ironic that they don't even realize it themselves; well except maybe Gina.

As I watched Gina primping and Megan reading I looked around for Dorothy.

"Where's your mom?" I asked.

"I don't know." Megan looked up from the book she had been reading. "She might be in the kitchen on the phone."

I remembered hearing a telephone ring as I walked through the door but didn't pay any attention to it. I was just happy it wasn't my phone.

"I'll go see what's keeping her," I responded.

I briskly walked into the kitchen. Time was clicking by and we had to go. When I got to the doorway Dorothy was just hanging up the phone. Her face was pale and her hands were shaking. Her face had a look of anguish on it. This look was much more agonizing than the one last time we were here.

"Aunt, Dorothy what's wrong?" I couldn't help the worry that came out in my tone, she just looked awful.

Tears started to gather in her eyes and then stream down her cheeks and she choked trying to get the words out.

"It's Ally. She's dead." She broke out into a full sob.

I stood there stunned, not knowing what to say. Could this be true? There had to be something more. Things don't just happen like that. I threw my arms around her, trying to console her the best I could. By this time her sobs had caught the attention of everyone in the other room.

"Wha's wong with Aunt Dorophy?" Amy asked innocently.

I looked up and everyone was standing in the doorway. Amy's angelic face was confused as she looked up at Megan who was holding her hand.

"I don't know," Megan answered.

Her face was much more confused than Amy's ever could be. She looked as though she could have been holding her breath as little as she moved. Gina's face had terror in it as she watched her mother crumble in grief; then tears started to form in her own eyes.

My arms were still around Dorothy. "Boys, can you take Amy and go play? I need to talk to Gina and Megan."

They both nodded, trying to be good. They grabbed Amy's hands and gently pulled her toward the living room again.

"Amy, do you want to color?" Ryan's voice trailed off.

"What's going on?" Gina asked. Her voice was just above a whisper.

"Ally's dead!" Dorothy was so distraught that she could hardly get the words out.

"What?" Gina screeched.

"Wait a minute, let's not jump to conclusions." I tried to sound steady and compassionate. "Tell us what's going on. Why do you think Ally is dead?"

"The... the phone call, it was the Sydney police. Ally took a small plane to Ayers Rock the other day and the plane never made it back. The man on the phone said they left the airport at about 10:00 a.m. yesterday and they should have gotten in sometime last night, but they never showed up."

She paused, trying to get any kind of composure, then grabbed a napkin that was sitting in the middle of the table in its wicker holder.

She continued, "He said the pilot attempted a distress call, but it was too broken up to make it out." She couldn't go on. The tears started to flow again.

I sat there with one arm embracing her shoulder, my opposite hand stroking her arm. I tried not to think of Ally's fate; that would be too hard to deal with. I had to be strong.

"Did they find the plane?" Megan asked, wiping the moisture from her eyes.

All Dorothy could do was shake her head.

"They didn't find the plane?" I asked, puzzled.

"They said they were sending out search parties, but there were no promises."

"So they don't know for certain if they are alive or not."

I was getting a little upset. *There* was still hope and my aunt had already given up.

"Yeah, I guess not, but how could someone survive..."

I cut her off before she could finish. "How do hundreds of people survive any of the tragedies that they go through? The human spirit can deal with amazing things."

"You're right," Megan chimed in. "We can't give up hope. Ally's tough."

"And stubborn." Gina added. "She can get through this."

Gina came over and put her arm around Dorothy's other shoulder, while Megan knelt down by her feet, her hands wrapped gently around her mother's hands.

Megan's face brightened up a little, her mouth forming a smirk. "You know, she'll be fine, she's really strong."

"Because she eats a lot," Both Megan and Gina sang together.

They both laughed at what I figured was a private family joke. It broke the tension and Dorothy's despair and she was able to manage a smile. I started to chuckle but really didn't have a clue what the joke was. I figured I could find out later.

"Okay," I automatically turned on my managerial voice. "They said they haven't found the plane yet, right?" Dorothy nodded. "And they're sending out search parties?"

"That's what they said."

"Do they know where to look?" Megan asked.

"I don't know. They didn't get into all that. They just said they would keep us updated."

"Great, how is that going to work with the time difference and our work schedules and everything?" Gina's voice was laced with sarcasm.

"I think someone should go over there and find out exactly what's going on," I suggested.

"Right, how are we going to pay for that?" Gina grimaced.

I could hear the discouragement and frustration in her voice.

"I was thinking I would go," I announced.

I knew things sometimes were a bit tight for Ally's family and I had a really well-paying job. It just made sense for me to go. I could afford it and I had vacation time built up. Besides, someone needed to keep their eye on Dorothy's health.

"Darci, I couldn't ask you to do that. What about the kids?" Dorothy said.

I looked over at my three wonderful kids. They were playing happily in the living room. Amy had gone from coloring to playing with her doll, and the boys had decided that the fireplace accessories made great swords as they challenged each other to duals. It would be hard to leave them, but I couldn't leave Ally's fate up in the air and my favorite aunt wondering if she would ever see her daughter again. Someone had to go.

Ally had always been there for me, especially when I was going through one of the hardest times of my life. I couldn't just abandoned her now, now when she needed someone more than ever.

"You'd watch them for me, wouldn't you?" I already knew her answer.

"Of course," Dorothy responded.

"Sure," Gina added.

"I don't know," Megan joked as she cracked a crooked grin.

"Then it's settled. I'll catch the earliest flight I can get. Hopefully I can leave tonight."

I looked at the kids playing again, my eyes furrowed, my nose crinkled.

"What?" Megan asked.

"I was just thinking, how I am going to tell the kids about the movie?" I sighed.

"We'll take them tomorrow. I promise." She crossed her heart and put her palm up for me to see.

"Thank you," I said gratefully. "Well I better get this over with. Kids!"

As I drove home I kept going over the plans in my head. Gina had gotten on the computer and found me a flight leaving tonight, which gave me just a few hours to pack and get to the airport. I was a little anxious if I was even going to make it. The next one wasn't until late tomorrow. My foot seemed to press down on the gas a little more as my anxiety grew.

Megan had volunteered to stay with the kids while I was gone. She and Gina planned on taking turns depending on how long I was gone, but they would be spending a lot of time at their house, especially since that's where I would call to give updates.

"Call us as soon as you get in and find out any information. I don't care how late or early it is," Dorothy exclaimed. "If you have to call collect, that's fine. Just keep me up-to-date with what's going on."

My aunt's words rang throughout my thoughts. I wanted so badly to make things right, to be there for Dorothy, for Gina and Megan. I wanted to be strong and be their shoulder to lean on, and I wanted to be a good mom and be there for my kids. So many things were pulling me in different directions. But at this moment I knew I had to pull myself together. There was one thing I wanted, not more than any other but just as emotionally powerful. I wanted to find Ally, find out if she was alive. I didn't believe she was gone; I couldn't believe it.

I pulled into the driveway a little too fast and everyone bounced as I hit the corner of the curb. I jumped out and raced into the house, leaving Megan to take care of the kids. I grabbed my suitcase from the top shelf of my closet and threw it onto my bed and opened it. It was the type that you would need if you were always going to go on business trips, but it looked as new as the first day I bought it. Except for a bit of dust on the top.

"Mom, do you need any help?" Ryan's voice caught my attention as he sat on my bed.

"Yeah, sweetie, can you grab my red sweater that's hanging on the back of the chair in the kitchen?"

"Okay." He jumped off my bed and hurried out the door, but before he could get too far I remembered something else.

"Can you also ask Miles to keep a lookout for the taxi? It should be coming pretty soon."

"Okay," he said again, smiling at that fact that he could help. "Miles!" he yelled as he left the room.

Miles was still pouting a little that they didn't get to go to the movies.

I continued to pack my bag, trying to think clearly of what I needed. Ryan brought me my sweater and I sent him on another errand to retrieve another article of clothing from the dryer.

"*Mom the taxi's here!*" Miles hollered at the bottom of the stairs.

"Ryan, can you go tell the driver that I'll be right there?" My tone was anxious again as he handed me my requested item.

I threw the last few things in my bag and zipped it up. I looked around the room frantically, my hand rubbing my forehead, trying to think of anything I might have missed. I yanked the bag off my bed and pulled out the handle. I started to head downstairs but a picture on my dresser caught my eye. I picked it up to look at the two smiling women.

Ally and I had so many good memories together but one in particular stood out. She had come to help me take care of the kids after SD (short for Stanley Davidson Thomas) left. I decided the boys needed some fun: it was a very hard time for them. So I took them to the zoo while Dorothy watched Amy who was one at the time. It was a good day. We laughed and joked and then Ryan asked if he could take our picture. It was a little off-center and a little too close but we both looked so happy, two big smiles shining through all that was going on. It quickly became one of my favorite pictures.

What seemed like minutes holding the picture were just seconds. A loud blast of a horn broke into my thoughts and Miles was yelling again.

"*Mom!*"

I hurried downstairs, my suitcase thumping as it hit each step, and met everyone on the front porch. I wrapped my arms around each one of my kids and kissed their soft cheeks. Then I gave Megan a reassuring hug, lingering for just a few short seconds.

"Don't worry, she's going to be fine," I said, trying to sound confident.

"I know." Her eyes starting to form a tear.

"Remember, she's strong." Her mouth stated to curl up on the sides. "One day you'll have to let me in on the joke," I mused as she laughed lightly.

I gave the kids a group hug. "Be good and don't get into too much trouble." I grabbed my bag and gave it to the driver.

The taxi headed down our quite street and I waved to my family out the window. Megan still had worry on her face but was quickly distracted by the small fight that was already breaking out between the two boys. Amy was waving sadly, very much aware that I was leaving her behind, and I thought that I saw her starting to cry as we turned the corner.

I turned back around and let out an exhausted sigh. As I faced forward I noticed a pair of dark eyes looking back at me in the rearview mirror.

"Long trip ahead of you?" The driver asked curiously after watching our farewell scene.

I looked up into the mirrored eyes "You have no idea."

10

Friend

✳✳

"How long have we been walking?" I asked as I cleared my throat. My throat felt scratchy from the heat and the lack of water.

"Only a couple of hours," Jack replied.

"That's it?"

The heat of the sun seemed even hotter than the day before. Maybe I was just getting too impatient with all the walking. Nothing but the same dry bush, half-dead trees, and rocks of all sizes and shapes to look at. Out in the distance nothing but the same mundane scene repeated itself over and over again. Jack was even starting to show the strain.

I didn't know why but I couldn't stand the quiet anymore. I was used to people talking to me. I never thought that I had many friends but it seemed like I always had someone to talk to, more than I had thought. Even on my quiet days.

I knew Jack didn't enjoy my happy little melody from earlier, but maybe I could get away with something a bit more up-to-date. I thought of a song that made me feel good and was upbeat to keep me going.

I started to sing a little to myself, then got louder as I started to feel the effects of the upbeat melody and lyrics. The second round of singing my song I couldn't help but start walking to my attempt at the beat. By the time I reached the chorus my voice had risen to a volume that irritated Jack.

"Ooo OooOoo Oooo…."

"Ally!" Jack snapped.

It didn't work. He hated this song more than the last one.

"Could ya jus' shu' it?" He turned and glared at me, his fist clenched in a ball. "For five minutes could ya jus' give me some quiet?"

I looked at him, puzzled, because that was all I'd been giving him. We had hardly spoken at all during this whole trip.

"What are you talking about? I just started singing now," I snapped back. "It's better than going mad from all the silence," I continued.

He ground his teeth and his jaw clenched; then he took a slow, deep breath through his nose.

"I need a break." I could hear the aggravation still in his voice as we stopped. "D'ya have any more of tha' water?" He asked—actually, demanded.

I took my backpack off and handed him the half-drunk bottle of water. Then I pulled out the granola bar and broke it in half and gave one to him. I was already feeling the stomach pains of not eating much. I pulled out of my pack a bag of beef jerky and offered Jack a piece as well. He took it reluctantly.

"Don't you like beef jerky?" I asked.

"Not really."

His face cringed and wrinkled as he chewed the sliced dehydrated meat. It was amusing to watch, but I soon could tell it wasn't food he wanted.

Jack finished his tiny meal and then swallowed another mouthful of water. He handed the bottle back to me and reached in his pocket for his pack of cigarettes.

Suddenly his face twisted into a strange, panicked-but-angry look. Then he turned and glowered at me. "Where's my smokes? Did ya do somethin with them?" he accused, his voice dark and hard.

"No."

He started to search every pocket; once he was done he searched again. With each pocket he checked I could hear the anxiety and aggravation filtering in as his colorful language became more harsh and expressive. I cringed at the sound of each word.

"The nicotine must be wearing off," I thought as Jack started having a full-on panic attack.

In a way it was kind of amusing to watch Jack slowly start to lose it. I seemed to always be the one that was the emotional wreck and he seemed to always be in control. Now for this brief moment, and I didn't know how brief this moment would last, I was in control.

While enjoying the moment I suddenly had a flash of memory, something that might not be good to share.

"Oh," escaped my lips before I even had a chance to stop it.

"Whit?" he asked, an edge in his voice.

"Nothing." I tried to play it off like I just had a regular thought. "Don't tell him. Don't say anything." My thoughts were warning me.

"Whit?" he asked again.

He knew something was up as he stood there, his hands still checking his pockets, waiting for me to talk.

"You'll regret it," I continued warning myself.

But the impulse to be honest with him got the better of me.

"When we headed out this morning I just happened to look back to make sure we didn't leave anything and I might have seen your lighter."

I cringed slightly, ready for his reaction. He started breathing heavier and his nostrils started to flare as his hands curled up into balls again. If I wasn't a woman I think he might have hit me right then.

"I didn't realize that that's what it was. I thought it was a rock," I said, trying to make amends.

"A rock? How many rocks do ya know tha' are square and made of me'al?" His jaw locked and he gritted his teeth as he tried to keep in control.

"I couldn't tell it was square. I just thought that it was a shiny rock that was reflecting the sun," I said defensively.

That was his limit. Just that little bit of attitude seemed to have pushed him over the edge. The volume of his voice reached a level that stunned me and his accent became almost completely unrecognizable. I covered my ears to block out the sound of his continual cursing. I didn't like to hear that kind of language, but the fact that it was directed toward me made it even harder to listen to. Then he did it; he took one step to far. His anger became just a slur of profanity and insults.

I could only make out a few words through his rant: *stupid, irresponsible, brainless, ugly, cow.* He turned his back to me, I figured so he didn't have to see me while he continued yelling, which made his accent harder to understand, but it didn't change the daggers of pain he caused me. I could hear each insult, each vile expression loud and clear as he threw each one toward me.

I clenched my teeth together to hold back the tears from his hurtful words, and then I quickly noticed that along with the hurt a part of me was angry. I wanted to yell at him, tell him what a jerk he was, that I had never met anyone so rude and callous and unfeeling in my whole life. I wanted to turn my fist into a ball and hit him square in the jaw, but I couldn't. I couldn't escape the hurt that he made me feel.

I could tell the tears were starting to form and I wasn't going to give him the satisfaction of seeing me cry. I turned and just started to run; I wanted to get as far away from him as possible.

He was so caught up in his anger that he didn't even see me leave; maybe he did but was happy that he didn't have to deal with me anymore. I was just this hideous obstacle that he had to endure.

I ran and ran while tears dried on my face as the air rushed past me, never stopping until I practically collapsed. I finally stopped when I heard my name being called. It sounded like a soft whisper in my ear, so close, but it had to be in the distance.

I didn't realize how far and long I had actually run until I turned and there was no one in sight—I was alone. Just the bush and the dirt surrounded me. I thought I would at least been able to see Jack, maybe just a speck in the distance, but still something.

I heard him calling out for me again, but this time his voice was faint and distant. It sounded intense and panicked.

For a brief second I felt guilty for running like I did, forcing him to come find me. But it only lasted for a second; his words echoed in my mind again.

"Good," I thought. "Let him try to find me."

I was determined not to go back. I didn't need him. I could find my way by myself. I just had to go in the same direction.

"Just keep going straight. I'm bound to run into some town." My inconceivable logic made perfect sense to me.

"Just go straight," I repeated to myself.

I walked along for I don't know how long, trying to be brave and not thinking about what I had done, but it was starting to get dark and I had to admit I was getting a little scared. Jack's voice faded and I knew the distance between us was a lot further than I really hoped. I was alone and I had to make it by myself.

I reached into my bag and pulled out my keys that happened to have a flashlight hooked on them. It was flat and small but powerful. I got it a while ago as a freebie when I signed up for some stupid drawing that no one ever really won.

I squeezed the sides of my little flashlight and tried to find a place that would give me some kind of protection. Then I saw a grouping of rocks and figured that was as good of place as any. I walked around, trying to find something to start a fire with—it was getting a bit cold again.

I gathered just a few sticks and broke off a few branches from a nearby bush. I reached over and grabbed my bag, rummaging through every pocket until I found the small book of matches that I had grabbed from the hotel lobby, thinking matches were always good to have on hand. But I couldn't get a fire going. The wind was blowing too hard. The matches I lit wouldn't stay lit. Frustrated, I gave up. It wasn't in my best interest to use all my matches anyway.

I pulled my bible out and opened it randomly. Using my little light I started reading the first verse I saw, hoping it would give me that same comfort I had the night before, but I couldn't concentrate. I kept reading the first line of the same verse I picked over and over. I growled to myself, frustrated, and closed it and set it next to me. Then I crossed my arms in front of me and stared down at the dirt and just sat there in my grouping of rocks, thinking about my life. About all the wrong decisions I had made, this being one of them.

"I'm always too hasty in my actions," I said out loud as I wrapped my arms tighter around me.

Realizing that my decision to run away wasn't the best idea. The thought of Jack looking for me now was making me feel guilty and stupid.

"What is he going to say to me when he finds me? Will he find me?" I continued talking to myself. The sound of my own voice helped break up the silence.

As the night started to get darker, the cold was starting to become more evident. My body started to shiver a bit. I put my scriptures back in my bag, pulled out my extra pair of clothes, and put then on as quick as I could, then zipped up my sweatshirt and tied the hood tight around my face.

"What is Jack going to do about the cold?" The thought bothered me.

He only had a leather jacket. He could build a fire except the fact that he didn't have his lighter anymore. The slight guilt I felt about running away was nothing to the anguish I felt now that we both might freeze to death. I thought of my family, then his. All of this could have been avoided if it wasn't for my abrupt decision.

As I stared out into the darkness of the night, I saw a dark figure move in the distance. My heart raced and the joy of being found was starting to warm me. But as the movement got closer I could see that the figure was a lot lower to the ground than Jack would be. I froze as I watched two eyes flicker in the moonlight and it stalked forward.

My body tensed and I stayed as motionless as possible, watching every movement the figure made as it came closer. When it was about ten feet away I could make out the shape of what looked like a dog. I thought my heart stopped beating as I held my breath.

A white dingo was looking right at me, his eyes glowing. He looked smaller than I would have thought—not a puppy, but not quite full-grown either. He stopped his advance and just stood there as though he was waiting for me to do something. I knew a little about dingoes. I had read about their dangerous, wild nature, how when they were hungry they were like wolves and would attack. But I thought they usually were in packs, not by themselves. Why was this one alone?

He sat down, still and motionless, and continued to watch me, softly whimpering. He looked so sweet just sitting there as if he were a neighbor's dog. I couldn't help feeling sorry for him.

"Are you hungry?" I asked as I slowly grabbed my bag.

I unzipped it carefully, trying not to make any sudden movements. I felt sorry for him but I was still cautious. I reached in and pulled out the bag of beef jerky that I had, opened it, and threw him a piece. He crawled over to it, sniffed at it, then ate it quickly. This was good. If he ate the beef jerky maybe he wouldn't eat me. I threw another piece and again he ate it. I continued throwing piece after piece until the bag was empty.

"Sorry, that's all I have." I said nervously.

Was that enough to satisfy him or was it just an appetizer to his main course? I continued to stay as still as I could. Then he suddenly got up and walked back into the darkness. I started to breath a little easier but knew he probably wasn't far. I wouldn't be getting much sleep.

The night seemed to drag on forever. I kept thinking about Jack and wondered if he was okay. My eyes kept wanting to close but I kept forcing them open, afraid to go to sleep. I would just about drift off when I would hear a noise that would startle me. And of course the cry of my furry friend in the distance didn't help.

My eyelids finally couldn't stay open any longer and I slowly leaned over until I was laying on my side. For just a few more minutes I was aware of the noises around me. I thought I heard something coming closer to me, but I was so tired that I couldn't get myself to get up and run. If something was going to kill me, at least I was pretty much out of it. But nothing was attacking; I was still alive. And even better than that, I was actually getting warmer as I drifted in and out of consciousness.

I dreamed of someone placing a heavy fur coat over me. I stroked it automatically, letting the fur run between my fingers. It reminded me of my black-and-white Luck at home—I really needed luck tonight.

Suddenly my dreams led me to my home. I was with my mom and sisters and Darci, but they couldn't see me. I tried to talk to them but they couldn't hear me, either. Then I was alone again and I felt like I was a child. I turned and a stranger was there grabbing at me. I struggled to get away and ran. I saw Jack in the distance but this time I ran toward him, wanting his protection. But just before I could reach him he turned into the white dingo. My heart jumped and my eyes popped open wide and I was completely awake.

My body automatically jumped when I realized that my furry friend was laying peacefully against my body, his paws under his chin. I quickly realized that he was the one keeping me warm through the night. I wasn't quite sure how to react. His actions were just like a regular dog, but *he* wasn't. I reached down cautiously, and stroked his coarse fur; it felt softer in my dream. He started to stir and stretch, and then he got up and walked away. As he started to walk away he paused and looked back at me.

"Thank you," I called out to him. And I could have sworn that he smiled. "I need to get back to civilization," I said as I watched him walk out into the distance.

11
Repentant
※❀※

I removed the extra clothing that I had put on during the night, stuffed them into my bag, and pulled out my apple. It was bruised up a bit, but it was food and I was getting really hungry.

As I ate my apple I figured I should start looking for Jack. I wasn't totally over what he had said, but my guilt from taking off had gotten the best of me. And despite what he said I didn't want to spend another night out on my own.

"Maybe if we are both looking, we'll find each other," I thought as I finished the apple. "Crap," I looked down at the bare apple core. "I should have saved some for Jack." I groaned at my selfishness.

Well, there wasn't much I could do now, so I threw the core back to nature, snatched my bag off the ground, and put my arms through the straps. I wasn't sure where to go. I wasn't paying much attention to details as I ran from him the night before, plus it had been getting dark.

My first thought was to not go the same direction as the dingo went this morning. I looked around, trying to find my bearings. Suddenly a gust of wind blew past me, blowing my tangled curls into my face, and I heard my name being called.

I thought it was Jack at first, but then I realized it was different. It was soft, almost musical, the same whisper that I heard last night. It seemed to come from the direction I didn't want to go. I stood there trying to figure out what I was hearing. The wind blew past me again and this time I thought I heard Jack's name in it.

I hesitated. "Am I going crazy?" I wondered.

The lack of food, water, and sleep must have been getting to me. Then another thought came to me, something that I wanted to brush off. I remembered the story of the Dreamtime and the aboriginal version of the creation, how everything has a spirit: the land, the wind, the animals.

"Could this be true? No," I chuckled, but that would explain a lot. I couldn't help but start to believe my own thoughts. "Okay then," I said out loud to the emptiness. "Where can I find Jack?"

I shook my head in slight disbelief in what I was saying. Suddenly the wind started to blow again as soon as the words escaped my lips. I stuck my index finger in my mouth to wet it and then held it up in the air reluctantly to feel which direction the wind was blowing.

"I must be crazy," I said, shaking my head again. "Okay, I'll go this way."

I started walking as the wind whipped my hair up around my face, surrounding me, helping to push me along, guiding me carefully to my desired objective.

I probably walked in the direction of the wind for about twenty minutes when I heard my name again. This time I could tell it was Jack.

"It's him." I sighed in relief.

As I got closer I could hear so many moods in his voice—frustration, panic, annoyance, and worry. My guilt was coming back strong. I was also a little leery of his attitude. I knew he didn't really like me that much and when I left he was furious. What would he be like now? Now that I had been missing all night.

"Well, I better get this over with." I sighed again.

I started to pick up my pace, not watching where I was going. Without warning I felt my toe catch on something hard and I was suddenly falling forward, my hands grasping at the empty space around me, trying to find something to hold on to.

My body plunged downward in what seemed so much longer than what I would have imagined. A high-pitched scream flew out of my mouth and to my surprise Jack's name was attached to it. I finally came to an abrupt stop with a loud thud.

It took a few seconds until I could breathe; there was no air left to breathe with. I gasped for any kind of oxygen to fill my lungs. Finally I was able to breathe normally again. I looked around, still a little stunned, and realized that I was surrounded by dirt. I had fallen in a hole as deep as a cemetery plot, but I figured with a little effort I could get out.

I rolled over onto my knees and tried to push myself to my feet. As soon as I put pressure on my right ankle a surge of pain shot through my foot and straight up my leg. The pain was so excruciating that it made me dizzy and my stomach started to turn.

I was stuck and I knew it. The only way I was going to get out was with Jack's help. I was so embarrassed I didn't want him to see me like this—weak and helpless. But I didn't have a choice.

"Jack!" I yelled, desperate and humble. "Jack, help." I managed to exhort a little more volume.

I was starting to feel a little anxious. "Where is he? Is he further then I thought he was?"

I stood up the best I could so my voice would travel out of my surroundings.

"*Jack!*" I screamed his name as loud as I could, the sound of urgency and fear intertwined in his name.

The pain race furiously through my leg again and I crumbled back to the ground. My body's reaction to the pain automatically turned on the waterworks and my eyes started to moisten. I sat holding my ankle, thinking maybe somehow if I held it just right the pain would subside.

I was about to call out for help again when I heard what sounded like running coming toward me. I hoped it was him but worried it might be something else. I held my breath, waiting.

His dark, wavy hair and his stunning jewel eyes peered over the edge of the hole, a look of relief on his face, then he grinned as if he couldn't help himself.

"Dig'in for truffle?" he said casually, a bit of humor to his voice.

"Did he really just say that?" I thought. "Did he just call me a pig?"

I started to fume as I glared up at him.

"Here I am stuck in a hole with maybe a broken ankle and he has the nerve to insult me? What kind of person is he?" I grumbled to myself.

I was just about to give him a piece of my mind when he jumped down beside me and started to check out the damage. His face turned swiftly to a soft, concerned look as he gently examined my ankle. His strong hands turned it so carefully and then touched certain areas to see were the damage was. Each touch sent a chill through me, and I shivered just a bit.

"Ya migh be in a li"le shock," he said, mistaking the shiver. "I' could be broken, bu' I can't be sure. Let's git ya ou' of this hole firs'." His voice was unusually calming.

"How?" I asked.

"I'll pull ya up."

"Great, that's all I need, as if I don't feel self-conscious enough." I thought.

He climbed out and reached down his hand for mine. I grabbed it and locked my fingers the best I could around his wrist. He grunted a little as he pulled me up. The muscles on his forearms flexed as the veins became more prominent, but besides that he pulled me out without much effort at all. I was relieved and surprised at the same time. I thought that my weight would be an issue, but he pulled me up easily, hardly breaking a sweat.

I stumbled on my good leg while he helped me over to a tree that look dry and thirsty for water, and then set me down carefully. I was astonished that he was being so sweet.

"Give me yer bag." I pulled my bag off my shoulders and handed it to him, wondering what he needed.

He pulled out my extra shirt that I had shoved in it earlier and started ripping the cotton fabric into strips.

"I hope ya weren't fond of this," he mused.

"Uh," was the only thing I could get out before he had it completely shredded. "It doesn't matter now." I stared at him stunned.

I could see that a smile had crept up onto his face. He looked around where we were sitting and picked up a few sturdy twigs and put the two largest on either side of my ankle. Then he wrapped it securely with the makeshift bandages that he made out of my shirt.

"Well, I don't know if i's broken or not, bu' ya defini'ly have a pre"y bad sprain. This will hopefully stabilize i' until we can git ta a hospi'al."

"Thank you," I said.

As I leaned back against the tree, trying to get comfortable, pain raced through my leg again and my face cringed, as I tried to endure it.

"We'll stay here through the nigh'; give tha' ankle a chance ta res' up."

Suddenly my stubborn side kicked in. "I can still walk on it," I said, trying to stand. "I heard once that you shouldn't baby a sprain because it will get stiff, that you need to walk on it, keep it moving." I got to my feet and took one step. My ankle gave out under me and I stumbled forward. Jack reached out quickly and caught me, easing me back down by the tree.

"Like I said, we'll be stayin' here for the nigh'."

His sapphire eyes gleamed as he stared down at me, and I caught myself staring back dreamily—they were so hypnotic.

I quickly looked away and moved wrong. Even though Jack had bound my ankle pretty tightly it still didn't take much for pain to surge through my foot and travel up my leg, hitting each nerve as it went along.

"Okay," I said as I winced.

I kept waiting for the other Jack to return. The mean Jack, the rude, insensitive Jack. Where was the anger that was sure to come from my escape last night? Was he waiting until I was more relaxed to pounce or did he actually feel bad about the whole situation? I wasn't going to take any chances. I was partly to blame so I was at least going to try to be civil and make amends.

"I should git some firewood for tonigh'," he said casually.

"But you don't have your lighter anymore."

I couldn't help the apologetic tone that seemed to be seeping through my statement. I grinned slightly and grabbed my bag. My pathetic attempt to start a fire last night left me with only a half a book of matches. Hopefully it would be enough for him to be able to start one. He took the book from me and shook his head, and I could hear a soft chuckle as he smiled with amusement.

"Ya have everythin in there, don' ya?"

"Better safe than sorry I always say." I smiled back.

"Well, I guess I be"er go find some wood. I's goin' ta be as cool as last nigh'."

"About that."

"Yeah?" He looked at me with a curious expression in his eyes.

I wanted to tell him how sorry I was, that it was stupid for me to run off. I wanted to tell him about the dingo and how it kept me warm through the night but I didn't think he would believe me. And I wanted to ask him about how he stayed warm himself but I figured he could tell me later. I had so much to say but I didn't know how.

"Never mind."

He shrugged as he turned and headed toward a group of bushes.

"Ye're goin ta be okay without me, aren't ya?" His voice was a little anxious as he turned back and looked down at my ankle and makeshift splint.

"I'm fine."

He walked a few more steps and then paused. I waited for him to say something but he stood motionless, as if he had turned to stone. Finally he looked back over his shoulder at me, regret on his face.

"Sorry abou' all I said yesterday, I didn't mean i'." His voice was soft and tortured.

"Yes, you did."

He took a deep breath, even more somber, and glanced downward, ashamed, searching for the right words.

"Sorry I did." He finally said repentant.

He turned back away from me and took a few more steps and then hesitated.

"Jus' for the record, I was wrong."

Then he disappeared behind a clump of bushes and dead, twisted trees to look for wood, his head bowed a little.

That was it for me—the fight was over. In my eyes he had made amends. Anyway, I couldn't afford to continue to be mad. Jack was my security, my safeguard, and if I was going to make it home, I was going to have to rely on him almost completely. What was the point of holding any kind of grudge? I reached down and rubbed my ankle, trying not to move as I waited for Jack to return.

I was resting my head back on the trunk of the tree. My eyes closed as I thought about the dingo and the crazy wind. Was I just imagining the whole thing? I knew the dingo was real; I felt his warm body and stroked his coarse fur. But what was up with the wind?

"That I had to of imagined." I thought out loud. "I was scared, and your mind plays funny tricks on you when you're scared."

Just then I heard the soft crackle of twigs beneath light steps coming toward me again—too soft to be Jack's. I smiled, expecting to see the white dingo coming back for more jerky, but to my surprise when I opened my eyes a dark-brown dog stalked toward me pacing a little as he carefully watched his prey—me. I didn't move, not even to breathe. I could tell he smelled the fear radiating off my body.

I saw something move in the corner of my eye. I carefully looked over without moving my head; another dingo had joined the party, then two more, all of them hovering just a few yards back as if waiting for some kind of sign to attack. Maybe they were just waiting for their prey to take flight to enjoy the thrill of the chase, which of course I couldn't do. Suddenly the big, dark leader crouched down, preparing to spring, teeth bared, his eyes narrowing.

I felt my mind starting to get light and dizzy as I contemplated my death. I knew I should scream or something, Jack wasn't that far away, but I couldn't even make the smallest noise.

I could see the pack starting to grow anxious, and they were about to attack when suddenly, somehow, Jack was standing in front of me. Grasping a long piece of wood in both hands as if he were holding a bat, swinging it side to side. The whole pack crouched, ready to spring, low, fierce growls coming from all four. The dark-brown one bounded forward at Jack. He managed to hit it hard enough that he knocked the animal down along with himself. It got up and got in position to charge again, but before it or any of the pack had a chance something white flew between Jack and me and the ravenous pack.

It took me a few moments to realize what was going on. My furry friend had appeared out of nowhere and was guarding us from the wild predators. He crouched, meeting their stance, and an even fiercer growl came from this beautiful white creature.

In an instant everything happened at once. The pack attacked the smaller white dingo and he fought back with so much vigor and strength, it was as though more than one dingo was on our side. Jack crawled over to me and wrapped his arms around me like a protective shield and pulled my head into his chest, blocking my view of the animals' snarling fight. I could just hear growls and snarls, teeth clamping down on each other. I cringed over and over again. Finally I heard a loud yelp and then the sound of paws running away from us. In the distance the sound of yelps and howls echoed again, and then it was quiet.

12

Changes

※◈※

Jack released his hold around me and I looked around his body to see if I could see anything.

"They're gone," he said. His voice was soft and gentle, trying to keep me calm.

They were gone, but my mind was still racing. What happened to my furry friend, my guardian who had saved me twice now? Did he lose his life to protect us? I couldn't stand the thought of that; tears gathered in my eyes as I started to cry.

Jack, thinking it was just the shock of what had happened, hesitantly put one arm around me again for comfort, and even though I sensed a little uneasiness I automatically leaned into him and laid my head against his chest.

The image of what I heard kept running through my mind. The last sound of the agonizing yelp rang loud and strong. I automatically covered my ears to try and block out the sound that wasn't there. Jack withdrew his arm from around me and gently pulled my hands away from my ears.

"Hey."

I looked away from him; I didn't want him to see the sadness in my eyes. He gently lifted my face, and then wiped the remaining tears off my cheek. I looked up into his eyes that were so warm and comfortable they made me feel safe, and I could feel the tension between us dissolve into the past. He paused and smiled for a brief second, staring back at me, his eyes fixed on mine, and then he blinked quickly and slowly let go of the hand he was still holding.

"I's ok, they're gone and they won't be back." His voice was full of assurance.

"How do you know that? They could be back later tonight when we're sleeping."

"Trus' me."

I wanted to trust him, but I didn't know him very well and it worried me. I thought about the dreams I'd been having and it made me even more apprehensive about who he was.

Jack stood up abruptly while brushing the dirt off his pants, and glanced at me wearily.

"I need ta go git the wood I found before i' gits dark."

I couldn't believe how quickly the day passed by.

"Are ye goin ta be okay?" He glanced at me, waiting for my response.

"I think so, but hurry back."

He nodded, acknowledging the fact that I was still pretty traumatized by the earlier event, and walked quickly out of sight.

While I waited I tried to get comfortable against the tree trunk. Finally I leaned over to my side and rested my ankle on the opposite leg, and my head on my arm. I closed my eyes and concentrated on ignoring the pain. I tried not to think of the white dingo, holding back tears.

I don't know if it was the day's events or the jet lag still hanging on or just the simple fact I didn't get much sleep during the night, but before I knew it I faded into a wistful dream.

I was standing alone out in the middle of nowhere, surrounded by the vicious dingoes as they circled me again and again, getting ready to attack. Suddenly my hero came to protect me. I could feel a tear rolling down my cheek. Then suddenly the attackers were gone as well as my protector and I was alone. My eyes snapped open and I sat up quickly.

"Jack!" I called frantically.

"I'm here." His voice rang out close to me.

I must have been asleep for quite awhile—it was right around dusk. The distant trees and bushes in the distance were nothing but a silhouette against the orange and pink cotton clouds as the sun melted into the horizon. Jack had a fire blazing in front of me and quite a bundle of wood—sticks and twigs actually—sitting next to him.

"Wow," I yawned, "how long have I been sleeping?" I stretched, forgetting about my ankle until a shot of pain ran up my leg. "Urrrr." I gritted my teeth.

"How's the ankle?" Jack put down the long, thin stick he was using to poke the fire and moved over closed to me to take a look.

During my nap it had grown twice, if not three times its normal size.

"The swelling is pre"y bad," he muttered. "I wish we had some ice ta control it." He sat thinking for a moment, his forehead wrinkled with contemplation.

Then he reached over me and snatched my bag from my side and started going though it, pulling everything out.

"Hey!" I huffed, annoyed, but he didn't pay any attention to me.

He pulled out the bottle of water and set it aside, then grabbed the leftover strips of fabric from my destroyed shirt and poured half the water on top of it.

"What are you doing?" I gasped as I watched him waste half of our only water supply.

"If I wet the rags and put i' around yer ankle i' migh' git cool enough ta help the swellin' especially since i' will be cooler tonigh'."

"But that's our only water." I couldn't help but be a little panicked.

"If we don't git the swellin' down yer ankle will be worse off."

He took the wet strips and arranged them around my ankle and through my splint, making sure it had the best coverage for what little he had to work with.

"Now we need ta elevate yer foot."

He held my feet very gently and placed them on a large rock near me. My feet were raised so high that I couldn't sit up and face the warmth of the fire. I looked like an oversized letter L. Jack's low chuckle made me laugh at the situation and the movement of my laughter brought a small surge of pain as my face winced.

He looked at me with a crooked grin, and then he did something very unexpected. He sat down next to me, leaning against the bolder my feet were on and pulled my legs carefully off and rested them on his lap.

"Is that be"er?" He smiled.

"Yeah, thanks."

It was better; besides his first-aid skills, the compassion he suddenly was showing me was very comfortable, and I started to feel something very natural between us. We were passing through the stranger faze and entering into friendship.

I lay still on my back, hands resting on my stomach, and my feet resting on Jack's lap, watching the fire dance. I looked up and saw that Jack was just as mesmerized with the flames as I was. His face seemed to radiate the glow of the fire. His amazing eyes were dark pools of water that I could easily drown in.

"Jack?" I turned back to the fire.

"Aye?"

"What do you think happened to that white dingo?" I concentrated on not allowing my voice to shake.

"I don't know." His response was a little hesitant.

I could tell he was being a little candid trying not to upset me.

"Seriously, what do you think? Do you think they killed him?"

He was quiet for a few seconds.

"Yes."

I looked up at him and his facial expression was bleak. I turned to the fire again and I felt a tear roll out from the corner of my eye and into my hair.

"That's why I don't think they'll bother us. He gave them quite a figh' though, before they…" He couldn't continue.

"I have to tell you something." I sat up the best I could, leaning back on my elbows. "That was the second time that dingo saved my life," I explained.

"Whit are ya talkin' abou'?"

"Last night after I…" I didn't want to bring up bad memories. "Well you know. I couldn't get a stupid fire started. It was so cold I thought I might freeze to death or something. I had fallen asleep and sometime during the night he came up to me and laid right against me to keep me warm."

"Ya must have been dreamin'. Dingoes don't act like tha', they're wild animals, not domestic."

"I wasn't dreaming, I thought I was at first too, but I felt his warmth and I stroked his fur."

"Why would he do tha'?"

"I don't know, that's what I was wondering. Maybe it was because I gave him my beef jerky."

"Ya whit?" His voice became a little scolding.

"Yeah, yeah, I know, don't feed the animals, move on," I replied mockingly.

He just shook his head in disbelief.

"The point is that he did and then he gave his life for us now. I just can't believe that he's gone. There was something special about him. Maybe he got away somehow." My eyes started to water again.

"Maybe he did," Jack replied.

But I could hear in his voice that he really didn't believe it.

I laid back down pulling, the hood of my sweatshirt over my head, and started watching the fire dance again as Jack tossed another piece of wood onto the flames. Tiny sparks jumped out in different directions. The pain in my ankle was starting to subside, and with Jack unconsciously gently massaging my legs I felt warm and safe, and hope that we were going to make it flooded every part of me.

"Jack." My voice broke the silence.

"Aye?"

"How did you get through the night?"

He grinned slightly. "I don't need my ligh'er or even matches ta start a fire. I jus' found a good spot for the nigh', made my fire, kept my coat on, and made i' through. I was actually more concerned abou' ya gittin' through the nigh' than myself."

"Oh," I said, feeling a little stupid that I couldn't even make it through the night without some kind of help.

"Hey." His voice was a little perky. "By any chance is tha' apple still any good? I'm pre"y hungry."

"Um," I hesitated, feeling quite guilty. "I kind of ate it this morning. Sorry." My apology seemed weak.

"So whit do ya have in tha' bag of yers?"

I grabbed my bag and looked through it. Everything was gone but the half bottle of water. Between the dingo and myself I had managed to eat all the snacks I had brought with me.

"Sorry, everything's gone."

I waited for some kind of repercussion of my selfishness, but all he did was look at me thoughtfully and smile. I couldn't help but wonder what that smile meant.

"What?" I asked.

"Nothin'," he answered, still smiling.

13
Tempting
❈❀❈

The sound of a soft inviting crackle woke me. I had slept through the night with no dreams interrupting my stillness. At least if I did dream I didn't remember it. The last thing I remembered was watching the fire blur into the soft waves of movement. And I scarcely remembered Jack moving from under my feet, but as I became aware of things around me I could feel my backpack was propping them up.

Before I could focus on opening my eyes the sweet smell of scrambled eggs with a hint of roasted nuts—maybe almonds—swirled slowly into my thoughts. My mouth started to salivate. My empty stomach growled in anticipation of something I didn't have to give it—food.

I thought I was waking up but I must have still been sleeping and having the best dream. My hunger was so prevalent that I could almost taste the dream on my tongue as it passed lightly over my lips.

I heard Jack move then and he cleared his throat. "He must know I'm awake," I grumbled. I didn't want to get up yet; I was enjoying my feast.

"Good mornin'," His gruff voice was cheerful.

"Good morning," I yawned and pushed myself up, still trying to wake up.

"Good dream?" He smirked.

"Why do you say that?"

"Well, jus' before ya woke ya were moanin' a li"le and ya kept lickin' yer lips."

"Moaning?" I asked, my face flushing into a bright shade of red.

"Well, maybe i' was a coo or ya were tryin' ta say somethin'. I couldn't really understand. But whitever i' was ya were really enjoying i'. I didn't want ta disturb ya." His smirk became more pronounced.

"Oh boy, I better explain before he gets the wrong idea," I thought. "Oh, I was dreaming about eating this really nice breakfast…"

All of the sudden I realized that Jack wasn't just stoking the fire; he was holding something over it. Slowly rotating a long, thin twig carefully over the fire, four large wavy lumps were pierced through one end to the other, spaced evenly down the stick. Ranging in different shades of brown.

"What is that?" I said crinkling my nose.

"I made breakfas', shish kebugs, my specialty."

"Shish ke what?" I asked in horror.

"They're called witchetty grubs. The aboriginals and ou'backers ea' em all the time. Usually they ea' em raw bu' I thought ye migh' like them cooked be"er. Here, try i'."

He handed me the stick with four large caterpillar-like worms on it. I looked at it questionably but didn't take it.

"Why are you cooking them?" I asked.

"Last nigh' ya said there wasn't any food left so I got up early and found us some grubs. Come on, try i'." He offered the stick to me again.

"You know, I think I'll pass, but thanks anyway." I turned my nose away from the cooked worms.

"Jus' try one li"le bite," He coaxed as he took a bite out of one—showing me they weren't bad. "After whit I saw this mornin' ye've got ta be pre"y hungry."

My face flushed again. He stood up and walked over to me and sat down while holding the stick in front of me, leaning to my side.

"Come on, ya know ya want i'." His voice taunting me. "Can't ya smell the sweet aroma?"

He passed the stick under my nose. "Ye've got ta be soooo hungry. Ya haven't ea'en for a long time."

He leaned in closer and took my hand and wrapped my fingers around the long stick. I could feel the heat of the fire still on his skin.

"Jus' take one li"le bite."

He teased again, but I still resisted, my lips closed in a hard line as he guided my hand closer to my mouth. Then he leaned over, his lips brushed against my ear and chills ran throughout my whole body. Did he realize he had this effect on me? Then he just spoke one word.

"Chicken!"

His voice was gentle but powerful. It was like he knew how much I hated that word, or *coward*—all of the common words. I turned and glared at him, our faces only a few inches apart. I pulled my hand away from his and with my eyes still glued to his—not thinking about what I was going to do—took a huge bite out of the middle of one of the plump, rippled worms.

Its roasted skin crackled as my teeth bit into its soft center and a milky residue ran into my mouth as I started to chew. The taste and texture was that of scrambled eggs—well, that explained my dream. I chewed purposely, still fixed on Jack's eyes. As I swallowed the corners of his mouth turned up into a satisfied grin.

"See, tha' wasn't tha' bad, was i'?" He couldn't help but be smug; he got what he wanted.

I didn't want to say anything, I didn't want to give him the satisfaction of being right, but it really wasn't that bad. Not that I want to eat this all the time, but it was something I could tolerate, I just had to not think of what I was eating. Maybe I was just really, really hungry. I continued to eat the rest of my breakfast as Jack ate his. Jack just laughed at my disgust as my nose crinkled every time I took a bite.

We sat there eating our grubs quietly when I looked over at Jack. He had a very satisfied grin on his face. I went back to eating.

"See, ya really do like them, don't ya?"

"They're tolerable, why?"

"Ya jus' sound like ye're really enjoyin' them." Jack chuckled.

I looked at him, a little puzzled.

"Ya're moaning," he explained, still smiling.

"No, I'm not."

"Yes, yes ya are. Every time you chew I can hear this soft, pleasurable moan jus' like when ya were dreamin'."

I could hear the enjoyment in his voice and his smile looked a little wicked. He was really getting a kick out of my little embarrassing habit, while I, on the other hand, could feel my face heat up with what I could only imagine was a very bright shade of red.

"So where did you learn how to cook something that's so disgusting into something edible?" I asked, trying to change the subject and get through the last few bites.

"Ah, told ya ye like i'." He grinned.

"I wouldn't say that. But it's something I can at least stomach. I can't believe you'll eat this but you don't like beef jerky." I gave him a slight smile as I forced the last bite down. "But seriously, where did all the knowledge come from?"

I threw my skewer into the fire as tiny sparks jumped and then looked up into his brilliant blue eyes, waiting for his response.

"When I was in the air force I had to participate in a lot of survival trainin'. I would have ta spend days ou' in the middle of nowhere with nothin' bu' whit I had on my fligh' suit, as if my plane had crashed."

"Oh, I see, you were in training for that fateful day when your plane would fall out of the sky with me in it," I tried to joke with him, chuckling at my attempt, but he didn't find it at all amusing. He just looked at me and then continued.

"I was very good at survivin' with what I had, usin' whit the land offered me. Cookin' with what ever I could find kind of became my thing. Then when I got ou', cookin' became my hobby."

His tone became content and relaxed as he finished the last of his grub; then he threw his stick into the fire as well, a little too hard as the sparks jumped out and landed inches away from me.

It finally made sense, how he knew what to do with my ankle, how he didn't need his lighter or matches to start a fire. The fact that he knew how to get between me and the ravenous dingoes without them noticing, even how he was able to put the faltering plane down safely without killing us. As my mind raced through my evaluation I felt suddenly grateful to Tom for his choice to send me with such a skilled pilot. Maybe he wasn't as malicious and sinister as I had perceived.

My mind was so caught up with my thoughts of Tom that I didn't hear the question Jack had asked me.

"I'm sorry, what?"

"Whit do ya do back home?" he repeated.

"Oh, I have the most exciting job ever, I do data entry," I said sarcastically.

Jack's voice was light as he held back a chuckle. "No wonder ya were runnin' away. If I had a job like tha' I would want ta run away, too."

"I'm not running away." I could hear my voice go on guard.

"Ally." His eyebrows rose, questioning my answer.

"I'm not." I shot back a defensive glare.

"Whit do ya call i'? Comin' clear ta Australia by yourself? When we were at Uluru and ya were walkin' around did ya happen ta notice anything abou' the other touris' there?"

His face smoothed out and his eyes seemed to linger attentively on me. I shifted uncomfortably, trying not to disturb my ankle. The question made me anxious; I didn't want to think about the conclusion I had already come up with.

"I don't know what you're talking about."

"Think abou' i'. Didn't ya notice the groups of people, the friends and families, the couples tha' were together. I didn't see one person by themselves the whole time we were there. Mos' people don't take this kind of trip alone." He watched for my reaction and then poked at the smoldering timbers, trying to act casual.

"Some people do," I responded, thinking of the elderly woman who I met on the trail. She was definitely alone. "What about the old woman that was there by herself?" I countered.

"Whit old woman?"

"The old aboriginal woman that was on the trail. You had to have seen her when you came looking for me."

He looked at me confused. "I didn't see any old woman on the trail."

"You would have passed right by her. She was wearing a bright floral shirt and red shorts down to her knees." I was starting to get irritated. He had to of seen her; how could any one miss her?

I shifted again, deciding that my position was still uncomfortable; it made my stomach a little uneasy. I sat for a few moments getting frustrated while thinking about how oblivious he had to have been to his surroundings.

"Well she was there," I grimaced.

"Okay, I guess I jus' didn't see her." He put his hands up, palms out, as if to surrender the point. "Le's talk abou' something else," Jack suggested while he started kicking dirt on the burned out timbers. "Tell me abou' yer job." He asked in such a way that he really did seem interested.

I looked down, trying to avoid the question. "There's nothing to tell; it's just a job."

"But whit d'ya do?"

"I sit at a desk typing on the computer all day. No one bothers me, no one talks to me. I get a lot done." I didn't want him to know that I was such a loser I didn't even have a job.

"No one talks ta ya?"

"Dang, Why did I say that," I thought.

My stomach started becoming even more uneasy. I rubbed it hoping that it would settle, then my mouth started to get dry and it felt like I had something caught in my throat.

"Why doesn't anyone speak ta ya?" he asked curiously.

"I don't know, why is the sky blue? That's just the way things are."

I cleared my throat, not able to help the feeling creeping up. I cleared my throat again trying to dislodge the uneasiness that had moved from my stomach and was now making its home in my throat. I tried rubbing my neck hoping the feeling that I was now immensely aware of would subside.

"Ally, are ya okay? Yer color looks quite off." Jack's tone was ranging from curiosity to concern.

"Yeah, I don't think your shish kebugs agreed with my stomach. I just need a drin...,"

Before the words even finished coming out of my mouth, I was bent over, sweat collecting on my brow, and a loud roar came from deep within out into the great outdoors. I could faintly hear a flock of birds taking flight—startled by the revolting sound that I couldn't control.

"Please let me die." I thought to myself as I remained hunched over—face flushed from the pure embarrassment of it all.

As I waited for the next round to hit I was vaguely aware that despite my position my hair wasn't hanging in my face. Then I realized that Jack had wrangled in my thick, wiry curls in his hands and was holding it gently so it wouldn't get in my way. The embarrassment whirled around my head as I continued a chorus of unpleasant melodies.

After what seemed like forever my stomach finally seemed to be back to normal. I stayed lying on my side, the last of the water in front of me, and my bad ankle once again propped up on my backpack. Jack was finishing up covering the last of the burnt embers of wood with dirt. He already did the job of covering up the remains of my breakfast.

He saw me watching him as he kicked and stomped on the extinguished fire.

"How ya feelin'?" His tone was light.

"I feel a little better. Sorry you had to see that."

"Don't ya worry, I've seen much worse. I remember this one time when a group of us from trainin' went ta this pub in Glasgow. Tom got so buttered tha' his head didn't leave the toilet for a whole day. Usually Aussis can really throw 'em down, but not like us Sco's." He started to laugh out loud at his memory.

He went to continue with his story then stopped when he noticed the awkward look on my face.

"Sorry, I forgot ye're not in ta drinkin' and havin' fun, are ya." His tone was a little mocking.

"No, well yes, I mean no, I don't drink and all that but I do like to have fun. It's just your description of Tom is bringing up not-so-fun recent memories."

"Oh, sorry," he said, then chuckled once. "I have ta say, fer not eatin' tha' much, ya had a lot come ou', I mean I had no idea…"

I quickly cut him off before he could go any further. "Well, thank you for noticing Jack, but can we not talk about it anymore?" I took the last gulp of our water and sighed.

"Now what are we going to do?"

"I've been thinkin' abou' tha'. I think there migh' be a river abou' a half day's walk—if I remember correc'ly."

"So you know where we are."

"Things are startin' ta look familiar, bu' I still can't tell ya exactly where we are."

He paused for a second and then changed the subject. "So what kind of fun do ya like?"

He was trying to keep things casual.

"You know, just your ordinary things. Going to dinner, going to the movies with my sisters. Once in a while going dancing."

"Ya like ta dance?" His voice had a certain lift to it and his eyebrows rose. I wasn't sure if he was intrigued or if he didn't believe me.

"Oh yeah, I'm a great dancer. I tell you, get me out on the floor and this girl has got it going on." I raised my hand and did a sorry attempt of a Z snap. Jack chuckled.

I jerked my body wrong and a slight twinge of pain shot through my foot—I cringed.

Jack crouched down to examine my ankle. "How's the foot?" he asked as he gently evaluated my injury.

"It's okay," I responded, trying not to seem anxious. "It still hurts a little, but I'm fine."

Jack carefully untied the scraps of fabric that he had wrapped around two large sticks when he had fabricated my splint the night before. He slightly twisted my ankle to one side then the other, carefully pressing down on different tender areas.

When he touched spots that were particularly sore, my body would automatically stiffen and my teeth would clench together to hold back the urge to voice my pain.

"Sorry," Jack said when he saw me stiffen up, and then he touched me even more carefully. "Well, yer swellin' has gone down some, bu' i' looks pretty black and blue. Can ya move i' at all?" His hands released my foot to give it the freedom to move around.

I slowly moved my foot up and down, trying hard not to inflict any more pain onto myself.

"Tha's good," he said with a smile. "Now try movin' i' around in circles."

I started to rotate my foot.

"Slowly," he advised.

I slowed my movement down and warily rotated my foot.

"How does tha' feel?" Jack's eyes were intense as he watched my movements.

"It hurts but it's more of a dull pain, not the sharp stabbing pain from before."

"Good." His smile got brighter. "Tha' means ya didn't break i'. If ya did ya wouldn't be able ta move i' at all."

I let out a sigh of relief and I thought I could almost hear a sigh come from Jack as well.

"Looks like I'm going to survive." I chuckled, thinking Jack would chuckle to, but his face got serious and his mouth had formed a hard line.

He quietly wrapped my ankle back up the same way as he did before. I noticed his face became intense and serious and I could sense that he was struggling with something. Something he wasn't sure he wanted to share.

"Jack, is something wrong?" I asked, mystified by his expression.

He finished tying the last of the fabrics and then just stared at my leg. Then he finally broke his silence.

"We need ta git goin'," He said apologetically.

"I know."

I could see the concern in his eyes. He didn't want to make me walk with my ankle.

"Ya know, we can't stay here all day. We need ta git ta a town as soon as poss…"

"Jack," I interrupted, "I know." I reached out and touched his wrist reassuringly. He smiled back in response.

"Can ya git up?" he asked as he stood.

"I think so."

I maneuvered myself into position. I felt that I could use my good leg to help push myself up. I didn't get enough push and failed.

"D'ya need some help?" Jack mused as he watched. I could see the corners of his mouth twitching as he held back a smile.

"I got it."

I maneuvered again, rearranging my position and trying to calculate how much strength I would have to exhort to push my body up onto one leg. I managed to use the large rock next to me and hoisted myself up.

I stumbled onto my good leg and tried to balance myself but lost my balance all together as my foot slipped from underneath me and I landed hard right on my butt. My face winced as I felt the hard thud on the ground. Jack could no longer help himself: He broke out with a huge gust of laughter. I could have sworn even the bushes around us were laughing at me. They seemed to start to rustle as soon as I hit the ground.

Jack extended his hand toward me. Embarrassed, I took it and he pulled me up gently onto my feet—well foot. I reached down to pick up my backpack but Jack was already there. He flung it over his shoulder as I looked at him in amazement.

"Okay, le's go," he announced.

I took one step, maybe two, and then Jack was by my side, his arm securely around my waist.

"Here, lean on me," he said, his eyes fixed on mine.

I looked at him attentively. Could this be the same person who seemed so mean and distasteful in the last twenty-some hours? He had shown me such compassion. The memory of his earlier remarks and attitude were slipping away into the distant past.

"Jack, thank you," I said softly.

"No problem." His tone was light, not understanding my meaning.

As he started to walk, I didn't move. He turned and his expression was confused.

"No," I shook my head, "thank you," I said with earnest.

This time he understood the meaning behind my words. Maybe he could see it in my eyes.

"You're welcome." His voice soothing and comfortable.

His eyes lingered on mine for a few moments, and I felt him lean toward me as if there was something he wanted to add but he quickly pulled himself back. We both smiled. Then automatically, as if we were one person, we started walking together.

14
Mutual Cause
⌘

As soon as my plane rolled into the terminal I could feel my anxiety flowing through my body. Before anyone around me had a chance to collect their belongings I had my carry-on and was already a few steps ahead of everyone else.

"Excuse me," I said while bumping into people as I tried to get close to the front as much as possible.

"Pushy American," a voice rang behind me, but I didn't pay to much attention to the criticism.

I rushed through customs at an amazing velocity and had my one extra bag of luggage as soon as it slid down onto the baggage carousal. The only wait time I made for myself was trying to figure out where to go first. Should I check into my hotel or go directly to the police station? I decided to go to the hotel first.

I checked into the same hotel as Ally, figuring that would be the best place to start. And if they cleaned out her room before she got back I could keep an eye on her things. I didn't want to think of the other reason I would need her belongings.

"Good day, welcome to Circular Quay Inn," The twenty-something male said as he smiled.

"I have reservations. Darci Thomas."

He started typing quickly and then smiled as he gave me my key.

"Here you go, Ms. Thomas, room 601."

I took the key hastily, my hands trembling slightly. Then I paused and took in a deep breath.

"You don't know how I get to the police station from here do you.?" I asked.

The young man looked up at me, bewildered. "I'm not exactly sure how to get there, but I can find out for you. Is something wrong?" he asked, trying to be helpful.

"No," I answered automatically, "thank you anyway."

I didn't have time and I didn't want to get into a long discussion about it. I just wanted to get the answers I needed. I rushed to my room just long enough to drop my bags off and ran back downstairs.

In front of the hotel cabs were coming and going and I figured they would know how to get to the police station. I was right. I was dropped off right in front of the local station.

As I walked in, there were a few officers and all sorts of people mulling around, most of them of their own free will, but some escorted in handcuffs. An older woman with an unhappy disposition was sitting at the front counter.

"Excuse me, can you help me?"

"Burglary, homicide, kidnapping or misdemeanor?" she drawled as she typed on her computer.

"I'm here about my missing cousin. She was in the plane..."

Before I had a chance to finish, without even looking up, she slapped a few pieces of paper stapled together in front of me.

"Fill these forms out, have a seat, and we'll call you."

I looked down at the paperwork, in bold letters at the top where written the words "Missing Person."

"No, I'm here about the two missing people from the plane crash. The young woman is my..."

Just then the phone rang, which didn't bother me until she walked away from the counter and left me standing there, still with no answers. Anger and frustration from my anxiety was starting to build up inside. Ally was lost out in the middle of nowhere or worse, I hadn't had much sleep in the last two days and this woman was being so unprofessional. I waited a few more seconds to see if she was going to help me. Then I couldn't handle it anymore.

Knocking hard on the counter. "Excuse me, the two people in the plane crash, can you help me? I'm the American's cousin." I was almost yelling the words at her.

The woman turned and glared at me and then mumbled something in the phone and put the person on the other end on hold.

"Ma'am, we aren't handling it. It is out of our jurisdiction," she said finally. "If you want to find anything out you're going to have to go to Wind Croft Airfield. That's where they are heading the search."

"Thank you, and how do I get there?"

She rolled her eyes, sighed with exasperation, then proceeded to give me vague directions on the back of the forms she had given me.

I walked back out determined to get to where I needed to go, but as I looked around I realized that my taxi had left. In my rush I had forgotten to ask him to wait. I hailed a passing cab and decided that it would be much more productive if I rented a car. I got back to my room and within a half hour had a rental and was headed to, what I assumed was a small, somewhat adequate airport.

As I drove my nerves were on edge and I didn't know exactly where I was going. I just had the very vague directions to a place in a very foreign country. And driving on the other side of the car on the wrong side of the road didn't help. I had to concentrate hard as each car passed, hoping they wouldn't hit me—flinching each time.

As I turned down a small street I could see the airport coming up. I stopped at the stoplight, waiting to continue down the road that would lead me to the front gate. As I sat there idling, waiting for the light to change, an elderly man passed in front of me—a strange look on his face—then shook his head in a critical manner.

"What's his problem?" I mumbled to myself as I watched him pass.

I started down the road toward the gate when I immediately realized the strange look I was given. I had automatically turned onto the right side of the road which of course was the wrong side. Grateful that a car wasn't headed my direction, I quickly got back to the correct lane.

When I got to the small airport the gate was closed.

"Now what am I going to do?"

Just then a car passed me and punched in some numbers on a keypad on a small metal box just outside the gate—this was my chance. The chain-linked gate slowly opened, and as the car drove through I raced in right behind it.

I drove around and looked for some kind official building, but all I could see were hangers after hangers. Finally on the far end corner of the rows of hangers I noticed a much smaller building. It was a nice, rustic brick building—it could have even been a home or some kind of lodge or community center. A well-kept lawn surrounded it and the Australian flag swayed in the wind out front.

The small parking lot seemed to be buzzing with activity as cars would come in and park and others would leave. I felt that this might be a good place to start.

As I parked my car I noticed a fair amount of official cars parked toward the front—not just police cars but what looked like airport security, as well as National Park vehicles.

Inside things seemed to be just as manic. In a large room that looked like it was usually used for banquets or other large functions, chairs were set up all around, with a few tables scattered among them. People were rushing around getting directions as they looked at maps and then grabbed what they needed and headed out the doors.

I walked up to a young man who was about to leave. "Excuse me, is this where I can find out about the missing plane?"

"Yes, are you here to volunteer?"

"Kind of, who's in charge?"

"Officer Roberts, that man over at the table." He pointed to a group of people standing around a long rectangular table. "See the map with the pins in it? You'll find him over there."

"Thank you." I sighed in relief.

There was a group surrounding the table intently listening to instructions when I walked up. Even though he was blocked from my view his low, gruff voice seemed to radiate his authority.

After they got their instructions the crowd dispersed and just two men were standing at the table. One was a tall man with a little bit of a bulge around his middle and broad shoulders. His dark wavy hair stuck out the sides of his hat. The official markings on his uniform told me this must be Officer Roberts. The other man was slightly shorter and slimmer, nice looking with straight, sandy-blond hair. He didn't look official but his attire made me think that he was perhaps with the National Park vehicles I had noticed outside. Both their faces seemed pleasant enough, although Officer Roberts had a harder edge to his face.

I spoke up, bold and determined. "Excuse me, Officer Roberts?" They both turned their heads to look at me.

"Yes?" He responded.

"My name is Darci Thomas.'

"What can I do for you, Mrs. Thomas?"

"It's Ms. Thomas, and I'm Ally Pierson's cousin. I'm here to find out what's going on and help in any way I can to find her."

"Well, Ms. Thomas, I really don't know what you can do. We have search teams out all day looking for your cousin. The best thing you can do is stay out of our way. Go back to your hotel and when we find something out we'll let you know." His voice was condescending and obviously irritated.

"Look," I said as I glowered at him, "I'm not leaving here until my cousin is safe and sound." I crossed my arms, daring him to make me leave. I could see in Officer Robert's eyes that he was about to dispute my words.

"Look, Ms. Thom…"

"Ms. Thomas," the blond man interrupted, "why don't we get you some coffee?" His request was gentle and pleading.

He softly place his hand on the small of my back and escorted me over to a table were an assortment of pastries were available and two big thermos containers held coffee—one decaf and the other caffeinated.

"I don't drink coffee," I explained.

"They also have juice." He poured me a cup and then handed it to me.

"Thank you." I smiled slightly as I took a drink.

"My name's Tom, Tom Bagner."

"Darci." I put my hand out for him to shake; He accepted the offer. "Are you with the police or are you with the National Park Service?" I asked, thinking how he seem to match the trucks that were parked outside.

"No, Jack McQuewen is my friend."

"Who's Jack McQuewen?" I asked curiously.

He cocked his head to the side and looked at me, his eyebrows scrunched together. Then just as quickly they smoothed out again as understanding hit him.

"Oh, I forgot you don't know any of the details. Jack McQuewen is the pilot of the plane."

"Oh." A slight gasp came out as I started to understand. "I'm sorry, you must be pretty worried as well."

"Of course, but I'm also concerned about your cousin." He glanced down, not wanting to meet my eyes. "You see," he continued, "I'm the one who arranged for Jack to take your cousin to Ayers Rock."

I looked up at him, lingering on that idea for a moment, not sure how to react to this new information. Should I be angry or sympathetic? After all, he wasn't to blame for the plane going down, was he? He seemed to be in the same boat I was, so of course I felt sympathy. He obviously felt responsible and guilty for arranging the trip. Why would I make him feel worse?

"Tom, did you have any idea that this would happen?" I asked.

"None. As far as I knew his plane was in perfect working order."

"Then don't beat yourself up about it," I said, trying to sound encouraging. "But how could this happen?" My voice was starting to get high and pitchy. I calmed myself down before I spoke again. "I'm sorry; I don't mean to be rude, I'm just worried about Ally."

"No worries," he said casually. "If anyone can keep them safe, it's Jack."

As I watched him the corners of his mouth turned up into an impish grin. It made me wonder what he was thinking.

I thought about the words he used. If anyone could keep them safe, not alive, but safe. As if he had no doubts that they would remain alive—they just had to stay safe. I knew there was more to this than he was telling me.

"How long have you known, Jack is it?" I asked curiously.

"About fifteen years. We were in the air force together."

"You must be pretty good friends?"

"Yeh, I guess you can say that he is my best mate."

I took another drink of my juice while I contemplated our conversation.

"Tom, can I ask you a question?"

"Go ahead."

"What do you think happened? When we got the call at home they didn't give us many details; we were just told the plane went down and they were looking for it. Ally's mom is frantic thinking Ally is dead." I gritted my teeth, holding back the emotion that was fighting to show through, but I was determined to be strong. I would break down later when I was alone.

"Well, from my understanding, Jack's plane instruments went out. And they couldn't see him on the radar. They got a short distress call from Jack; then there was nothing."

"I just don't understand. With today's technology, why can't they find them?" I set my cup down a little too hard—frustrated at it all.

Tom gently stroked my arm and then laid his hand inconspicuously on my shoulder.

"Don't worry, Darci, like I said, if anyone can keep them safe, it's Jack."

Just then a low, throaty voice came over the radio. His accent was so strong I could barely understand what he said.

"This is search team Blue-seven, come in."

"Go ahead, Blue-seven," Officer Roberts responded.

Tom and I rushed over to hear the conversation better.

"We found the missing plane, but there was no one in it. By the footprints it looks like they headed south."

"They're alive," I said, almost literally jumping for joy.

Officer Roberts put his hand up to shush me and I felt Tom's hands rest softly on my shoulders.

"Good job, Blue-seven. We should be able to find them fairly soon. They couldn't have gotten too far."

"We actually have to come in. We're running low on fuel and a storm is headed this way."

"Okay, come on in, Blue-seven."

My heart sank as I listened to his words and anger started to build inside.

"What are you doing? Have them keep looking!" I screeched.

"Ms Thomas…"

"They could be hurt or worse, dead. Tell them to keep looking!" I continued, the level of my voice starting to rise with each syllable.

"Darci," Tom called, his voice calm.

Officer Robert's face became stern and his voice serious as he spoke each word slowly and clearly making sure I understood each one.

"Ms. Thomas, the plane is out of fuel…"

"Send out another plane," I interrupted.

He ignored me, "And a storm is headed our way. We already have two people missing I don't need a whole search team missing as well. Now as soon as the storm passes we'll be right back out there. Until then you need to remain calm and let us do our job."

I couldn't stand the fact that he was right—as much as I wanted to find Ally, it was stupid to put others in danger. I walked away, my arms crossed in front of me, trying to control the frustration and anxiety that continued to grow.

I walked over to the other side of the room. The glass windows seemed to take up half the wall. As I stared out into the distance I could see dark clouds starting to gather. I wondered how long it would take for them to reach us, and how long it would take to reach Ally and her companion, Jack. Would they be stuck out in the rain or would they find the shelter they needed? My anxiety grew.

"Ally, where are you?" I whispered.

I closed my eyes to say a quick prayer for their safety and shelter as the thunder rolled in the distance.

15
Mud And River
❊❂❊

The pain in my ankle seemed to come and go. It came when I put any kind of pressure on it and it went as soon as I took the pressure off. Using Jack as a crutch did help but it was making our journey very slow.

I could tell that after a day or so without his cigarettes that Jack's new-found kind disposition was wearing thin and he was starting to get edgy, but even though I had to stop more than he wanted, he didn't say anything.

"Jack, can we stop for a few minutes?" I said breathlessly as the pain wrenched through my ankle. Clenching my teeth—jaw flexed, hoping to hide the pain. It didn't work.

He removed his arm from around my waist and slowly helped me to the ground. Holding both of my hands securely in his as I tried to maintain my balance, I couldn't help but notice how each muscle in his arms flexed as he lowered me gently down. I could feel the heat of embarrassment cover my face thinking that my weight could be somewhat of an issue, but he never seemed to have a problem with my weight. He moved me around with hardly any effort at all.

"Maybe he was just being extra vigilant," I thought. "Trying not to hurt me."

Once I was sitting down he bent over to examine the damage.

"Le's see whit's goin on here." His voice was soothing.

He held my leg over his bent knee and pressed his fingers around the splint without undoing any of the strips of cloth.

"I' looks like i's swelling up again. Lie back and I'll fine something ta prop yer feet up with."

He gently put my leg back on the ground. I bit my lip as a trace of the familiar ache came back.

"Sorry," His face creased into concern when he noticed my discomfort.

"I'm fine, it's not your fault, I'm the dope that ran off and fell in a hole."

He didn't seem to find any comfort in the reminder of the other day as he just grimaced and walked away. I quickly realized that I now had to remove my much-too-swollen foot out of my mouth.

I took my sweatshirt that I had wrapped around my waist and rolled it into a ball and put it under my head. I laid back and watched as the big, billowy clouds were connecting together one by one and starting to form one huge cloud. And as each one connected with the others their color seemed to change from a bright, glowing white to a soft, hazy gray.

Jack had gotten back carrying a good sized rock and placed it under my foot. Then he sat down next to me—legs stretched out, leaning back on his hands.

"How long are we going to stay here?" I asked.

"Jus' a few minutes. We want ta try and stay as far ahead of tha'," he pointed to a grouping of darker silver-gray clouds collecting in the distance, "as possible."

I looked in the direction he was pointing and shock filled my eyes. With the clouds above us and the ones in the distance there was no doubt a downpour was on its way. I could feel the tension starting to bubble up inside my body.

"There is no way we are going to outrun that."

"I never said we were goin' ta ou'run i'," he said, not missing a beat, "I just want ta get as far along as we can before i' hits."

We were both silent for a moment. I kept watching the clouds above me and Jack stared out into the distance. But it wasn't the uncomfortable silence from before. It felt calm and natural—this part of the journey had actually been better than the last few days, hurt ankle and all. Jack seemed to be more at ease talking with me and keeping up a conversation.

"So, ya have how many sis'ers?" he asked, picking up were an earlier conversation left off.

"Two: Gina and Megan," I explained, turning to look at him as he gazed at me.

"And ya live with them and yer mum?" It was more of a question than a statement.

"As roommates," I clarified.

His eyes seemed to be studying me, trying to understand something that I wasn't telling him.

"What?" I asked, my eyes narrowing on his. He was making me nervous.

"Why aren't ya married?"

"Ugh, that stupid question," I thought. "I always hated that question."

"You seem to be marriage material. Ye're smart, kind...attractive." I was very surprised by his last adjective and I could feel my skin start to flush.

Why was it that if you were over a certain age everyone always asked that question? Couldn't someone be single and happy or at least appear happy without everyone asking that same stupid question? I wanted to tell him exactly that, that I was single and happy and it was a stupid question. But the real reason was I didn't know. I was relatively happy, but the fact that I wasn't desirable to anyone enough for marriage material always stung just a bit. So instead of answering I countered his question with my own.

"Why aren't you?"

"Ally." He leaned in, his eyes staring into mine firm and superior trying to be all intimidating—it didn't work. "Why do ya thin...."

"Wow!"

I was suddenly distracted when a large group of kangaroos jumped past us, maybe only twenty feet away. They were so elegant as each one bounded at an amazing height and speed, flowing so smoothly you could hardly tell they were jumping.

"Whit?" Jack tuned and looked in the same direction. "Oh, now tha's a mob," he responded.

I propped myself up on my elbows and watched as they quickly darted side to side and forward. Each one an individual but as a whole—a family.

"Look there." Jack leaned in close to me, his cheek almost touching mine. "See the one in the front? I bet he's the head of this mob." He pointed out what looked like the biggest of the group. "The one at the point leading the way."

I watched them as they faded, one by one, out of sight. As the last one bounced past a group of bushes nestled together, something moved and caught my eye. I sat up quickly and stiffened. Fear seemed to enter the core of my body. For just an instant two dark eyes with pointed ears and four legs stared at me, then backed into the bush.

"Jack," I said breathless, grabbing his arm. As I turned to talk to him, we were closer than I thought—just a few inches away from each other. I paused awkwardly and let go of his arm, leaning back a few inches. "Look," I managed to choke out, pointing to the bushes.

He stared at the group of bushes, straining to see something.

"I don't see anything."

"I could have sworn I saw a dingo."

The thought of the group of dingoes coming to finish us off made me shiver.

"Ally, there's nothing ou' there." He slumped back into his original sitting position.

"I saw a dingo," I insisted.

"Whit did it look like?"

"I don't know, I just saw him for a second." I couldn't help the annoyance that was creeping into my voice. He didn't believe me. "We should go," I said quickly.

I pulled my foot off the rock, maneuvered myself onto my knees and then pushed myself up from the ground the best I could. As I stumbled on my good leg Jack quickly grabbed my arm to steady me before I had a chance to fall over. He picked up my bag and once again the long trek was before us.

After a while of walking we came to a riverbed that looked as if it had been dormant for who knows how long as it cried out for moisture through its cracked surface. Bushes and trees seemed to have lined the sides even though there was no water to give them nourishment.

Jack half-slid, half-jumped down the side and then reached his hand up to help me down—not an easy task with a hurt ankle. I pretty much sat down on my butt, my legs dangling over the side, and slid into Jack's half-opened arms. The slight impact made me cringe.

"Ya be"er lean on me again." He smiled at me.

It was only a few yards to go from one side to the other, but as Jack looked at the wall of dirt, he decided with my ankle it might be easier to find a lower point to try climbing.

As we walked along, side by side, I started thinking of this man who had started out as my pilot and was now becoming my friend. I didn't know him very well and certain things were making me curious. Besides, talking helped keep my mind off my pain.

"Jack, can I ask you a question?"

"Go ahead."

"It might be a little personal."

"Okay." He looked at me, a little wary as he continued to cling to my side—my personal crutch.

I paused, thinking about my question, then decided to ask a different one.

"You're Scottish, right?"

"Aye."

"Why isn't your accent very strong?"

He smiled and then chuckled once. "I haven't lived in Sco'land for a long time. And I've been all over the world. My accent is bound ta lose some of i's strength." He chuckled again. "Is that all?" he asked.

"Yeah," I lied. "Why?"

"I thought ya were goin' ta ask me somethin like, why do I like ta smoke or somethin' abou' my relationships with women. Maybe somethin abou' my childhood."

I could hear a slight sigh of relief in his voice.

"No that's it." I chuckled awkwardly, hoping he wouldn't notice and smiled. "I'll wait 'til later to quiz you on the more personal stuff," I joked.

One single drop of rain hit my cheek and rolled down my face like a tear that had escaped my eye. I looked up at the darken sky just as millions of drops fell quickly to the earth.

The rain was cold and wet I couldn't help myself. Walking for so long without any water had brought on such a thirst. I stopped where I was, letting go of Jack, tilted my face up toward heaven, and closed my eyes and opened my mouth wide. My tongue stuck out as far as it would go. It made me feel young, like a child trying to capture a snowflake on her tongue.

Raindrops sprinkled across my face, in my mouth, through my hair. Before long every part of me was wet. I didn't care; as I moved my tongue across the moisture on my lips the fresh taste of just the few drops seemed to help the aching thirst that had been growing deep in my throat.

I opened my eyes, figuring I would see a disapproving look on Jack's face—he'd been wanting to get moving. To my pleasant surprise he was participating in the same activity. Looking just as silly as I probably did—his tongue out as far—his thirst as great as mine.

I continued taking in each little drop of water as it coated the dryness of my throat.

Jack turned toward me and I to him and we both couldn't help but laugh at the juvenile way we looked. After four days of walking in the sun and the heat of the outback along with everything else we have gone through, a little laughter was so exhilarating I couldn't help myself—the bratty girl inside had to come out. For no reason at all I picked up a handful of mud and flung it at Jack. He ducked just in time as it whizzed right past him.

He looked at me, his eyes wide in amazement. "Ye're goin' ta get i' now," he warned.

He bent down and filled his hand full of mushy, wet dirt and with perfect aim hit me square in the chest. A soft squashy thud came from the mud ball as it flattened out in one big splotch on my shirt. I wiped the thick mud off and glared at him—a slight smirk on my face—and I bent down and gathered more mud for another round. This time my aim was better. I managed to hit his shoulder. This act seemed to be the call to war. Both of us instinctively started throwing mud at each other, covering each of us from head to foot.

We started laughing so hysterically that it got harder and harder to throw. Soon we were laughing so hard that we no longer could stand. We just fell to our knees in front of one another, smearing mud wherever we could. Finally, in Jack's determination to win our battle, he pushed me over onto my back, straddling across my stomach, pinning my arms useless to my side, and with his final blow took a handful of mud and smeared it into my hair and then wiped the remainder down my face.

"Truce, truce!" I screamed though my laughter.

Jack slid off my stomach and rolled onto his back. We both laid there in the mud, our laughter finally slowing and our breathing evening out as the rain continued to fall onto our muddy figures.

Jack sat up and pushed himself to his feet and then offered his hand to me. I took it graciously as he helped me stand. He looked at my mud-caked face and smiled, then wiped away the mud from one side with his fingers. Then he cupped my cheek with his hand and with his thumb cleared away the mud on the other side.

He held his hand on my cheek for a few moments, staring into my eyes as the rain starting to come down even harder. Mud was starting to wash away and his eyes looked bluer than any of the times I'd seen them. It wouldn't have made me so uncomfortable, but I was always so mesmerized every time he intently looked at me with his warm sapphire eyes. My heart seemed to beat faster and I could tell my breathing almost stopped as I looked back at him.

He started to lean toward me just a little as though he was going to say something, his lips parting slightly. Then his lips formed a perfect grin as he backed away and snapped out of whatever he was thinking. Then his voice was suddenly serious.

"We need ta git goin'."

He picked up my backpack that had fallen to the ground during our childish exhibition and flung it over his shoulder and went to put his arm around my waist again.

"That's okay, I've got it," I said as I hobbled next to him. I felt it was time to give him a break from helping the gimpy, though I never minded his arm around me.

As we sloshed along and the rain continued to increase Jack seemed to get more and more anxious. His speed started to increase, making my hobble a little more difficult, and he kept looking back past his shoulder as though he were waiting for someone to sneak up behind him.

"This looks pretty low," he said. "Can ya git up here?"

I looked at the side of the river wall, my eyes evaluating what Jack was talking about. We were looking for a low point that would be easy with my bad ankle and this was definitely not the place and not something I could really manage.

Jack's tone was so persuasive and urgent though that I didn't question his decision—I started to climb. I grabbed the roots and rocks that were protruding outward and tried to pull myself up, mainly using my good leg. Jack had already made his way to the top and had reached down to help pull me up. Again I tried using my good leg to push myself toward him but the rain made everything so muddy—my foot just slipped off whatever I stepped on and I would instinctively use my bad ankle to compensate for the wrong footing.

"Arrr," I groaned as I slipped for the third time. "Can we just walk down a little further and see if there is something lower?" I asked, looking frustrated and miffed.

He looked up the empty riverbed and then jumped down.

"Okay, bu' lets hurry, I don't trus' this river," he said, still looking back from where we had come from.

"Why? Its not like the rain is going to fill this thing up anytime soon." I snickered at the thought. "It would take a lot more rain than this to do that." I smiled at him, thinking he would be as amused as I was. But his face was strained—serious.

"I'm worried abou' a flash flood. The river can be immersed in jus' a few minutes from ou' of nowhere. Hence the name *flash* flood."

I felt dumb and embarrassed—if I hadn't had so much mud on my face you could have seen my face turn red. Of course he would be aware of something like that; another advantage of his training.

Our pace increased as Jack kept searching for a way up, looking side to side. There was a sound of soft rolling thunder coming from behind us along with the piercing crack and crunch like something big being mangled by something hideous. We stopped and looked at each other and then slowly in unison looked back over our shoulders. An enormous wall of water and debris was coming straight toward us.

"*Run!*" Jack yelled.

We both took off, our feet sloshing through the mud as fast as we could. Our bodies' heavy from the mud and rain that covered every part of us. My ankle gave out on me and I fell palms first before the rest of my body had a chance to hit the ground. Jack realized I wasn't by his side and raced back and grabbed my hand, pulling so hard that I landed on my knees again. He helped me up and while still holding my hand took off running—dragging me behind him.

He climbed up the side of the riverbank so fast I didn't even know how he did it. he reached down to me so I could take his hand.

"*Come on!*" his voice was frantic.

I grabbed his hand and started to scale the wall of mud—not thinking about my ankle—as the intruding danger got closer. As I climbed I lost my footing, let go of Jack's hand, and slid down the side.

"I can't," I cried.

Jack jumped down and linked his fingers together, making a step for me to use. I put my good foot in his hands for help but it was too late. Before I knew it I was being whirled around in every direction, my arms and legs feeling disjointed from my body. My brain disoriented by the lack of sight and sound as the muffled, whooshing water rushed over me, dragging me under as it pulled me further down the river.

I finally broke through the surface and gasped for air. I reached frantically around me, trying to find something to keep me afloat. As I started to go under the second time Jack wrapped his arm around my chest and swam to the side, then hoisted me onto the bank. I started to cough and spit out water, trying to regain my composure.

A dull but loud thud and a strange sound from Jack caught my attention. My head snapped up just in time to see the large tree trunk that had hit Jack from behind float away. Jack fell back lifeless into the water.

"*Jack!*" I screamed.

I ran along the side of the river, watching his body float along motionless, calling out his name.

"*Jack, Jack!*" I wished I could do something. I couldn't jump in to save him; I couldn't swim. I had never felt so hopeless in my life. Tears started to flow as I trailed further and further behind.

"Please save him," was the only thought that came to my mind—it was the only thing I could do—pray.

Out of the corner of my eye something zipped past me and then I heard a loud splash in the water. It took me a moment to focus on the figure swimming out to Jack. A white clump of fur was moving in his direction. My furry protector had come out of nowhere.

"Get him, boy!"

Relief filled every part of me as I watched him catch up to Jack. By the time the dingo reached him, Jack had regained consciousness and was trying to swim to shore, but the current was too strong. The furry life preserver finally made it to him and he took the help. Jack wrapped his arm around the dingo and they both swam to the river's edge.

As I caught up with them I immediately dropped to my stomach and stretched my hand out as far as I could.

"Jack, Jack, grab my hand."

When he got within reach he locked his hand around my wrist. I pulled as hard as I could using every ounce of energy I had left in me. Between my pulling and our friend, Jack pulled himself up onto the solid ground. The soaked white dingo, just as exhausted as Jack, dug his claws into the dirt and pulled himself out of the raging river behind Jack. We both laid there our hands still locked together, trying to catch our breath—both weak and trembling.

"Thank you," I whispered breathlessly as I glanced upward.

I managed to pull myself up onto my knees and moved closer to check if Jack was okay. I reached out to him as he pushed himself onto his knees and looked at me. My emotions were too strong to hold back. I through my arms around him and he responded in the same way—his arms tight around my waist.

"Are you okay?" I softly spoke in his ear—tears filling my eyes. "I'm fine," he whispered back—his arms tightening around me. At that moment, I never wanted to let go.

16
Flattered
※❖※

"Darci."

In the back of my mind I thought I heard a soft, gruff voice calling my name. So soft that it didn't completely register, but then a firm but gentle hand lightly shook my shoulder.

"Darci."

I opened my eyes and Tom was standing over me with a smile on his face. I sat up quickly, realizing I had fallen asleep sometime during the day while waiting for the storm to pass.

"Are they back?" I said, my voice anxious.

"No, it's still pretty wet out there."

He sat down facing me on the other side of the couch as I stretched my arms over my head while yawning, still trying to wake up completely.

"How long was I asleep?"

"Maybe an hour. You looked completely knackered. I thought you must have really needed the sleep."

"Oh great," I thought, "that probably means I was snoring." I shifted uncomfortably.

Tom grinned as though he could read my mind but he probably just read my horrified expression.

"Don't worry, you didn't do or say anything too embarrassing." He let out one amused chuckle. "But you did say something about you wanting me to take you out for some tucker." His grin got wider as he winked at me.

"What?" My voice squeaked when I spoke. I cleared my throat and tried again. "What?"

Tom laughed at my reaction as he pulled a bag out from behind him.

"I thought you might be hungry so I bought you a cut lunch."

"A what?"

"A sanger," I looked up at him still confused. "A sandwich."

"Oh," I smiled feeling slightly embarrassed.

"I didn't know what you would like on it so I had then put everything on." He smiled back as he held his hand out, offering me the sandwich.

"Thank you, but I really couldn't eat right now."

He looked at me, examining my expression, shrugged, and set the sandwich down between us.

"How long can it keep raining?" I complained as I looked out the window, watching the sheet pound against the glass.

"Can't really say, it's the rainy season. It could end anytime or it could go on for hours. But the weather report says it's going to be a long one."

I sighed and rubbed my forehead—the stress of everything was starting to give me a headache.

"Darci, you need to relax. Tell me about Ally. I only met her for a short time. She seems very…" he paused, "interesting. We sat by each other on the way here when I boarded the plane in Fiji."

"Fiji?" I marveled, "What were you doing in Fiji?" I couldn't help but sound curious. He was the one who seemed interesting.

"I was there on holiday." He shrugged. "My business is in the travel industry—so I travel. Now back to your cousin. You two are close?"

"Very. You see, I don't have any sisters, so she's the next best thing." I smiled at the thought.

I reached down absentmindedly and grabbed the sandwich between us, unwrapped it, and took a bite—realizing I was a lot hungrier than I had thought.

The unfamiliar flavors left a bitter, earthy taste in my mouth—I had to spit it out. The taste of chicken was definitely present, but some of the others I was wary about. I took off the top slice and carefully dissected the contents and was surprised by the mix of colors and flavors that came between the two white slices of bread. As I discarded each unwanted layer my nose scrunched in disgust.

"Sprouts, carrots, cucumbers," my eyes widened as I listed the ingredients in my head, "asparagus, *beets?*" As I picked the slimy burgundy disk off my sandwich with just my fingertips and laid it on the wrapper with all the other unwanted items, I couldn't help but wince.

"Yuck." I muttered. I left only the bread, chicken, and lettuce.

Tom watched my careful operation with amusement—trying to hold back whatever comment he was dying to say.

"What?" I asked defensively.

"Well, I guess next time I won't get you the chicken salad." He chuckled. "Just the chicken."

"This wasn't a chicken salad sandwich," I opposed, reassembling what was left of my sandwich.

"It is here." He paused, shaking his head as he examined my pile. "I can't believe you Americans don't like anything between your bread."

"Well, excuse me for being American," I snapped.

I regretted the words as soon as they passed my lips. But I felt irritated that I had to defend my choice of sandwich toppings. I wanted to put the sandwich down and not eat anymore, just out of plain stubbornness, but I was much too hungry.

"Sorry, I'm just stressed, and I think the jet lag is catching up to me. I went from taking my kids to karate to jumping on a plane in just a few days. And then I came here almost directly from the airport—I'm exhausted."

I could almost see Tom's thoughts turn a different direction as his eyes suddenly narrowed and the small space between his brows creased.

"That's okay, I understand." He took a couple of seconds before he continued. "So what does Mr. Thomas think about all of this? You coming clear across the world at a moment's notice."

"Not much since it's none of his business what I do anymore. I divorced that mistake a long time ago."

Tom's face seemed to shift again and he seemed to emulate some kind of excitement. The crease seemed to smooth and his eyes beamed a bright smile.

"Sorry to hear that." There was no sincerity in his voice.

I gave him a half-smile back. "Thanks."

"So when did you break those ties?"

His curiosity was a bit unsettling. I didn't want to get into my whole marital history, especially with a stranger and especially when there were more important things going on. So I don't know what made me start.

"After my youngest was born we decided it was for the best. We'd been having problems, and when I got pregnant they seemed to escalate to a point where it was better for the kids for us not to be together."

"How many kids do you have?" he asked curiously.

"Three." I reached in my purse and grabbed a wallet-size folder and opened it proudly. "Ryan is the oldest; he's nine. Then there's Miles; he's the handful," I couldn't help but grin, "and he's seven. And then there's my sweet angel, Amy," as I spoke I could hear a devotion for my kids coming out. "She's going to be four in about a month." I lingered on Amy's picture for a few moments, missing her and the boys terribly.

"So you've been divorced about three years now," Tom interjected.

"Boy, he doesn't miss a thing," I thought as I put my pictures back in the safety of my purse.

"Yeah, that's about right." My voice was wary from his observation. "Why?"

"I just wanted to make sure you were free and clear before I ask you to have a real meal with me." He smiled a wide, Cheshire cat smile.

I blinked madly, trying to understand what had just happened. Did he just hit on me? It had been so long I wasn't quite sure. A few different emotions flooded my mind as I assessed his words. One was anger. How could he be hitting on me when I was so concerned about Ally? The second was embarrassment. How could he want to go out with me, a middle-aged, minivan mom of three? Third was flattery, for the same reason as two. There were others but after the third emotion I kind of forgot the rest.

"Thanks, Tom, maybe once Ally's back safe." I smiled sheepishly at him, my face blushing for the first time in who knew how many years.

"Great, I'm looking forward to it."

He slouched back into the couch and finished the last bite of his sandwich. I could tell by the size and the multiple colors sticking out that he also got the chicken salad.

"So what about you?" All the questions made me a little curious about him. "Were you ever married?"

"No, I was never lucky enough to find anyone I loved as much as the outdoors. I guess I like the solitude too much."

"I wouldn't mind some solitude once in a while, but I think I would eventually miss the crying and whining, the pestering, the laughter and the hugs."

Tom shifted his weight, seeming a little uncomfortable with the conversation. I thought I would let him off the hook and change the subject back to the present situation.

"Tom, you said you met Ally on the plane. So you talked to her?"

I was a little surprised. Ally never really talked to anyone she didn't know.

"Yeah, she was asleep when I first boarded. When she woke up I could tell that she was really nervous about flying so I tried to keep her mind off it. She was a little hesitant at first..."

I interrupted, "I can see that. Ally is pretty quiet if you don't know her."

"That's the feeling that I got, but she seemed to warm up to me quickly and then she just opened up. It was strange, it was almost like we had been friends for a very long time. I guess she just needed someone to talk to."

"That is strange." I felt a little hurt. "She usually doesn't trust people enough to open up right at first. It takes a while and even then she usually keeps them at arm's length."

I leaned back on the couch, staring at the wall, trying to wrap my mind around Ally's unusual behavior.

"What did you mean when you said she was interesting? It sounded like there was a double meaning in that," I asked.

"Well, I think you're right about her keeping people at arm's length. Even though we got along great and she opened up, I could tell there's something more to her. Something that is hidden. She may not even know what it is. She's holding back the best part of herself."

"You sound like a shrink," I said with a laugh.

"I used to be one." His reaction was serious. "Well a therapist. I had to get out of it—it was too stressful of a job."

"Sorry, I don't mean to offend you."

"You're fine."

I sat up and leaned toward him, my hands clasped together and resting on my lap. "Too stressful—how—if you don't mind me asking?"

"No," he said casually. "It just got too hard sometimes. I had a hard time leaving my work at the office. I guess I just cared too much. That's why I like the solitude. The only one I have to worry about is me."

I could see that there was a small glint of pain in his eyes as he reflected back on his memories. I felt bad that I brought a sore subject to the surface. But then he snapped out of it and his eyes smiled again.

"So anyway, I tried to dig a little but she seems to be guarded without even realizing it. Then we arrived in Sydney and we went our separate ways. But when she came into my agency looking for a tour trip to Ayers Rock, I realized I had a perfect opportunity standing in front of me."

I looked at him curiously, my mind again racing at all the information he was giving me.

"What are you talking about?" I asked, stiffening a little.

"You see, Jack has his share of issues as well. I know a lot of it has to do with his past. His father used to use him as his personal sparring partner when he was just a boy after his mother passed away. He left home when he was about fourteen and had to make it on his own. He got into a lot of trouble just trying to survive. When I met him he seemed a bit of a bludger, but by the time he got out of the air force he had matured and straightened up a lot. I think he found a kind of family in the air force that he didn't have before. It brought out the best in him. That's why I know that they're okay." He paused, and took a drink of coffee. "I thought this might be the perfect opportunity to help him, as well as Ally."

Suddenly the pieces of an unlikely jigsaw started to fit into place. My eyes got wide as I stiffened.

"Tom, you're not seriously saying that the plane going down was your doing, are you?" I whispered somewhat in shock.

"No," he huffed, "I just thought that they might hit it off."

I sighed in relief.

"From what I learned from your cousin and what I know about Jack I thought they would be great together. They're the perfect unlikely pair that are a lot alike. So I convinced him to take her."

"How did you do that?"

"Well I'm not proud of it," his lips turned up into a sly smirk, "okay maybe I am. I told him she was one of his typical conquests. He fell for it like a rock falling off a cliff."

"One of his conquests," I muttered, then slid back against the back of the couch and ate a few more bites of my sandwich, listening to his explanation.

"Well, she's not Jack's typical type—he usually goes for the obvious when it comes to the good looks department. Long, slender bodies, the blond hair, and everything cosmetically proportioned perfectly. They usually got it all except…"

"Brains," I interrupted again.

"That and depth." He chuckled once. "He's my best mate, but sometimes he can be a bit on the shallow side, but he is a good bloke. So Ally may not have the obvious…" he held his hand up, his fingers making quotations, "good looks, but she has a lot to offer."

"Well that's nice," I thought as I sat there listening.

"When I first met your cousin, I couldn't help but be totally captivated by her once she opened up to me. She's a very charming and beautiful woman on the inside as well as out. And her eyes are amazing; the contrast between her dark hair and her sky blue eyes are just stunning. It's like they just capture you, and you bring her right into your heart. You can almost see the joy as well as the sorrow in them."

I looked at him a little begrudgingly.

"It sounds like you have quite an admiration for her."

I couldn't help the edge in my voice, and I didn't know why, just that the way he was talking about Ally seemed to bother me a little. I collected my thoughts and erased whatever expression my face was making and waited for his response.

"Yeh, but she's not my type, I like the more maternal, career type." He looked up and winked.

And I couldn't help the girlish smile that curled up on my lips. "Smooth," I thought adjusting my position. "Now what were you saying about helping Jack and Ally?"

"Well, I figured once they were at Uluru's base they would be able to break though their walls and talk, and get to know each other."

My eyebrows raised a little as I listened to him continue his explanation. Something in the way he chose his words made me feel like there was a secret he didn't want to share. I tried to read his expression to see if I could figure it out, but he just had the same grin on his face like he did when I told him I was divorced.

"What is Uluru?" I finally asked. "And why would you think they would have to wait until they got there to talk?"

His smile finally faded and he sighed; then he pushed himself to the edge of the couch and leaned toward me. I automatically leaned toward him—our faces only a foot apart.

"Okay, but this might sound strange to you."

"Why, because I'm American?"

"Yes," he retorted.

His reaction made me flinch just a little. And I sat back a few inches from his glare.

"Uluru is the aboriginal name for Ayers Rock. Some legends say that the Rock or Uluru is a very mystical place. It's a place where you can be healed."

"Like if you can't walk suddenly you can walk again?" I scoffed. "Not exactly. It's more like healing of your heart or your spirit. You see, Uluru is the place that the aborigines believe is the starting of time and everything in it, the place where everything got its name." He paused and scooted closer to me and spoke a little softer. "Some old folks say that because it is the place where the land began that the spirits of the land are connected to every spirit that comes there and that they know the intent of your heart. They can help you find the lost part of yourself and heal you."

I sat there motionless, dazed for a few seconds, taking in everything that Tom had just told me. After mentally analyzing every possible aspect of his story, I snapped out of my thoughts, blinked quickly, and shook my head slightly. I couldn't help the wide smile I shot in Tom's direction.

"Yeah, right, I may be American, but I'm not gullible," I snorted.

"Believe what you will, but people have said once they've been to the Rock they were like a new person."

"So you think that these spirits would have gotten Jack and Ally together?" I asked halfheartedly.

Tom shrugged. "I thought maybe if it is true they would help them both find what they were looking for. Maybe they would find it in each other."

"And I guess you think that them crashing the plane is all part of these spirits' involvement as well?"

"You never know, but I don't actually think that. I think they crashed because Jack has a hard time keeping his plane in perfect condition."

"I thought you said the last time you knew the plane was in good condition?"

"Yeh, but it's been awhile since I've seen his plane and the last time it was in good condition."

Frustrated, I slouched back into the couch and finished the last few bites of my sandwich. Tom had given me a lot to think about, but none of it seemed plausible. I've never been a believer of legends or myths. But I guess people might feel the same about my religious belief. Who was I to judge someone else's beliefs or something so mystical and even magical?

Truth was I did believe the whole concept of things magical, but I called it having faith in miracles. Hoping in thing not seen that are true. And I had to hope, I had to believe. Everything in me had to hold on to that little bit of magical faith that Ally was all right.

17
Sheltered
❊❊❊

Jack and I walked steadily behind our unlikely guide, his white tail swishing back and forth, his tongue hanging out as he trotted along happily.

"Whit's up with this dingo?" Jack said. "I've never seen anythin' like i' in my life. They aren't suppose ta be domes'ic." He shook his head in confusion.

I couldn't help but smile at our new companion, Hero, as I liked to call him. His loyalty to my friendship was truly a gift.

As we walked my feet started to feel like my shoes had turned to cement and the pain in my ankle throbbed dully. My legs were nothing but two very wet noodles. I stopped abruptly as rain poured down around me. Exhausted, I allowed the noodles under me to yield to that exhaustion and I slumped down on the wet, soggy ground.

It took Jack about three seconds to realize I was no longer hobbling next to him, and Hero four. Jack's eyes were wary as he saw me sitting, my legs slightly crossed, with my bad leg out in front of me and leaning back on my hands.

"Ally, whit's wrong?" He knelt down to check my ankle, while Hero walked over and sat at my side, resting his chin on my lap.

"I can't do this anymore. I can't go any further." My voice cracked as I held back the tears that were coming out through the frustration.

"Whit are ya talkin abou'?" His voice was light and almost mocking. "le's go."

Hero raised his head and his ears straightened.

I looked up, still holding back my tears, and shook my head definitely. "No."

I knew it was stupid to just sit there in the mud and rain, we had to keep going, but I was too exhausted to care.

"I'm sure we don't have tha' much further ta go. Maybe jus' one more nigh'."

"That's what you keep saying, but we just keep walking. We're lost and you know it. We'll probably die out here."

My voice started to tremble just a little and the onset of hysteria was starting to come out as I wiped the first tear to leak out.

"We're not goin' ta die ou' here, bu' le's get goin' and find some kind of shel'er before i' gets ta dark."

"No, I can't. I'm wet, I'm tired, and I hurt. I'm going to stay right here."

"In the rain?" Jack asked as he raised his eyebrows.

"It's not raining as hard. I should be fine." I looked around, trying to find a rock that would work as a pillow.

"Look, I'm tired and wet too, bu' staying ou' here isn't the bes' idea. I's goin ta be a Baltic nigh'."

"What?"

"Really cold, so if we stay ou' here—well le's jus' say i' won't be good, so le's go."

Jack waited as I just sat there. My furry friend looked between me and Jack watching the conversation, and then rested his chin on my leg again.

"Ally! Get up off yer …" He stopped his own exclamation as he gritted his teeth and sighed, realizing that maybe he should take a different approach.

"So ye're jus' goin' ta sit here all nigh' in the rain, not movin' or doin' anything? Allowing yourself ta freeze and not even try ta find someplace ta keep ya drier and warmer through the nigh'?"

I could see where he was headed with this, what he was trying to do.

"Whit are ya, a qui"er?"

I looked up at him, determined not to show any of my doubts and fears, and spoke strong and confident.

"Yes."

He threw his hands up exasperated, giving up the battle. I couldn't help but feel a little smug. I knew what he was doing, and it irritated me more than his cursing did. Using reverse physiology just felt so condescending.

"Fine," he finally said.

He turned to walk away and I could hear some slight grumbling under his breath and a little of the unpleasant vocabulary he had a tendency to use.

He looked back over his shoulder. "Ya stay here and freeze then. Enjoy yer pi'y par'y."

I stayed sitting in the mud watching Jack walk further and further away from me. Hero whimpered as I stroked his course, wet fur waiting for Jack to come back. Even though he was still in sight and Hero was next to me I suddenly felt very alone. The stubborn side of me wanted him to walk away as far as possible but the realist part of me knew I needed him.

Suddenly the ground felt hot, really hot, as though I were sitting on asphalt on a hot summer's day. It was no longer comfortable sitting on the ground. Then it was as if something had shocked me. I couldn't help but jump to my feet—well, stumble to my feet.

I started walking toward Jack, still yards away, with Hero at my side. I tried to hobble quickly so I could catch up. Before long we were side by side again. Jack had obviously slowed down, taking his time, to allow me to catch up. I looked over at him—his jaw was clenched and his eyes focused out in front of him. I was a little afraid that I would have to deal with his anger all night, but instead I could see a slight smirk rising up on his lips. Then he nonchalantly slipped his arm around my waist to help me walk, and I knew I wasn't in that much trouble.

For the longest time the sky had been the same charcoal gray without any sign of the sun. My watch read that it was clearly in the early evening and the sun should just be starting to descend behind the horizon, but the only change we could see was the cloud coverage that had become darker.

As we continued to slosh along a brisk bite of cool air seemed to seep straight to my bones. I wrapped my arms around myself as my teeth started to chatter. Suddenly Hero stopped, his ears alert.

"Whit is i' boy?" Jack said. He crouched down to try and see what Hero might be looking at.

There in the distance stood a large, solid figure. This seemed to be out of place in the openness of the surrounding area. It was good sized, but not huge, rectangle in shape, and as we got closer I could make out the angles of a small house—very small.

In the distance and headed in our direction the dark clouds started to spark with light. Flashes and rods filled up the surrounding areas. The following rumbles warned that another major down pour was on its way.

"Come on," Jack urged as we picked up our pace toward the tiny building.

I turned to my side and noticed that Hero wasn't next to me. I stopped and turned back. The white figure stood motionless, his eyes fixed on me.

"Come on, come on boy," My voice started to shake, as I got more desperate for Hero to follow me. "Come on boy, its okay." Clapping my hand on my knees.

He turned his head, looking toward the open land around him, and then back at me for just a moment. Then he rushed off into the darkness and as suddenly as he came he was gone.

Even though I knew he wasn't mine to keep, I felt as though I had lost something very special and close to my heart. I wiped my eyes and walked back over to Jack.

"He's meant ta be free and roam," he said.

Jack pulled me in close and wrapped his arms around me, letting me have my moment of sadness.

"I know," I said, swallowing back the large lump that had formed in my throat as I buried my face against his chest.

When we reached the small structure the sunlight that had been hiding behind the cover of charcoal clouds had already sunk into the horizon. Jack peeked in the small window on the side and then tried the door handle. The door swung open as we stepped in out of the rain—shivering.

To say the place was dry was true, but it was definitely not any kind of living quarters. It was basically an eight-by-eight storage shed out in the middle of nowhere. It was adorned with bridles, ropes, and a stock whip on the walls, and an old, dusty saddle on a sawhorse in the corner. Old lanterns were lying around the floor and on a back shelf, and a big bag of dog food that had been sitting in the corner for who knows how long was collecting dust.

"Well, at leas' we have shel'er," Jack mused as he brushed some cobwebs out from in front of him.

"What is this?" I asked, confused.

"I think i's a herder's shack."

"A what?"

"When herders are drivin' their stock across the bush from point A ta point B, they can stop here take a break and fix or replace whit they need before they go on."

"Do people really do that anymore?" I asked curiously.

"I's not very common, and by the looks of i', this one hasn't been used in a long time."

Jack picked up one of the lanterns that had fallen to its side from the ground and blew the dust off it.

"D'ya have anymore matches?"

Just then I realized that I didn't have my backpack.

"Where's my backpack?"

I could see in Jack's expression that he suddenly realized he didn't have it either.

"I must have lost i' in the river."

"Oh man, all my stuff was in there. My money, my passport, some personal items." I started to panic as I glared at Jack. "Now what am I going to do?"

"I'm sorry; I thought saving our lives was a little more important at the time," Jack said a little irritated.

I could feel my face flush as I calmed myself down. It was stupid to worry about something so trivial when we had gone through so much.

"No, I'm sorry; it's just everything I need was in there."

I turned away as a feeling of awkwardness and embarrassment flooded my mind. How could I be so thoughtless? Jack almost died saving me and I was worried about a few replaceable items? Even the most important thing I had brought with me on this trip—my scriptures—could be replaced.

While contemplating how to get my foot out of my mouth again I noticed one of the lanterns used batteries instead of a wick.

"Hey, does this work?" I reached over, grabbing the lantern off the dust-caked shelf, and wiped what I could off its casing. "Please work," I mumbled as I pushed the button, and to my happy surprise a small light flickered on. "And then there was light." I smiled at Jack, which seemed to ease the little bit of tension that was still lingering in the air.

"Now le's see whit we got here," Jack said as he looked around the small space.

In the far corner was a pile of crumpled up blankets that looked like they hadn't seen a washer for quite a few years. Jack grabbed a couple and threw them to me.

"They may not be clean bu' at leas' they're dry," he said as he chuckled.

My nose crinkled as the smell of dirt and mildew filtered out of the fabric. I grabbed the end of the bigger of the two and shook it out as hard as I could in front of me, making sure that any insects that might have made their home there were gone. Then I wrapped it tight around me, trying to stop the shiver.

"Ya'd be a lot warmer if ya got ou' of yer wet clothes," Jack suggested as he grabbed a couple blankets for himself.

Shocked at his suggestion, I couldn't help but laugh.

"You're kidding right?"

Jack looked at me, his expression serious, as he raised one eyebrow.

"No!" I squealed.

"Ally, look at yerself, ye're so cold ya can't stop shiverin'. Trus' me, ge"in' ou' of yer wet clothes will help," he explained.

I stood there trying to control my shaking body to prove he was wrong, but it was a loosing battle, so reluctantly I agreed.

"Okay, but first turn around."

"Ally, ya don't have ta worry abou' me lookin'," he teased.

"Good, turn around."

"Fine, then ya turn around too."

We both turned our backs to each other as we took off our wet, muddy clothes. As I removed each piece I couldn't help but think that he was doing the same. Then without warning I couldn't help myself. I'd seen his body outlined so perfectly under the cover of his drenched shirt as it clung purposely to his chest in the rain. The temptation to just take a quick peek outweighed the reserved image I usually portrayed.

I turned inconspicuously, peeking over my shoulder, a jolt of electricity flowed through me as I watched each muscle in his arm flex as he removed his shirt. And as I watched his muscles roll effortlessly along his golden-tan back I couldn't help my wicked little smirk as I enjoyed him.

When he reach down to grab his blanket I couldn't help but marvel at how perfect his build was. I immediately felt insecure about my own body—it being far from perfect. No wonder he was so disgusted with me when we first met.

I was caught up in my own thoughts when I suddenly noticed Jack reaching back further than I expected for his blanket. I snapped my head back around, hoping that he didn't catch me looking.

I finished getting out of my wet clothes and wrapped the blanket securely around me, then hung them up the best I could so that they might dry. When I turned back around to Jack, he had a playful grin on his face and his color seemed a little more red than just from the sun.

"Dang, he caught me," I thought as I bit my lower lip. "Just act normal, don't say anything and maybe he won't bring it up." I pulled my blanket tighter around me and then sat down, leaning against the wall.

The awkward silence between us seemed to fill the air. Still embarrassed, all I wanted was for the earth to just open up and swallow me whole. I glanced over at Jack and he seemed almost as uncomfortable as I was, even though his smile still lingered on his face. As I quickly looked away I noticed a square box with dials.

"Hey, a radio," I said, finally breaking the silence.

"Does i' work?" he asked.

I flipped the switch and loud static bellowed out.

Holding his hands over his ears, Jack yelled, "Turn i' down!"

"Well duh," I thought.

I twisted the dial to lower the volume to a faint humming static and then started playing with the other dial, moving it back and forth. I pulled the long rabbit ears out and moved them around, hoping that something would come through. Just when I was about to give up a voice broke through the static.

"The two passengers of the missing Cessna aircraft that we reported to you yesterday have still not been located." The distinguished male voice echoed through the small space. "Search parties are still looking but had to cut their search short due to a bad weather front that moved in earlier today. Search will resume as soon as the weather clears. Local authorities are still hopeful on finding survivors. In other news..."

"Well at leas' we know they're still lookin' for us." Jack leaned back as he sighed in relief and closed his eyes.

My fingers slipped a little on the dial as I processed Jack's comment. "Were you worried that no one would?"

"Ta be hones' I wasn't sure."

"But you always were sure we would make it."

"I still am, i's jus' nice ta have the backup."

He opened his eyes again and looked over at me. I couldn't help rolling my eyes at his confidence. I wasn't as sure. I continued to play with the radio, hoping that I could catch more news about us, or at least be able to listen to some good music. It had just been the sound of Jack's groggy breathing, and the unsteadiness of mine, since my peek at Jack for just a little too long. It was nice to have something to break it up.

I quickly passed the smooth sound of an unfamiliar Jazz song. The male voice singing a melancholy melody with a backdrop of trumpets, and a saxophone caught Jack's attention just as I passed it.

"Wait, turn i' back."

"You like this?" I asked.

"Aye, whit wrong with i'?"

"Nothing, I love this kind of music, I just didn't think you would."

He leaned closer to me. "Why, whit kind of music d'ya think I would like?"

I shrugged casually. "I don't know, something with more of an edge to it."

"I do like tha' a bit bu' I think I'm gi"ing' a bit too old for the head banger stuff."

"I think we all are," I agreed.

He leaned back and pulled his blanket tighter around himself, still leaving one arm exposed, then yawned and stretched out his exposed arm. Then pulled it back into his blanket.

"Burrr," he shivered. "I' is defini'ly gi"in' colder tonigh'. I' usually doesn't git this cold this time of year—strange." He stared off thoughtfully for a moment. "How are ya doin'?" he asked.

"I'm fine," I lied as my teeth quietly clicked together.

I grabbed the second blanket that Jack threw to me and shook it briefly, wrapping it around my shoulders. Jack watched me—his expression weary, then continued the conversation.

"So whit other things did ya assume abou' me?"

I looked at him, studying him intently. "Well, to me, you seem the type that likes to go to the local pub and hang out with your mates and get totally wasted while watching a good soccer—I mean football game."

He laughed at my description of him.

"And then you are constantly going out with every beautiful woman that you can, but you never get serious with any of them."

Jack shifted a little and I knew I pretty much had him nailed.

"Well, I have ta say tha's a pre"y good analogy of me. I do like a good game, and the women." He got that same wicked smile that I'd seen when we were at Ayers Rock. "Well...d'ya blame me?" he asked.

I rolled my eyes.

"Now i's my turn," he said. "Le' me see."

He scooted closer to me—so close that we seemed to be only inches apart, and he stared into my eyes so long that it made me uncomfortable. I had to look away from his gaze and looked down at the ground instead.

"No, nothin', I can't figure ya ou' at all."

"What?" My voice a little high.

His mouth had a slight crooked grin to it as though he were holding back something more. "Ya are defini'ely a mystery."

"Oh, come on, there's got to be something you assume about me," I said. Throwing his own words back at him.

"Alrigh', le' me see." His smile was more pronounced as he gazed into my eyes again. This time I didn't look away.

As we sat there, our eyes locked on each other, Jack's smile faded and he became more serious.

"Ye're very kept." My eyebrows pulled together. "I don't mean that in a bad way," he explained, "ye're very reserved, and ya like ta keep ta yerself. Ye're also very cautious abou' yerself and those around ya." He pulled back as if to get a better look at me. "There's a par' of ya tha' ya hold back a par' tha' ya don't want anyone ta know. Ya don't trus' anyone because tha' scares ya."

My eyes started to water and I tried to wipe them without Jack noticing. I couldn't believe how close he came to all the feelings I had running around in my head.

"How do you know all that?" I asked, still stunned.

He looked up at me from under his long lashes. "I lis'en."

I didn't know what to say. I felt exposed. I tightened the blanket around me again as if that would help. But for as vulnerable as I felt I might as well have been standing in front of him nude with nothing wrapped around me. I had to change the subject and I had to do it fast. I looked around the room, trying to think of anything to talk about, when I noticed the stock whip on the wall.

"Here's something you don't know about me," I said. "I can break a twig in two by using a whip."

"Really?"

"Uhh... no, but I do know how to use one. I can really make it crack," I bragged, proud of my accomplishment.

"I can juggle," Jack added.

"I can balance a pencil on the bridge of my nose roll it down and catch it in my mouth." I continued.

"I can pick objec's up with my toes."

"What, do you have monkey toes or something?"

"No, watch."

He stood up and walked over to the bag of dog food in the corner and reached in and grabbed a few pieces and dropped them on the floor. Then he proceeded to pick each piece up with his toes until he had each one in his hand again. When he finished he bowed triumphantly.

"Well done," I applauded. "Okay, I can tie a cherry stem into a knot with my tongue."

"Really," he said slyly, "I wouldn't mind seeing tha'."

Feeling a little self-conscious I decided to turn our small banter in a different direction.

"I can also name all seven dwarfs."

"Anyone can do tha'."

"Okay, name them," I challenged.

Jack looked at me and rolled his eyes. I could see in his face that he thought my challenge was stupid.

"Grumpy, Dopey, Sleepy, Sneezy, Happy, and Doc." He grinned at me.

I chuckled softly. "That's only six."

Jack's eyebrows scrunched together and he focused on a spot on the ground.

"Grumpy, Dopey, Sneezy, Sleepy, Happy, Grumpy, Doc," he said out loud to himself.

"Uh, you said *Grumpy* twice. Do you need me to help you?" I asked a little smug.

"No, I got i'."

Jack started to sound a little frustrated as he began repeating each name under his breath and used his fingers to count out each dwarf. The exhilaration of being right was kind of a high and Jack's frustration made it even better. What was it about men always having to be right and not wanting a woman's help?

"You know, it's not that big of a deal." I said.

He just glared at me, frustration clear on his face. I just started to laugh.

"Grumpy, Dopey, Sleepy, Sneezy, Happy, Goofy, Doc," he tried again.

"Nope."

"Okay miss perfec', whit is i'?"

I sat up straight and full of confidence. "Grumpy, Dopey, Sleepy, Sneezy, Happy, *Bashful*, Doc."

"Bashful, I should've known ya would remember Bashful."

We both started to lightly laugh at the situation.

"Ya know, ye're not tha' bad, Miss Alison Pierson."

"Neither are you, Mr. Jackson McQuewen. I especially like you when you don't have a cigarette hanging out of your mouth."

"And I like you much better without a song coming out of yours."

We both broke out into a much harder laugh, neither of us taking what the other said too literally. Our laughter died down and we both sat quietly listening to the music on the radio that was starting to fade as the batteries were starting to die.

I suddenly let out a big yawn and rubbed my eyes. It had been a very long day and my exhaustion was catching up with me.

I stood up and started looking around for a small place to lie down. "Well, I'm going to bed," I announced.

"Ya know, we may want ta sleep together."

My neck popped as my head quickly snapped in Jack's direction. "Excuse me?" My voice almost a shriek.

"Whit I mean is i' feels like i's goin ta git pre"y cold tonigh'. We may want ta sleep nex' ta each other ta stay warm," he explained as he shifted awkwardly.

Once again I automatically tightened the blanket around me like a mummy ready to be put in a tomb.

"You know, thanks for the offer, but I think I'll be okay."

"Ally, ye're goin' ta freeze. Survival 101, we can make more body heat together. I'm not goin' ta try anythin'."

"No, really, I'll be fine." I couldn't help the awkward self-conscious feeling that came through my voice.

I shuffled over to a small area and laid down, facing away from Jack. I could hear Jack give an exasperated sigh as he found his own spot on the floor.

"Good night, Jack," I whispered, still feeling a bit self-conscious.

"Good nigh', Ally"

18
The Dance
✖✖✖

The night was bitterly cold, so much colder than any night so far. I had been so wet that it seemed as though I had never completely dried, and it didn't help that the wet humid air continued to seep straight into my bones.

The cold seemed to bring on a new edge to the strange dreams that seemed to be plaguing my nights lately. Tonight my dreams seemed stronger and more real than ever.

I was standing alone in the vastness of nowhere, disoriented, when a dark figure approached me. I tried to run but my legs didn't want to move. It was as though they were stuck in some kind of thick mud.

My legs finally began to move slowly, one foot in front of the other, but before I knew it the dark figure was right there forcing me down. I could feel my body tense as I felt the weight of the darkness completely envelop me.

I wanted to scream and wake up from my nightmare but nothing would come out—I couldn't even breath. It was as though I were being smothered, but there was no one there.

My body twisted and turned, trying to break free from the hold that was keeping me down. Suddenly my body started to tremble as a strange sensation ran through me. I pulled my blanket tighter around me and curled up into a ball as memories that I had long since forgotten started showing their ugly self in all directions, flooding all my thoughts. My tremble grew stronger as each sensation pulsed through my body, and the memories grew more prominent.

Half awake, I tried to control the images and the thoughts running through my head—not wanting to wake Jack. I laid there shaking as the darkness continued to overshadow me, and the cold night continued to pass through the thin blankets. My teeth began to chatter in addition to the shivering that I couldn't control.

I heard Jack stirring in his little space in the darkness, and then suddenly I was aware of everything around me. The cold air sneaking though each little crack—as if it were purposely making sure it didn't miss one. I could feel the cold, hard floor under me, like lying on cold, smooth marble instead of the dirty, worn-out wood. And then there was the sound of the wind whipping fiercely against the shed, singing some strange song that I couldn't understand.

When I heard Jack move again I was afraid that I had woken him. I didn't hear any terrified screams come from me, but then again I was still half asleep. It had to be the chatter of my teeth. They were so loud that you could hear them even over the sound of the wind. This cold night was probably nothing to him, being a master at survival skills.

I laid there waiting to hear a groan or a sigh or a smug snicker, as if to say "I told you so"—but nothing. The next thing I knew I felt his broad body scoot next to mine, pulling half his extra blanket over me, and then his muscular arm wrapped around me, pulling me into him. I was surprised that his touch didn't frighten me. Instead it had the opposite effect. I felt safe and comfortable next to him. I just laid still, allowing the heat of his body to warm mine.

It only took a few minutes for my teeth to stop clicking together and for my body to stop shivering. I began to completely relax and my breathing flowed into a much steadier pace. I opened my eyes, looking forward into the darkness, and let out a quiet sigh of relief. I could see the white steam of my breath flow out past my lips, and I felt relieved that my nightmare was over for now. The strange sensation that pulsed through me was gone, and the images from my forgotten memories were once again tucked away in the back of my mind.

I don't know if Jack sensed my uneasiness consciously or unconsciously, but he pulled me closer to him—his hold more secure, almost protective. I could feel his breath against my cheek.

I was finally starting to fall back to sleep again, my eyelids getting heavier by the moment, now that I felt warm and safe. Just as my eyes were closing for the final time before I allowed myself to completely drift into slumber, I listened to the peaceful steady rhythm of Jack's breathing. Then he suddenly nuzzled his face in the curve of my neck and inhaled long and deep, as if he were taking in the sweet bouquet of a beautiful flower. Then he gave me a tight squeeze, crushing my body against his. I trembled as a new sensation flowed through me and made my heart beat so loud I was sure he could hear it. As his grip loosened his breathing was steady and peaceful again. My heart calmed and I fell asleep to his rhythm.

I woke up, relaxed, to a balmy morning. The weather had calmed down and I could see streaks of sunlight shining through the cracks. The sound of a kookaburra sang in the distance. I continued to lie still, enjoying this peaceful moment. Jack's arm was still wrapped around me and his hold was so tight that we were almost one.

I didn't feel any need to rush getting up. The only thing we had on our agenda was more walking and it was nice to be able to give my ankle a long rest. So I closed my eyes and remained motionless, allowing myself to slip back into a restful sleep.

I was nearly completely gone when I felt Jack move. I figured he was adjusting his position since there was no longer a need to keep me warm. But instead of backing up or rolling away from me I felt him sit up. I could tell by the way his body felt along my back that he was lying on his side, his upper torso probably propped up on his forearms. He just laid there as if he were waiting for me to wake.

I was just about to open my eyes when he softly pulled back the hair that loosely covered my face and tucked it behind my ear. Then I felt the soft touch of his fingers as he gently grazed my cheek. His touch instantly sent butterflies straight to my stomach.

This very sweet action seemed as if he were admiring me, and all I could think of was, why? The questioned lingered in my mind. I knew I could never be Jack's type and I knew he felt the same—at least I thought I did. I thought he had made that perfectly clear a few different times. Then why was he being so sweet?

I couldn't bear it anymore; my curiosity peaked and I had to find out what was going on. I rolled myself around to look at him—still wrapped up like a cocoon with only one arm exposed. When I rolled over he didn't move much except to position himself directly over me, the full impact of his amazing jeweled eyes gazing into mine in wonderment and curiosity, sending my heart racing.

I was about to speak, ask him what was going on, or thank him for keeping me warm and safe last night, something, but before I could say anything he bent down and kissed me softly on the lips, lingering there for just a moment. It caught me off guard and my body tensed, but I have to admit I enjoyed it. His lips were surprisingly soft next to his rugged face.

Even though I tensed in surprise it seemed too short as he pulled back to look at me, a charming coy smile on his face. I must have had a look of desire or curiosity of my own because he bent down to kiss me again, but this time I was ready for it—I kissed him back.

Our lips started to move softly with each other like a slow dance—romantic and smooth—knowing each move the other would make.

My heartbeat picked up once again as I pulled my covered arm out from my tightly wrapped cocoon and pressed my hand against his chest, feeling the warmth of his body on my palm, and then I wrapped my other arm around his neck.

Jack gently laid his hand on my face and then slowly moved it to the nape of my neck. His fingers intertwining through my dark curls, his other hand eagerly grasping at the fabric at the small of my back, pulling me closer. At that moment all my defenses were down and something took over. Our dance became more passionate as our lips continued to move perfectly with each other.

I pulled away to catch my breath as his lips moved to my throat. He moved slowly up my neck and as he grazed my ear with his teeth a strange intensity pulsed through me, making it apparent that my breathing was very unsteady.

I twisted myself just right and managed to move his lips back to mine as they melted eagerly with each other again and I could feel the warmth of his breath against my mouth as he slowly opened my lips with his.

He pulled me tight against his body as he gently lowered me back onto the ground, his weight barely pressing against me.

Suddenly I felt like I was in some other place, feeling vulnerable but secure, anxious but excited. I felt like this was a place I wanted to stay, and I realized that this was someone I wanted to stay with, even with all that had happened and all that was said and done. This felt right; he felt right.

As our lips continued to dance I couldn't help but think, "Is this what it's like? Am I falling in…"

Just as these thoughts entered my mind a sense of pure fear and panic surged through my whole body.

"What am I doing?" I thought. "This isn't me."

I pushed Jack away gasping, trying to catch my breath. I quickly sat up straight and secured my blanket around me. Fear radiating from every pore in my body.

"I can't do this it's wrong." My voice barley above a whisper.

I stood up, tightening my blanket even more, trying to make sense of my actions.

"Ally, whit's wrong?"

Jack stood up, tucking the edge of the fabric tightly around his waist, leaving his bare chest exposed. It made it hard to concentrate. I turned away from his confused face.

"I'm sorry, but I can't do this."

"Do whit?" he asked.

"This." I turned back to look at him, trying to convey some kind of message without having to actually say it.

"Ally, ye're not makin' any sense."

"I know, I just…"

My eyes began to mist over as I tried not to show my emotions. Jack had his arms around me in just two short steps.

"Hey, i's okay," he said. His head rested on mine as he gently stroked the middle of my back.

I pushed away from his hold. "No, it's not, you don't understand."

"Then help me ta understand," he said, confused.

"Don't you get it? I can't be with you. I don't…get involved."

"Whit are ya talkin abou'?" His face furrowed and there was even more confusion in his eyes.

"I don't believe in getting serious with anyone."

"Whoa, wait a second." he shook his head, stunned, and held his hand out to stop my comment. "Whit makes ya think that tha's whit I want?"

"Don't you?" I asked, starting to feel a little embarrassed.

"No! I mean I like ya, sure, bu' I wouldn't go tha' far."

"But the way you kissed me?"

"Ally, haven't ya ever been kissed before? Sometimes a kiss is jus' tha', a kiss." His tone sounded cold and indifferent.

"Yes, I've been kissed before," I snapped, "and that wasn't just a kiss. You have feelings for me."

"Whit," Jack scoffed, "Ya know, Ally, I think ya might have go"en a little ta much water on the brain in tha' river."

I glared at him, anger building up inside. "So this is how he wants to play this." I thought. "Fine!"

I stiffened and adjusted my stance as the feelings of rejection filtered through me.

"Well it doesn't matter anyway." I said curtly. "Even if you did have feelings for me I wouldn't be with you." I cringed inside at my own words. "I mean, look at you. Look at how you live your life."

I regretted my words as soon as I spoke them, but I felt so angry and embarrassed from his denial that I couldn't stop. I wasn't going to allow myself to get hurt from this.

"Whit's wrong with my life?" he said defensively, an edge to his voice.

He took a step back from me, his hands balling up into fists.

"It's so empty, you have nothing—nothing in your life that is solid, nothing that you can hold on to."

I stood there glaring at him with a disgusted look on my face as I crossed my arms in front of me.

"You go from one woman to the next, not wanting anything emotional from them, just using them for your own selfish gratification. You use sarcasm and bitterness as a way of communication and you drink to avoid any kind of connection, just like your father."

I went too far and I knew it but I couldn't stop myself and kept going. "And your best friends are your cigarettes, and they even left you."

"Look, ya know nothin' abou' my life. Ya think jus' by talkin' ta me for a few days ya know me. Ya don't know anything. Who d'ya think ya are?"

His voice was harsh and rough as he continued and shouted out a line of profanities at me. I just stood there motionless, glaring into his eyes, but cringing on the inside, waiting for it to end.

I hated how I seemed to have a gift for bringing out so much anger and hurt in someone, knowing the right words to hit that one sensitive spot that hurt more than anything. I couldn't stand the pain I had inflicted on Jack—I finally had to look away.

"Why did ya come here, Ally?" he asked suddenly, his voice calmer but stern. "Why are ya by yerself? And don't tell me i's because no one would come. I'm not the only one who's empty. Ya act like ya have everything under control, bu' the truth is ye're so empty tha' ya don't have anything ta give. Ya won't even let anyone close enough ta ya ta find ou' who ya are."

My head snapped up from the spot on the floor I was focused on.

"You want to know how I am?" My voice a little shaky but hard. "I'm someone that is so messed up in her own head that she can't even keep a stupid office job, someone who is afraid to go to sleep at night, someone who is afraid of being alone, but can be in a crowded room and feel completely alone, someone who feels so lost that she may never be found. I wake up every day wondering what happened to my life, and why am I still here. That's who I am."

Tears slowly filled my eyes and crept down my cheeks even though I tried to hold them back. Jack's face seemed to soften as he listened to my rant. Then as if something prodded him he crossed the small space between us and tried to put his arms around me again, but my emotions hit their limit. I stepped back from him.

"I can't."

I turned, tears now racing down my face, grabbed my clothes that I had hung up to dry, and ran out of the shed. Away from Jack, away from the hurt, and away from myself.

There was a grouping of trees not too far from our shelter. It had been too dark in the night that I didn't notice them. Just as I got behind the cover of the trees an uncontrollable sob came flooding out. I leaned against the trunk, both hands covering my face to help muffle the sound as I slid down into a sitting position—my legs slightly crossed in front of me. All the emotions from the past few days spilled over and I suddenly was dealing with it all at once. Crashing, the dingoes, my ankle, the river and Jack, especially Jack.

From the moment we met til this morning, so much had change for me, and I thought for him to, but the realization of how different we were was evident.

I finally got hold of my composure and started to get dressed. My clothes were still a little damp—well more than a little, but at least they weren't dripping. As I put them on the moist fabric rubbed again my skin, and I could still feel a heaviness in them. But there wasn't much I could do. With the sun out I hoped they would continue to dry.

When I finished I wiped my eyes and fanned them vigorously with my hands, hoping they would dry enough and the redness would disappear. I didn't want Jack to know how upset I really was. I let out a big sigh in preparation for facing Jack again and walked back slowly to the shed.

Jack was also dressed when I walked in—his beautiful build covered. He had folded up the blankets and placed them on the back shelf, which I found odd. It also looked like he had straightened up a little. He reached out and took the blankets I had draped over my arms and proceeded to fold them as well and then placed them on top of the others.

"What are you doing?" I asked. "It's not like we're at someone's house."

"When I have a lo' on my mind I have ta do somethin'."

"A lot on his mind? So do I," I thought. "But it can't be for the same reason."

All sorts of scenarios ran through my head, none of them happy ones.

"Well, le's go." His tone was businesslike; he was my pilot again. That was the last thing he said.

We had to have been walking for hours. The sun moved across the sky until it was shining directly above us. My clothes finally dry except a few places in the creases. We didn't talk and even with the uncomfortable silence I didn't even think about singing.

Jack stopped abruptly, his head cocked slightly.

"What's wrong?" I asked.

"Shhhh. D'ya hear tha'?" I shook my head. "Listen."

Then I heard a low thrumming noise coming in our direction, getting louder and louder. A helicopter was heading toward us. We both started waving frantically screaming at the top of our lungs.

"Hey, were here!" I yelled.

"Down here!" Jack roared.

In a few seconds the search helicopter landed quite a ways away from us. The wind from the rotor blades picking up the dust and getting it in our eyes. A man in a dark leather jacket and a red baseball cap climbed out of the front and rushed over to us.

"Are you Jackson McQuewen and Alison Pierson?" he asked, yelling over the sound of the propellers.

"Well that's a stupid question," I thought, "how many people do they have lost and roaming around the outback of Australia?" I wanted to say this out loud, but we both just answered "Yes!"

"Boy am I happy to find you," He said cheerfully. "We found your plane just yesterday, but because of the storm we had to wait to continue to look. Well, let's get you home. There are a lot of people that are going to be happy you're okay." He grinned warmly at us.

We automatically crouched down under the blades and then took our seats and strapped ourselves in. Jack, not having any problems of course, had to reach over and help me out. We took off quickly almost completely vertical, and it felt like I was on a ride at an amusement park, my stomach feeling the weightlessness.

As I watched the landscape pass beneath me I couldn't help but feel relieved that we were headed back to Sydney, but then why when I brushed the hair away from my face did I feel a single wet drop on my cheek? I turned and glanced at Jack, who was staring out his own window. I wiped the tear away casually and then leaned against the window, closed my eyes, and let my mind drift.

19

Darci's Restlessness
✖⊙✖

Big drops of water collected on the corner of the overhang of the hotel and dropped evenly six stories down onto the wet pavement. The heavy rain was finally turning into a slow drizzle. Restlessly I counted each drop as they fell.

"One hundred and forty-eight, one hundred and forty-nine, one hundred and fifty…"

Knock knock—two firm knocks on my hotel door broke my concentration. I quickly got up from the somewhat uncomfortable armchair that sat in front of the window and walked to the door.

"Who is it?" I asked through the crack.

"Darci, it's me, Tom." His warm, pleasant voice made me smile.

It was always so easy to be cheerful around Tom; he always seemed so positive even when it seemed like things were at their worst. I opened the door and was surprised to see him out of his tour guide khakis and into a pair of dark-navy Dockers and a white T under a gray flannel shirt that he had cuffed a few inches past his wrist. I never really realized what an attractive man he was, but with his sandy-blond hair and sage-colored eyes he was quite a nice-looking man.

"Hey, come on in. I just have to get my purse."

"Did you get a chance to call your family?" he asked as he entered the small room, his hands in his pocket.

"No," I answered.

"And why not?"

I grabbed my bag and threw it around my shoulder as I walked past him to the door.

"I just don't know what to say to them right now. Can we go?"

He looked at me without budging and raised one eyebrow as he crossed his arms in front of him. It was somewhat irritating.

"My aunt is already so upset I just don't want to call without any good news. It will just upset her even more."

"What about your kids?"

"Yeah, that's killing me. I do want to talk to them." My tone became slightly solemn.

Tom walked to my side and pulled my bag off my shoulder. "I'll wait."

I sighed and walked back into the room, grabbed the phone, and started to dial. All I could get was an empty sound coming from the other end.

"There must be something wrong with the phone. I can't get anything."

"Use your cell," Tom said casually.

"I don't have international use on my plan."

Tom reached in his pocket and pulled out his cell phone. "Here, you can use mine. I use international as much as local."

I looked at him a little puzzled.

"Travel business, remember?"

I grinned slightly at my embarrassment and took his phone from his hands as he flopped down on the bed, his hands linked behind his head.

I waited excitedly as the phone rang.

"Wait! What time would it be there?"

"Don't worry, its only eight here so it's about six o'clock last night there."

Just then the sweet sound of my angel's voice came through the receiver.

"Helwo?"

"Amy, its Mommy."

"Mommy!" she squealed with excitement.

"What are you doing answering the phone, sweetie? Where is Aunt Megan or Gina? Where are your brothers?"

Just then I could hear some commotion on the other end and then Amy started to cry. Then it sounded like someone was consoling her.

"Hello, Darci? Sorry about that, we were in the other room and she grabbed the phone before we had a chance to get it," Megan panted.

"That's okay," I lightly chuckled, "it just took me by surprise. So how are things? Is everything going okay? Are the boys behaving?"

"Yeah, for the most part," Megan answered, a slight lift in her voice.

"Hi, mom!" Miles and Ryan both yelled in the background.

Megan chuckled. "No, I'm kidding, they both have been very helpful."

"Well I'm glad to hear that, surprised, but glad."

Just then I heard a loud scream come from Amy in the background.

"I want to talk to my mommy!"

"You can in just a few minutes. Let Aunt Megan talk, then you can, okay?"

I could hear Gina's comforting voice. I imagined her wiping Amy's tears and then giving her a tight quick squeeze and I wished I was with them. There wasn't anything as important as my kids, but I knew I wouldn't be gone long and they were in good hands.

"You better let me talk to her quick or we'll never get anything discussed."

I looked over at Tom. He just nodded in approval.

"Mommy?'

"Hey, sweetie, are you being a good girl for your aunties?"

"Yes. Mommy, guess what? We went to the park and found a bug and Ryan squished it and it was yucky." She laughed.

"Really, that's nice," I responded.

"And Miles, he watched a movie and cried because he was mad cause it's not what he liked."

"I did not, Amy," Miles hollered in the background.

"Well, I'll talk to him when I get home."

"And I saw Aunt Megan kiss a yucky boy. When you be home, Mommy?" Amy asked in her sweet soprano.

"As soon as I find Aunt Ally, okay? Can I talk to Megan again, sweetie?"

"Okay, Bye."

"Bye, I love you."

Amy was already off the phone and playing with her toys before I even finished.

"Hey," Megan answered a little awkwardly.

"A yucky boy?" I chuckled.

She quickly changed the subject. "So what's the story, have you heard anything?"

"Well, they found the plane and it looks like they've been walking. It's been raining cats and dogs here so they have to wait to send out search parties again. But everyone here seems pretty optimistic." I glanced over at Tom and grinned slightly. "I guess the pilot is an ex-air force pilot with a lot of training."

"Well, that sounds pretty hopeful." Her voice sounded enthusiastic.

"Yeah, I'm feeling pretty optimistic myself, but until she's back safe, I'm not taking anything for granted. I just wish I had more news to give you," I responded with a sigh. "Well. I hate to make this short, but I actually have to get back over to the airport where they're heading up the search efforts. I'll call back as soon as I find out more information. Talk to you later."

"Wait, before you go, do you have time to talk to the boys?"

I wanted to tell her I had all the time in the world, because it was killing me not being able to talk to my boys, but I only had a few minutes. I didn't want to take advantage of Tom's generosity and add so much to his phone bill.

"I don't think so; I'll talk to them later."

Without my noticing, Tom had gotten off the bed and was right beside me. He took the phone right out of my hand and spoke in his always pleasant voice, "She can talk to whoever she needs to," and then handed the phone back to me.

For the next forty-five minutes I spoke to the boys, finding out everything that they were doing clear down to the whole movie incident. I spoke with Gina and Dorothy, explaining the same information I shared with Megan, being even more positive when I spoke to Dorothy. Finally it was time to say good-by and I hung up the phone and handed it back to Tom.

"Thank you, Tom, you know you didn't need to do that."

"Well, I figured you had enough to worry about here you didn't need to worry about your family as well."

He gave me the same bright, wide smile that was constantly on his face and handed me my purse.

"Shall we?"

When we walked into the centre there was so much commotion going on it made me anxious. Officer Roberts quickly passed us, an airport official by his side. Tom and I looked at each other and followed them back into the main hall—maps still adorning the walls. As I took a closer look at each map it looked as though sections were marked off except one or two sections on each map.

"Officer Roberts," I said. "What's going on?"

"The weather has eased up and we got one team out and the second one is going out now."

"I want to go with them." My tone was sharp.

"Ms. Thomas, didn't we already have this conversation? You staying out of our way is the best way you can help." His voice sounded kind, but his tone was patronizing. "Just be patient; we'll let you know when we know something."

Tom gently wrapped his arm around my shoulder and escorted me into the familiar room from the night before. I sat down exasperated on the couch next to Tom—his arm still around my shoulder—and rested my head against him.

Time seemed to drag as the clock stared straight at me from the other side of the room, ticking by slowly as we waiting for any kind of news. The sun had been shining for awhile so there wouldn't be any weather problems, and yesterday after they found the plane they said it would only be a matter of time. So what was taking them so long?

I sat up and turned to Tom. "Surely even if they just found their bodies they would call it in."

"Shh."

He tried to comfort me as he pulled me back against him and tightened his arms around my shoulder, but I couldn't seem to sit still. I got up from the couch and walked over to the window, pacing back and forth in front of it. Then I crossed back over to the couch and sat for a few seconds. Then I would start the whole routine over again.

You would think that my manic behavior would really start getting on Tom's nerves, but he just sat there calmly and quietly watching me with a slightly amused look on his face.

I was just about to make another around to the window when a young woman, who I had met earlier when I introduced myself to a group of volunteers, came running in from the other room.

"Darci, Tom, they have something. Come on." Her voice was breathless but full of excitement.

We rushed into the main room to see a group of volunteers surrounding a table with maps and assorted papers scattered everywhere and a big metal two-way radio in the center, along with Officer Roberts right in the middle of it all.

"Say that again Blue-two," Officer Roberts's voice reverberated.

"We found them." A male voice said.

I could feel the electricity in the air as everyone started to get excited, and cheers started to irrupt. Officer Roberts put his hand up briefly, silencing the excitement.

"How do they look?" Officer Roberts asked.

The man on the other end started to speak, but the radio started to break up with static.

"Th…ook… goo…ape…siderin…at…through."

Roberts hit the top of the radio and the static vanished.

"Blue-two, can you repeat that? We didn't quite get all of that."

"They look like they're in pretty good shape. Miss Pierson does have a hurt ankle and they seem a little dehydrated, but considering what they've been through. They're good." His voice was loud over the radio.

"Well, we'll have an ambulance standing by when they get here. Bring them home. Roberts out."

He clicked off his end of the conversation and turned to the waiting crowd of volunteers, police officials, and news reporters that had collected slowly during the last few days.

"They're on their way home," he announced.

All at once the room's electricity that had been building erupted in a chorus of cheers and celebration. A few men standing around Officer Roberts shook his hand in appreciation, while another confidently patted him on the shoulder. I could tell that all his worries were gone. He turned and looked at me, nodded, and then grinned. I nodded back in response.

As the celebration continued the relief from all my dread started to overcome me and was replaced with the excitement in the air. I threw my arms around Tom in pure delight of the moment before I even knew what I was doing. Tom put his arm around my waist enthusiastically and squeezed me tightly. I suddenly felt awkward and pulled away as my face started to turn pink, but I was still grinning from the excitement.

20
Frenzy

Sunlight radiated off the curved white shape of the Opera House, beaming a brilliant almost blinding spectacle as we flew past, headed in the direction of the small airport where my adventure began.

My stomach turned as we got closer and I wondered how much my family knew. I would have to call them as soon as I could in case they heard the worst.

As we approached the landing strip I noticed that there was some kind of commotion going on. People were milling around and there were police cars, a couple of ambulances, and I even noticed a news van or two.

"Wow," I thought, "something is going on down there. Huh, I wonder what it is."

I was just about to turn and say something to Jack when it hit me. We were the something big. Then I was grateful I kept my mouth shut and my thoughts to myself; I felt pretty stupid. I wasn't used to people making a big deal about me; usually I was the one that got overlooked or got in the way when the real issue was with someone else. But this was about me, and it was about Jack.

I wanted to reach out and grab his hand, no more than that. I wanted to wrap my arms around him and have him wrap his around me. I felt so safe in his arms. I wanted to press my lips against his and feel the soft contours of his mouth as they molded with mine, but things were different, and our differences were what kept my arms to my side.

When we landed the frenzy of our rescue seemed to intensify. Emergency crews from both ambulances came rushing over: one for me and one for Jack.

They helped me out of the helicopter and onto a stretcher, which seemed to be quite necessary. Despite all the walking and everything else, my ankle, which seemed before to be just a nuisance with its soft throbbing, was suddenly burning in pain.

They wheeled me over to the back of their vehicle, opened the doors wide, and were about to push me in.

"Wait!" I yelled.

Through all the commotion of the crowd a familiar face stood out brighter than anyone else's.

"Darci?" I called in amazement. She pushed her way through the crowd and made her way over to me.

"Hey," she said cheerfully, a big smile on her face as she leaned down to give me a hug.

"What are you doing here?"

"When your plane went missing the authorities called your mom."

I groaned at the image of what it must have done to her. "Was she pretty upset?"

"Of course, she was going to fly here to help look for you, but with her health—"

I interrupted. "She couldn't do that."

"Exactly, so I came in her place."

I shook my head, slightly still in shock. "I just can't believe you're here."

She just smiled and then reached down and hugged me again the best she could, then grabbed my hand.

"Do you want to come with her?" the EMT asked.

I nodded my head and looked at her with pleading eyes.

She hesitated, "Oh, I guess if I have to," she teased. Her face brightened and a big smile formed, showing all her teeth.

As I was pushed into the ambulance I could see a crowd of news reporters surrounding the man in the red cap—our rescuer—and standing next to him was Jack.

I sat up onto my elbows and watched him obviously tell our story. He turned and looked over in our direction and I happened to catch his eye. He didn't look angry any more; instead he looked remorseful. It made me a little insecure. I turned away from his intense gazes and contemplated the many questions he was probably being asked. What happened? Where did things go wrong? Will you take those chances again? The thought of these questions rang in my head so loud. I couldn't concentrate; everything seemed to be whirling around me. I closed my eyes and laid back down, trying to stop the spinning.

Suddenly through all the surrounding commotion I could hear Jack's soft brogue so close he had to be just outside the door.

"How is she? Will she be alrigh'?" he asked.

My heart skipped as I listened to his voice and the concern in it. I opened my eyes, wanting to look in his and sat up just in time to see the doors close before we sped away. I turned and looked at Darci who was still grinning at me, but I could see questions in her eyes. She was waiting for me to fill in all the details of what happened. The crash, our journey, and probably my sudden reaction to Jack's voice. I grinned back and laid back down, turning my head the other direction. I didn't want her to see the tears that were slowly coming out and hitting the white sheet of the stretcher. I usually shared everything with Darci, but I couldn't this time, at least not now.

When the ambulance pulled up to the hospital emergency entrance, there seemed to be much more chaos than at the airport. Police officials were holding back the swarm of reporters that seemed to have multiplied quite a bit from the handful that I saw talking to Jack.

As they wheeled me in I could hear the sound of cameras going off and see their flashes coming from every direction, with different voices shouting out questions so fast I couldn't answer them before the next one was thrown at me.

"So how does it feel to be back?" was shouted from my right.

"Did you think you were going to survive?" came out of the crowd from my left.

"So what kind of relationship do you have with Mr. McQuewen?" That question came straight at me, stinging me just a bit.

"What kept you going?"

"Why do you think you crashed? Are you going to sue?"

I was about to answer the last absurd question when Darci broke in.

"Back off people, she'll give a full interview later."

I looked up at Darci, shocked. "I will?" I asked, a little annoyed.

She bent down and whispered. "Trust me, if you don't make it official and cut them off at the knees they won't leave you alone." She squeezed my hand and gave me a reassuring grin as I was wheeled into the emergency room.

When the doctor came in I was surprised by how young and attractive he was. He reminded me a character from one of those teenage romance vampire novels.

"G-day, I'm Doctor Carmichael. How are you feeling today?"

He looked down at my ankle, which had turned an ugly shade of grayish purple in the last few days.

"Well, from the looks of things, not well." He grinned.

He picked up my chart and quickly skimmed through it, then carefully examined my hurt ankle.

"Tell me if this hurts."

He gently pushed my ankle upwards. I cringed as pain shot through my foot; then he rotated it one direction, then the other.

"How does that feel?" he asked.

"It hurts."

"On a scale from one to ten, what's the pain like?"

"I guess maybe a six or seven," I explained, keeping my voice even as he continued to poke and squeeze and rotate my foot.

He turned to the nurse that was assisting him. "Let's get some X-rays, and just to be on the safe side, some blood work. I want to make sure there's not any kind of infection."

With a dazzling smile he turned to me again. "Well, Ms. Pierson, we'll get those X-rays and then we can see what were working with. I'll be back."

Both the doctor and the nurse walked out together, discussing my condition as they left, leaving Darci and I alone together.

"So?" She looked at me curiously.

"Soooo, what?" I answered back.

"Are you going to tell me what happened or do I have to hear it on the news like everyone else?"

"Well, you're the one that said I would give an interview," I said, annoyed again.

"Like you're not dying to give me all the details." She sat down in the chair by my bed and made herself comfortable, waiting for my response.

I hesitated. "What do you want to know?"

"Well, first and foremost, what in the world possess you to come here?"

Her question took me by surprise. I was expecting any of the questions that the reporters were asking, or questions about Jack, but not that. I still wasn't completely sure myself.

"Well, my mom told you I got fired right?" I asked, my head lowering at the question, still disgusted with myself.

"Yeah."

"I just had to get out of town."

"But to Australia? Why didn't you just go to Disney World or something? This was pretty irresponsible of you."

"Urrr," I groaned in frustration. "I don't know how to explain it. You just won't understand."

"Then help me to understand."

Her words seemed to slash through my heart like a hot knife as I remembered Jack's voice repeating those exact words. How could I explain to Jack and now Darci what was going on in my head when I didn't know myself? I let out a big sigh and decided that if I didn't try, she wouldn't let it go.

"Okay, you know I got let go but you don't know why." Darci pulled herself forward and leaned in to hear me better.

"For the last few months I haven't been myself, well the last year or so. I was doing pretty good, but I don't know, something was blocking me. I couldn't concentrate, I kept messing up, and I didn't even want to be here anymore,' I quickly corrected myself, "I mean there anymore." I shifted uncomfortably hoping she didn't catch my underline meaning.

"The day I got fired had to be the worst day ever. I had never been fired in my life and it was something that I could have avoided. I realized that I had to do something. I didn't know what, until that night when I went to sleep. I dreamed about when I was here last time, which had to be one of the hardest but happiest times of my life. I felt so in control of things. I felt like I was really making a difference in people's lives and they were making a difference in mine. I also learned a lot about myself during that time—things I never realized and things I'd forgotten." I sighed.

I looked away from her intense gaze, as I started remembering my nightmare from the other night.

"I woke up the next morning and felt this pull to come here. I needed to have that feeling back. I wanted to make a difference, I wanted to feel happy, I wanted to feel—something. So I drew out my savings and here I am."

Darci didn't say a word, she just leaned back in her chair again and looked thoughtful, but her expression told me that whatever she wanted to hear came out and she was satisfied with my explanation.

I sighed quietly, relieved. There was so much more but that was something I still had to figure out. At least she hadn't pressed me about Jack.

"So what about this Jack guy?" she asked in her motherly tone.

"Great, now what do I say?" I thought, not wanting to get into that whole thing.

"What about him?" I answered casually.

"Well, what happened out there?"

I decided to just fill her in on the basic but vital details. I told her about seeing Ayers Rock and the beauty and majesty of it all. And the little old woman and how she helped me out, but I didn't mention how I was so upset when she did help me. I told her about the crash and most every incident that happened and about Hero and how he was always there saving us. Funny, how whenever I could avoid mentioning Jack, I did.

She listened intently and laughed at the appropriate times and was thoughtful at others. Then she looked at me, questions in her eyes again.

"So what about Jack?"

Just then the nurse came in with a wheelchair.

"Okay Ms. Pierson, I'm going to take you to X-rays now."

"Are you going to stay here and wait for me?" I asked.

"I think I'll go try to call your mom. I told her I would let her know when you were safely back."

"My mom, dang, so much has been going on that I didn't even think about calling her. Will you tell her that I will call her as soon as I can and that I love her?"

"Sure."

The nurse helped me down into the chair and Darci started to head out the door.

"Darci?"

She turned and gazed at me halfway out. "Yeah?"

"Thank you. Thanks for coming to get me. I know what a hassle it must have been." My tone apologetic.

"Are you kidding? A chance to come to Australia and get away from the kids for a few days?"

Her tone was light, but I know Darci well enough to not take her seriously. She was dying to see her kids as soon as she could.

"Besides, you're like my sister. I had to come. Just don't ever let it happen again."

She smiled her wide smile and held the door open for the nurse and I to go through.

"I'll be here when you get back," she said, her voice relaxed and cheerful.

I just looked back over my shoulder and smiled at her as the nurse pushed me down the hall.

21
Darci's Distraction
※◈※

Watching Ally roll away to X-rays down the long corridor, I stood there realizing that it was over, she was okay and that we were going home soon. I couldn't help the smile that came over my face. I missed my kids and I couldn't wait to see them. My next thought was, where's a phone?

I decided to go ask a nurse at the front desk. If anyone should know, they would.

As I turned the corner to the main lobby I could hear Tom's low, cheerful voice. His accent was always very distinctive. I could tell he was talking to someone: this mysterious voice was lower and more gruff. The accent was similar but definitely different, Scottish or Irish, I guessed.

I peeked around the corner to see who the other voice belonged to. A man about two or three inches taller than Tom with dark, wavy hair and a scruffy appearance but well-built was leaning over the desk filling out paper work. I recognized him from the airport. It was Ally's pilot, Jack. There was so much going on when they flew in I didn't even notice him until I heard him ask about Ally. I had turned to see who it was, but after seeing Ally's reaction to his voice I knew who it was.

I was going to introduce myself when I realized that they were having a pretty intense conversation. I took a step back behind the corner but was still in hearing range.

"Hey, it's not my fault the plane went down," Tom said defensively.

"No, bu' i's yer fault tha' ya tricked me into takin' her. Ya know I would have never taken the job if I knew she was…"

"Was what?"

Jack shook his head and his jaw clenched. "Ya know whit? I' doesn't ma"er."

As I listened to this candid conversation between the two men, anger started to build in me. Was this jerk actually blaming Ally for his lack of maintenance on his plane?

"You know you didn't have to take the job, especially if it wasn't in flying condition," Tom added.

"When we left my plane was fine. Besides ya know I needed the money, and ya made me think…" Jack trailed off, not finishing his thought again.

Tom leaned against the desk with a mischievous grin on his face. "So?"

"Whit?" Jack asked, a scowl on his face.

"What happened?"

"I don't know. I won't know until I can git a good look at the instrumen's."

"No, between the two of you?"

"Whit are ya talkin abou'?"

"Come on Jack, I know you—you can charm any woman, any time, anywhere."

"Yeah, well, tha's when I want ta."

"Come on," Tom said, trying to coax more information out. "I know how you are with beautiful women and you have to admit she's not bad looking." Tom's voice turned more serious, trying to make a point. "There's something special about her, and she has the most amazing eyes."

Jack stopped writing as he gripped the pen tightly in his fingers. His face twisted in frustration as he glared at Tom.

"Look, she was annoying and obnoxious. Basically she was a pain, and I'm glad ta git rid of her. Can we jus' drop i'? I jus' want ta git back ta the airfield so I can figure ou' whit ta do abou' my plane."

My anger that was starting to boil was now flowing over the top. How dare he talk that way about Ally! She's one of the kindest, most warmhearted people I know and for him to stand there and say such disrespectful things made me angrier than I had been in the last three years.

I rapidly realized why Ally was so reluctant to talk about Jack. If I had to deal with someone with that attitude for the last four days trying to survive, I would try and block it out too. How could someone be so coldhearted?

I was about to confront him when he grabbed his leather jacket off the desk and left. Tom still leaned against the counter. His face was confused and frustrated as he looked off the other direction.

As I watched this jerk of a person walk away, I wondered how Tom could ever think that this person and Ally would ever be good for each other, and how he could even be friends with a person like this, but then he stopped unexpectedly.

Jack stood motionless, staring down one of the long drab corridors, and his face changed from the harsh scowl he seemed to be accustomed to wearing to a soft, solemn expression. His eyes seemed to have some kind of longing in them. He briefly looked away, glancing down at the floor, but whatever he was staring at he couldn't keep his eyes off of for long. When he looked back his face became tortured, like he was in some kind of emotional agony. I couldn't help but feel for him as I wondered what could bring on such misery. He lingered there for only a few minutes; then his body tensed and the harsh expression was back. He stalked outside as he thrust the door wide open, lit a cigarette, and then he was gone.

Curious, I was about to look down the hall to see whatever he was so intently looking at when a cheery voice called my name.

"Darci!"

Tom was almost by my side by the time I turned around.

"Hello, Tom." My voice was a little stale.

"Hey, what's wrong?" he asked.

"Nothing," I lied. I didn't want him to know I was eavesdropping on his conversation. "I'm just really worn out; it's been a long few days."

"Yeh it has, but it's been worth it." He winked and then flashed his wide smile.

I could feel a slight blush turn my cheeks pink, which made me feel a little awkward, but I wanted to tell him something and I knew if I didn't do it now I wouldn't get the opportunity or I might change my mind.

"I was hoping I would see you before we left. I just wanted to thank you for all your support these last couple of days. It meant so much having a friend. I don't know how I would have handled things without you."

"Well, from what I've learned and seen from you I'm pretty sure you would have done just fine without me, but I'm very grateful I had a chance to get to know you too." We both stood quietly for a moment, and then Tom broke the silence.

"So where's Ally?"

"They took her to get X-rays on her foot. I was actually trying to find a phone to call her family and let them know she's okay. You haven't seen a phone around here, have you?"

I looked around, searching for any sign of a phone.

"Sure have."

"Where?" I said anxiously.

Tom had pulled his cell phone from out of his pocket and handed it to me.

"Tom, I can't use your phone again. It costs too much and I'm using all your minutes."

He smiled. "Don't argue, just call."

I took the phone reluctantly from his hand and quickly dialed the number. A very groggy voice answered the phone.

"Hello?"

"Aunt Dorothy?"

"Darci!" Her voice changed to an excited but worried tone in an instant. "What's going on?"

"It's okay, they found her and she's safe."

The other end got very quiet until I heard the soft sobs of a mother's love coming through the receiver.

"Thank you, thank you," she whispered so softly I almost didn't hear it, and I knew that her gratitude wasn't directed to me.

I couldn't help the moisture that filled my eyes as I listened to all her emotions flow out. Another voice entered the background and I could barely make out the voice.

"Mom, what's wrong?" It was Megan.

"They found Ally and she's okay."

I heard some rustling and then the voices seemed muffled for a few moments. I listened and wished I could be hugging my own children as I was sure Dorothy was hugging hers.

"Hello, Darci." Megan's voice, bright and happy, interrupted my contemplation. "So what's the scoop?"

"They found her earlier today. She's a little banged up and she has a hurt ankle, but besides that she's good. They're getting X-rays now so we'll know how bad it is pretty soon. She told me to tell you that she will call later and she'll tell you everything, and boy does she have a story to tell. Well, I'm going to make this short. I'm using someone's cell and I don't want to rack up his bill."

"Okay, Thanks for calling," she said gratefully.

"You're welcome," I answered back. "Oh, before I forget. She wanted me to tell you she loves you."

"Tell her we love her too. And we can't wait to see her. Bye."

"Bye." I hung up and handed the phone back to Tom. "Thanks again, Tom. Like I said, what would I do without you?"

He just grinned and put his phone back in his pocket.

"I suppose you're going home soon," He said.

"We leave tomorrow night." I self-consciously glanced down at the floor.

"That's what I figured." He sighed. "I never did get to take you out for a real meal."

I looked up from the floor and gazed directly into his eyes. His tone was disappointed but his eyes were optimistic. Without warning I threw my arms around his neck and passionately crushed my lips against his, practically knocking him into the front desk. I started to twist my fingers into his hair...

"Darci?"

Tom's voice sounded so distant and a little anxious. I felt a hand gently squeeze my arm as my mind snapped back to reality.

"Are you okay; you kind of drifted off there for a second. What were you thinking about?"

I realized my mouth was halfway open as if I were attempting to say something, but it wouldn't come out. I could feel the blood rush to my face—probably turning it a scarlet red.

"Oh, nothing," I said, trying to sound nonchalant. "Just about the things I have to do when I get home." I was hoping he wouldn't think any more of my distraction.

"What were you about to say?" he asked.

"Oh, just that if you ever get to California I'd lov...like to show you around," I said as I automatically grinned at the possibility.

"Well then, I'll have to take another holiday soon. I've always wanted to visit California," he cheerfully responded, his face beaming in delight.

We stood there silent for a moment when he unexpectedly reached over and pulled off a piece of lint that was connected to a string hanging from my sleeve, and then he pushed the small piece of string back in place. As he pulled his arm back he allowed his fingers to lightly brush down my arm, and I shivered slightly.

"Cold?" he asked.

"No," I responded automatically.

I should have thought of a better answer, because he grinned slyly. Then he softly took my hand in his. I couldn't stop the smile that spread over my face as we stood there, speechless.

As I was taking in Tom's charm, I heard the sound of a throat being cleared behind me. Ally was sitting in her wheelchair grinning from ear to ear, her nurse standing behind her waiting patiently.

"Am I interrupting anything?" Ally asked, a puzzled look on her face.

I was so distracted I didn't even see the nurse wheel her over to us. I quickly pulled my hand away from Tom's and bent down to hug her.

"Hey," I managed to choke out and then turned to whisper in her ear. "How long have you been there?"

"Just a few seconds. I just came from X-rays."

As I stood up she pointed at an opening to a long corridor between the desk and the front doors.

"I'll be right back Miss Pierson, I forgot your paperwork," The nurse said, disgruntled.

"Okay, I'm not going anywhere." Ally responded as the nurse hurried away.

"Ally, you look almost as good as new," Tom said.

She chuckled slightly. "I don't quite feel that way." Then she paused and her voice turned serious. "Tom, is Jack still here by any chance?"

"I'm sorry, you just missed him."

Her face turned solemn as she turned away from us. Just then the nurse came back a little breathless from rushing to get the forgotten paperwork.

"We better get you back to your room so we can find out when you can go home," She said cheerfully.

I stood there motionless as Ally, the nurse, and Tom headed toward Ally's room. My brain was trying to pieces something together that was all muddled with the moment I had with Tom and then Ally's sudden appearance.

"I'm sorry, where did you come from again?"

Ally sighed, "X-rays, over there," she said, pointing again.

I turned to see where Ally was pointing and realized what I was trying to piece together. Ally had just come from the same direction Jack had been staring at so intently.

"Oh," I gasped.

"What?" Ally asked curiously.

I was too caught up in my thoughts to answer. Then my mind started running through everything so quickly. Jack's attitude, the way he looked down the corridor, and the look on his face when he did.

"Nothing," I lied, not wanting to say anything until my assumptions were confirmed, after all, we were leaving the next day anyway. What if I was wrong?

"So are you coming with us or what?" Ally interrupted my thoughts.

I snapped back to the present. "Oh, I guess so, if I have to." I looked over at Ally and smiled.

When we got back to her room the nurse helped her back onto the bed while we waited for her doctor.

"I have to say Miss Pierson it's amazing you walked all that way with your ankle as bad as it is. I don't know if I could do it." The nurse said, as she helped Ally get comfortable.

Ally got quite and I could see her face turn a pale shade of pink.

"Well, that because she's strong, right?" She looked at me, grateful but confused. "That's what your family told me." Suddenly she smiled and her face turned crimson. "What is up with that saying?" I asked.

She chuckled once. "I'll tell you later."

I looked over at Tom who had been quietly sitting, watching our interaction with each other with an amused look on his face. Then he slapped his hands on the arms of his chair and pushed himself up with a slight grunt.

"Well I better go; I do have a business to run. Ally, take care of yourself and I'm sorry about your trip. I'll talk to Jack and get you your money back," Tom said apologetic.

"Don't worry about it Tom, it wasn't your fault." Ally's face was calm and there was a bit of sadness in her voice.

"Bye, Darci." His tone was a little reluctant as he opened the door to leave.

"Tom, wait. Ally, I'll be right back." I walked over to Tom, pulling him just outside Ally's door.

"You know, everything I said I meant. Thank you so much for everything."

I reached in my purse and pulled out one of my conservative business cards and scrawled my personal number quickly on the back and handed it to him. He flashed a warm smile at me, nodded, and placed it in his pocket.

"Thank you," he said softly.

He leaned into me and lightly pressed his lips against my cheek, lingering for just a moment, and then smiled his warm, cheerful smile as he pulled away, looking into my eyes, and then winked as he turned and walked down the long corridor. As I watched him walk away I couldn't help but feel that this friendship wasn't over. Our two days together made a lasting impression on both of us, and I would hear from him again and probably pretty soon. Wrapping my mind around that idea made me smile and my heart jumped.

22
Revealed

When Dr. Cutie came in with my X-rays in hand, my stomach seemed to flutter just a bit. Not because I couldn't help but be attracted to him, but what the films would reveal. I didn't want to go home with a big old cast on my leg. Then again if there were more to my leg than just being sprained, I would need to stay longer.

The idea of staying longer was good and bad. Good because I would love to see the rest of what I wanted to see, and bad because I still wanted to see Jack. Maybe if things had ended differently with Jack this anxiety that I felt wouldn't be so hard.

"Well Ms Pierson, it looks like you have got a small stress fracture on the fifth metatarsal," Dr. Carmichael said as he put my X-rays up on the lighted board next to my bed.

"What's the fifth metatarsal?" I asked glumly.

"The fifth metatarsal is the bone right behind your smallest toe." He pointed out exactly where he was talking about. "You'll need to be in a brace for a few weeks to let it heal, but just take it easy for a few days and you should be as good as new in no time." He paused for a moment, looking at the films that were casting a light glow across his face. "It's a good thing Mr. McQuewen secured your ankle as well as he did: you could have been a lot worse."

"I don't understand," I murmured. "If I had a fracture, how was I able to get around as well as I did without a lot of pain?"

"You didn't get the fracture when you fell. I'm sure you got it when you did all that walking. Putting pressure over and over again on an already injured area would have caused even more stress than normal which in turn would cause the bones to have more stress and cause the fracture. And you probably don't feel it as much because you have had a lot of adrenalin flowing through you right now. When it wears off you'll start to feel it, but don't worry, I'll prescribe you some good meds to take care of that," He said lightly and winked.

"Oh," was my brilliant response.

He flipped off the lighted board and placed the X-rays back into the file.

"So we'll get you your brace and you're welcome to leave anytime. Have a safe trip home," he said as he flashed his perfect smile.

"Thank you, doctor," Darci said in a gracious voice and then shook his hand before he turned to leave. She turned back to me with an exhausted look in her face.

"You look so tired, Darci, have you been able to sleep at all since you got here?" I asked.

"A little, but I have to admit I couldn't really sleep worrying about what was going on with you. What about you? I bet you didn't get much sleep the last few nights, either?"

I couldn't help the coy smile that came over me thinking about the last night Jack and I were together. That had to be one of the best nights I've ever had despite the conditions.

"They weren't too bad."

I looked up at Darci and I could tell she knew I was holding something back. Her eyes were narrowed and her mouth was pulled up to one side and one eyebrow was lifted higher than the other. But I couldn't say anything. The time I had with Jack seemed so personal and intimate and it was mine to hold onto and I didn't want anything or anyone to intrude on my memories.

Finally breaking our quiet moment she picked up her bag and threw it over her shoulder.

"While you get your stuff together I'll go and get the car."

"You have a car?" I asked, surprised.

"Of course, you didn't think I was going to be in a foreign country without any way to get around, did you?"

I couldn't help chuckling to myself at the difference between us. I had no problem walking around and taking public transportation like she did. That was the fun part of the whole experience.

"Well thanks again, Darci," I said thoughtfully.

Within just a few moments of Darci leaving a nurse came in with a brace and helped me put it on and then helped me into the wheelchair. She handed me a few pieces of paper that had all my instructions on it as well as the prescriptions I would have to pick up before I left for home. She wheeled me out the door and up to the front desk. She paused for a moment before stepping out of the main doors.

"Are you ready?" she said glumly as she hesitated.

Not understanding her remark I just answered, "Sure."

Just like a school of piranhas on a fresh piece of meat, as soon as we passed through the main doors, reporters where shouting at me from every direction. The flash from the cameras were more visible since the sun had gone down. The nurse tried to push me through the crowd but since Darci had already volunteered my statement I figured now was as good a time as any, and I probably wasn't going to have an official press conference anyway since I was leaving for home so soon.

"It's okay," I said as I turned my head toward her slightly.

She parked my chair and put the breaks on, still standing behind me.

"Miss Pierson, how does it feel to be back safe?" the first reporter asked.

"Great."

What else could I say? I liked being out in the middle of nowhere thinking I might die?

"What was the worst part of being stranded in the outback?"

I thought for a moment, and then I couldn't help but grin. "The food." I chuckled to myself. Everyone had a confused look on their face. I decided to let them in on my private joke.

"While we were out there Jack...Mr. McQuewen introduced me to grubs, and even though I was quite hungry I didn't care for them much. Neither did my stomach."

My face turned red as everyone laughed at my explanation. I had a few more questions thrown at me and I answered them the best I could, trying to sound intelligent while trying to be funny—most of the laughs were mercy laughs. Then one reporter asked me a question that turned everything serious.

"So now that you're back will you keep in contact with Jack McQuewen?"

I sat there thinking about my answer. I didn't know how to answer it because I didn't know myself.

Just then I was saved by Darci as she made her way through the sea of reporters and camera crews.

"Thank you, everyone, she needs to get some sleep. I'm sure you understand." Darci's voice had a firm and authoritative tone that I was very familiar with.

She pushed me through the crowd and up to the car. As we drove away I could still see some flashes of cameras going off in our direction.

When I entered my hotel room—Darci on my side helping me—I was shocked to see the overwhelming love and support for my well-being from complete strangers. I couldn't believe the amount of flowers, balloons, and cards that showered the whole room.

I hobbled over to the small table in the corner, the brochures still lying loosely across the top where I had left them days earlier, and on top of them sat a small mountain of unopened envelopes of every size and color.

"Wow, this is amazing," Darci said as she sat down at the end of my bed.

I picked up one of the cards at random and opened the crisp, light-green envelope. Inside written in a shiny red gloss above a picture of a rainbow stretching out from a field of clovers were the words "To Someone Special." I opened the card and continued to read the small message inside.

"Luck will always find you if you have a little faith. Luck will always find you if you look in the right place. We are happy you made it back. The Meta family."

I grabbed a few more cards and sat down on the edge of the bed next to Darci and read the same kind of sentiment and well-wishes as the card before. With each card all I could think of was how could so many people care about someone they didn't even know when I had a hard time even caring about myself? I had to wipe the slight moisture from my eyes.

I noticed one card that seemed to stand out from the others on the pile. The paper seemed rustic and grainy as if the paper itself were made by hand. The color seemed to reflect the beautiful earth tones that I spent the last four days surrounded by. There was no address, just my name on the front of the envelope. I opened the card and it only had one sentence. "One may find themselves where they do not look." No signature, nothing.

I stared at the mystery card, a little baffled, but it seemed innocent enough to make too much out of it. I had more pressing things on my mind, such as the growling in my stomach. So much had been going on I didn't think about eating, but now that I was back in the comfort of the hotel I realized that my last meal was nothing but three disgusting thick worms and they didn't stay down for very long.

"Hey, do you mind if we order room service? I'm starved," I asked as my stomach growled again.

"Of course not, that's much better than you trying to go out. You're supposed to stay in and take it easy, remember," Darci said in her motherly tone.

"Yeah, that's my plan, no late-night clubbing for me," I said sarcastic. "But first I think I'll jump in the shower. You can't believe how much I miss being clean."

Darci leaned toward me and sniffed quickly and then waved her hand in front of her face and scrunched her nose.

"Whoo, please go take a shower," she teased, plugging her nose.

Her sad attempt at humor made me laugh. Things had gotten so tense and serious since this morning it felt good to laugh and have that release and I couldn't help but think, this was how thing were suppose to be, sitting around with Darci, taking it easy and laughing at stupid stuff.

"Do you mind ordering for me?" I asked.

"I suppose I can do that, what do you want?"

I gave Darci my order and then grabbed my toiletries from my carry-on and my pajamas. The hot water felt amazing as the liquid streams ran down every part of my body, washing away all the dirt and tension, but not the memories. I hung my head as thousands of tiny beads of water cascaded over the top of me and then tilted my head back in the stream to wash my face. The constant rhythm of the running water along with its comforting warmth was almost hypnotic.

My mind began to open up and become clear as I started thinking about my adventure, actually the whole trip, and then drifted further back long before I got fired. Suddenly tears were intermixed with the drops that flowed over me.

Thoughts started to race through my mind and missing pieces of my fragmented life started to piece together. The main thought that I tried to ignore was my dreams. I finally realized the connection that I wondered about when I first decided to come to Australia, and the pull that brought me here.

Repressed memories were somehow triggered the last time I was here, but I ignored them as though they weren't real, but whatever it was about this place resurfaced my hidden childhood nightmare.

I had stuffed those memories down so tight that subconsciously I never thought I would have to remember them again, but my mind wasn't going to let it go. It was out there ready to be dealt with.

Being here in Australia with Jack and letting so many defenses down brought out a need that I didn't even know I had, but it also brought back those stuffed memories. Memories of a child alone and an intruder taking away a young girl's virtue.

As I started to think more of my new revelation I suddenly felt sick as a strange sense of pain came over me. It wasn't true physical pain, but something more internal. My body crumbled to the floor and I sat with my knees bent close to my body, leaning against the shower wall. My arms crossed over the front of me, while the hot water enveloped me, helping to muffle my sobs. After a while a knock on the bathroom door startled me.

"Ally, the food's here." Darci's cheerful voice called.

"Okay, I'll be right there," I managed to choke out.

I pulled myself together and got out of the shower, wrapping towels around both my body and my hair. I dried myself off and put my pajamas on, then ran a brush through my wet curls.

The steam was so thick I could see it swirling around as I moved through it. I tried wiping the residue off the mirror but it didn't do much good. Finally I was able to make a small circle to see my face. I pulled down and then pushed up on my cheeks with the tips of my fingers, looking intently at myself.

"Yep, I'm still…"

I stopped myself and leaned closer into the mirror, making the circle bigger. I was still me in a way, but there was something different. I studied my reflection, trying to figure out any kind of change. My hair was the same, my eye, nose, mouth. The only difference that I could physically see was the apparent redness of my skin from the days I spent out in the sun. But there was something different; I just couldn't put my finger on it.

"Ally, are you okay?" Darci asked through the door, a little concerned. "The food is getting cold."

"I'm coming," I answered.

I checked myself to make sure my eyes weren't teary any more and hoped she wouldn't notice the redness or at least think it was from being in the shower for so long. As I opened the door a gust of steam flowed around me.

"I think you might have used all the hot water in the building," she teased.

I half smiled at another of her attempts at a joke and took my food from the cart and plopped down on my bed. The smell of just basic roasted chicken made my mouth water and my stomach dance. Getting normal food after eating nothing but a few pieces of beef jerky, an apple and three grubs in four days was more like getting filet mignon.

Darci already had the TV on and was watching some old movie she happened to find while channel surfing. She turned the volume down and sat quietly watching me start to scarf my food down.

"I have a question for you," she said, putting down the remote.

I stiffened and stared down at my food, hoping she didn't notice my tear-dried eyes.

"What's that?" I asked cautiously.

"What's the joke about you being strong because you eat a lot?"

I laughed with relief that her question was so not what I was expecting.

"A few years ago I came over for dinner and we were talking about how I had to be strong because of all the files and boxes of files I had to move around at my job. Well Ryan popped in and said something like, 'Ally, I know why you're so strong, because you eat a lot.'" I chuckle as I explained. "It's been kind of a private family joke ever since. I'm surprised you don't remember."

"I don't, but then again you always see things in a different way than I do. You're strong because you eat a lot. That is pretty good." She laughed and then we both were laughing together.

Her laughter slowed as she became more serious. "Do you want me to stay here with you tonight or are you okay?" she asked, finishing her food.

"No, I'm okay. You don't need to stay with me, but you don't have to leave, either. Relax and watch the movie." I couldn't help yawning.

All that hot water made me so relaxed, or maybe I was coming down off of all the adrenaline or it could have been the medication they gave me at the hospital for my pain. But it was probably just simply the fact that I'd been lost out in the middle of nowhere for the last four days. But whatever the reason it was making me very sleepy. My eyelids kept closing involuntarily and before I knew it they stayed closed. The last thing I remembered was seeing the time on the clock—8:45.

I woke unexpectedly to a dark silent room and sat up looking around. Darci had obviously gone back to her own room. But before she left she managed to get me under the bedspread and cleaned up our dinner, although I didn't eat much of mine.

She must have thought about that because my plate was sitting on the table next to the pile of unopened cards, probably just in case I got hungry. She was right to leave it.

As I sat staring at the cold food on the table a familiar sound rumbled in my stomach. I limped over to the table and grabbed a cold piece of chicken and started to devour it, along with the cold green beans, but I couldn't get myself to eat the cold mashed pumpkin. As I sat there eating like some kind of rabid animal I realized that I never called home to talk to my mom.

I looked at the clock by my bed. Squinting to focus on the numbers then flipped on the light next to me. "2:52 a.m. We're fourteen hours ahead, that would make it around one in the afternoon there." I limped back over to my bed, grabbed the phone and dial my home number.

One ring, two rings, three rings, finally someone picked up.

"Hello?"

I recognized the voice immediately.

"Mom."

"Ally," her voice was bright and excited. "How are you sweetheart, are you okay?"

"I'm fine, sorry I didn't call earlier but I fell asleep."

"Well sure, I can understand that. What time is it there?" she added.

"About three."

Shouldn't you be sleeping?"

"I woke up hungry, and as I was eating my leftovers I remembered I was going to call you."

"Well, even though it's late there I'm glad you did. I've been waiting for your call. So tell me what happened," she asked anxiously.

I knew telling her every detail would probably stress her out, especially since I wasn't home yet. So I downplayed most of the drama and focused more on the lighter events of the trip, again leaving out any major details about Jack. Once I told my story and she was pretty satisfied with my answers to her questions she delivered her regular, but loving mother's advice about how my little excursion to go clear across the world may not have been the best idea. But even with what had happened I knew it was worth it.

"Well, let's talk about something else, how is everyone doing?" I yawned.

"Are you getting tired again?" she asked.

"Yeah, just a bit, But I'm okay." I yawned again.

"I'm going to let you go. Get some sleep and we'll see you soon."

"Okay, I love you, Mom."

"I love you, too." she said softly.

"Bye."

"Bye."

We both hung up around the same time and I rolled back onto the bed—happy and satisfied. I turned my light out to sleep, but stared into the darkness instead—wide awake.

My thoughts lingered on Jack's face, his dark wavy hair, his sapphire eyes, his perfectly proportioned body. Then I could feel his arms around my waist, his lips on mine. I shook my head, trying to dislodge the images from my mind, but the more I tried to ignore them the stronger they became. I threw my arms over my face and started singing, trying not to think of him. Finally I sat up, giving up on my efforts, and decided that I would go and see him and talk some things out. I took a deep breath and laid back down and allowed my mind to be filled with everything Jack.

23
Confession

❈❂❈

The loud blare of the phone startled me and I jumped as the ring continued to shriek. I reached over, trying to grab the receiver with half-opened eyes.

"Hello?" I said groggy.

No one answered for a brief second: then I could hear the soft click as a recording started.

"Good morning, this is your wake-up call. The time is now nine o'clock a.m. Have a great day." Another soft click ended the call.

"Well, that was polite," I thought as I hung the phone up and rolled back over in bed. "Darci," I mumbled out loud. "She must have called the front desk after I fell asleep."

I closed my eyes and thought about going back to sleep—I was never a morning person, but chances were that Darci would be knocking on my door soon to make sure I was up. I figured I'd call her and let her off the hook so she didn't have to waste time coming to my room. I dialed her room number, but there was no answer. Even after I let it ring five or six times.

"That's strange," I thought. I looked at the instructions on the phone to make sure I dialed correctly. I did. "Do I have her right room number?" I started to doubt my memory so I decided to call the front desk to make sure.

"Good morning, can I help you?" A cheerful female voice answered.

"Good morning, this is Ally Pierson in room 1112. Can you tell me what room number Darci Thomas is in?"

"Yes, Ms. Pierson she is in room 601."

"Thank you," I said as I hung up.

The room number was right too. I thought about where she might be and figured since she was an early riser that she probably was having breakfast. That made sense. I decided that I probably should go ahead and get up since I was pretty much up anyway. I stretched and then threw my legs over the side of the bed. I winced as a hint of pain reminded me of my fractured foot, and then I started thinking about what to wear.

I knew I had to see Jack again, but I didn't know what I was going to say. The fact that Darci wasn't around gave me the perfect opportunity to go talk to him. I decided to get dressed and leave as soon as I could before Darci came back. I would leave her a note, but this was something I had to do on my own.

I shuffled through the few clothes I had in my bag and found the blue silk blouse I brought in case I went somewhere a little nicer than just the corner fish-and-chips shop. It buttoned up the front and it was a little too sheer for me, so I had a matching blue cami that I wore underneath. I held up my blouse and decided that a quick touch of a warm iron would help the wrinkles, and then I hung it up 'til I was ready to get dressed.

When I looked in the vanity mirror my hair seemed to have created its own personality overnight. A snarling creature sat on top of my head, so the only thing I could do was wet it and start again.

As I started my ritual of wet, scrunch, and go I noticed my styling gel in my carry-on. I usually only used the mousse I brought to keep my hair under control, but since my clothes were a bit dressier I figured I should do the same on my hair and take an extra moment or two.

I put the hair dryer back on its holder and checked to make sure each curl was in the right place. Then not even thinking I grabbed the one tube of lipstick out of my bag and applied it lightly to my lips. I looked in the mirror, somewhat pleased with my appearance, and finished applying the rest of what little make-up I had.

I put on my cami and blouse and pulled on my jeans, which seemed to fit just a bit more loosely than before, and I couldn't help the grin that came across my face, and then slipped on a black strappy sandal on my good foot.

I looked at the combination of the sandal and brace and sighed. Besides my tennis shoes these were all I had. When I packed I didn't know I would be wearing a brace, and after four days in the outback my tennis shoes had gotten as much wear as they could.

I wrote a quick note for Darci, which read simply, "Darci, had to run an errand, be back soon."

I put the note in the crease of her door and then hurried down and hailed a cab and gave the driver the address that I managed to get from information.

As we drove and got closer the butterflies in my stomach kept getting bigger and my heart started to beat faster. I was starting to get a lump in my throat so big that I was having a hard time breathing. I knew what I had to do; I just didn't know how to do it.

When I reached Jack's house I took a deep breath and asked the driver to wait. I didn't know how long I would be, but I knew it wouldn't be long. I hobbled up to the door slowly, trying to organize my thoughts, then took another deep breath and knocked.

"Comin,'" Jack's irresistible brogue called through the door.

When he opened it I could see the shock and confusion on his face, and I couldn't be sure but there seemed to be a little of something else in his eyes. He didn't say a word; he just stood there staring at me.

"Hi, can I come in?" I asked.

He pulled the door wide open to let me pass. I walked in and looked around the medium-sized living space. The room looked as though he took a page right out of a home-style magazine and copied it perfectly, except for the same scene as my hotel room: his very clean and stylish front room was filled with floral arrangements, balloons, and a pile of open cards on the coffee table. As I continued taking everything in the warmth of the browns, blues, and cream that furnished his home helped make me feel at ease.

He closed the door then finally broke his silence. "Whit da ya want, Ally?" A touch of harshness to his voice.

"I'm leaving tonight and I wanted to say good-bye."

"Say yer good-bye then, I have a lo' ta do." He reached over and opened the door again.

I took a step toward him. "Look, Jack, I didn't come here just to say good-bye. I wanted to explain about the other morning."

Jack closed the door using, a bit more force than needed, then walked toward the kitchen and leaned against the counter bar, crossing his arms in front of him.

"There's nothin ta explain."

"Yes, there is." I paused, trying to get the right words out. "Jack, yesterday morning meant a lot to me. The whole trip did. You see, for the last few months, actually for the last few years, I really haven't been living, I've just been existing."

I took a deep breath. "When I was a young girl I was home alone and a man came in and raped me. I didn't even remember it until I was an adult and I've tried to just block it out. I managed to stuff it away in the back of my mind pretty good. But there was something about being here that brought it all up to the surface." I turned away embarrassed, not wanting to look at him.

"You were right when you said I was running away from something. I've been running away my whole life. Not getting close too anyone, not trusting anyone. So when I lost my job and felt completely hopeless I ran to the one place in my life that I felt whole; I ran away to here. Then I met you and everything went wrong, the crash, my ankle, the dingoes, us.

"I don't know what it was, but something happened out there and you were part of it. I had to trust someone and for the first time in a long time I did." I tuned back around and looked into his dark-blue eyes. They looked baffled.

"But when we kissed I realized what was happening and I had to make a choice. You see, I would've been giving you a part of me that I only want to give to one man, one person whom I'm going to spend forever with."

"Whit's tha'?" he asked indignant.

I paused and looked down away from him. Then as I sighed I took another step forward, looking up into his eyes.

"My heart."

I waited for some kind of response, but he just stood there speechless, looking at me, so I continued.

"I just couldn't give that up. Not yet."

I still wasn't getting any response from him and my embarrassment from my confession was starting to show more in the color of my skin.

"Well, I better go; I just wanted you to know why I acted the way I did."

I walked over to the counter where he was still motionless and silent. I leaned into him and softly kissed his cheek, lingering for a moment, taking in the memory of everything about him. Everything that I could process in just a few seconds.

"Bye, Jack," I whispered in his ear just before pulling away.

I turned and headed for the door, trying to get out before my tears started to flow. Suddenly Jack reached out and grabbed my hand, stopping me.

"Ally," Jack's tone had turned soft. "How d'ya know tha' I'm not tha' someone?"

I couldn't look at him, it was too hard.

"We're too different: our lives, who we are, are too different. It would never work."

I painfully pulled my hand away and then opened the door and practically ran out to the cab, not looking back.

I had to leave. There was a part of me that was broken and I wasn't going to put anyone through those repairs. I couldn't do that to him, I couldn't do that to me.

When I fall in love it wasn't going to be partners for life it was going to be companions for eternity. I knew what my goals were and as much as I was hurting, as much as I wanted to run back into Jack's arms, the reality of what would happen helped me stay away.

I watched what happened to Darci, my mom, and so many others, and I would rather leave him and have the memories, then love him and lose him later.

As the taxi pulled away I took one last glance at his house. Jack was looking out his window. I turned back around as tears welled up in my eyes, and the pain was so strong I could no longer keep them in. Tears rolled quickly down my cheek and a muffled sob escaped my lips. The driver glanced only once in the rearview mirror, his expression sympathetic, and then just allowed me my tortured moment.

By the time we got back to the hotel I regained my composure, but I was still wiping my eyes, trying to dry them as much as possible before I saw Darci again. I still wasn't ready to share about Jack.

As I paid the driver—giving him double his tip for having to listen to my sobs—I was glad I already had my excuse for where I was. On the way back I asked the driver to stop by the pharmacy so I could get my other prescriptions.

When I got back to my room I checked for any messages from Darci. I had been gone at least an hour and a half, maybe two, but there weren't any messages.

"That's strange," I thought as I dialed her room number.

Just then someone knocked on the door. It was a loud but happy knock, almost musical. I put the phone down and hobbled over to the door. Darci was standing there all smiles like a kid that just got back from getting ice cream.

"Hey there, sleepy head, you finally decided to get up," she said, quite chipper.

"Uh, I've been up for a while now," I answered back, questioning her mood.

"You have?"

My answer seemed to have surprised her and then I noticed her cheeks started to turn a little pink. Something was going on and since I didn't feel like I had to worry about my own excuse at the moment I decided I would have a little fun with her.

"Yeah, as a matter of fact I was really worried." I frowned and pulled my eyebrows together and than went back to my bed and sat down on the end. "I called your room and you weren't there. I actually called a couple of times. When you didn't pick up and with everything that's been going on I was so afraid that something happened to you." I couldn't help the slight smile that was creeping out. "I finally called the front desk and told them to file a missing person report."

"Ha, ha, very funny," she said sarcastically.

I snickered at my own joke.

"So seriously, where were you this morning?" I asked curious.

"Oh," she paused as her eyes shifted avoiding looking in mine. Her face started turning more red than pink. "Sorry about that. I thought you were going to sleep longer so I went out to breakfast." She paused again. "With Tom."

"Tom." I said, shocked. "How did that happen?"

"Well, last night after you fell asleep I went back to my room and there was a message from Tom to call him, so I did. Anyway, he invited me out to breakfast this morning. He said it was probably the only chance he had to buy me a decent meal." She smiled thoughtfully. "I meant to get back before you woke but I guess I just lost track of time, sorry."

"That's okay, I figured you went out to breakfast, but never did I even imagine you would be with Tom. So what's really going on with you two? First I catch you all goo-goo at the hospital, now breakfast?"

I could see something in her grin that I hadn't seen before—it made her seem ten years younger, although it made me a bit uncomfortable, like I was intruding in something personal.

"To tell you the truth I really don't know. We really got along great while we waited to find out if you and Jack were safe and something just clicked." She turned away smiling and was thoughtful for a moment. "I think we're going to be great friends."

I smiled at her choice of words. It seemed that they were already more than just friends. I decided that I would leave it alone; I had my own issues to think about.

We packed our belongings and arrived at the airport much too early than we needed to be, but the hotel had already extended our checkout time longer than normal without a fee and we didn't want to take too much advantage of it, which meant we had a lot of time to talk. And I had a lot of time to think.

Darci kept asking me about my journey, trying to get more solid details out of me, which I tried to give her the best I could, but then her questions would eventually turn to questions about Jack and I would answer them as vaguely as possible or change the subject altogether.

It wasn't that I just didn't want to talk about Jack; I couldn't help the feelings I had when I did. There was so much emotion wrapped around everything about him. Joy and happiness, sadness, fear, pain, want, love. Yes, even love. That was the main reason I didn't want to talk about him. It was hard enough trying to keep these feeling in control without bringing him up in conversation every few minutes.

Finally Darci decided that she was tired of me skirting around the Jack topic and asked me straight out about him.

"So did you and Jack get to together when you were out there alone?"

She was trying to be casual about the whole thing, but I knew what she was asking. There was more than one meaning in her words. I tried to play it off as casual as she was being.

"I don't know what you're talking about." I couldn't look at her.

"Come on, you know what I mean." she said, more anxious for my response.

I looked up, holding back whatever tear was trying to sneak out, and gave her the best answer I could.

"There's nothing between me and Jack," I said as convincingly as I could.

"I think you're wrong," she answered just as convincingly. "I need to tell you something, something about Jack. When you were getting your X-rays..."

"I need to get something to drink," I interrupted.

"Ally, I need to tell you this."

"Darci," I paused trying to think of the best way to put it. "Let's just leave it here. Whatever it is it doesn't matter. Did you know that if you take a piece of Ayers Rock with you it's supposed to bring you back luck? So let's just treat it like the rock and leave it all here." I grabbed my bag and walked away.

"Ally, where are you going? Ally!" She called out, concerned.

I passed one fast food kiosk after another to get my drink, because I didn't really need something to drink, what I really needed was air. Just talking about Jack was starting to constrict the air in my lungs and I had to get out and away from everything and have a chance to breathe.

I raced through the doors at the main entrance and gasped once I was outside, filling my lungs with fresh air. Then I could suddenly feel the cool breeze on my face even though the sun was still out. I looked around to see if anyone noticed me. A few people around me looked, but most people didn't pay much attention to my need to breathe.

I sat down on the first bench I saw just outside the doors, and took in a slow, controlled, deep breath and slowly let it out. I tilted my head back slightly and closed my eyes. The streaks of sunlight warmed me as the sun started to descend from another day, and even with my eyes closed the brightness of the late afternoon sun automatically made me want to squint.

Suddenly the sun was blocked completely and I could open my eyes easier. Standing in front of me was a motionless dark figure in silhouette. I couldn't make out the face at first. Then as my eyes adjusted I couldn't help the look of amazement and disbelief that came over me.

24
Survived
❊⊙❊

The sun behind her seemed to make the little elderly aboriginal woman's white hair glow around her face, and even though her face was somewhat in silhouette I could make out that her sweet wrinkled face was smiling at me—I smiled back.

I blinked a few times as her whole frame started to come more into focus, and I recognized her floral shirt and bright capri pants at once.

"You," I said, stunned as I stood up to face her better.

"Nhuma maln'marama buku walma batjiwarr," she said sweetly.

"I'm sorry, I don't understand you," I said, leaning in closer automatically as if I couldn't hear her.

"Did you find your way?" She answered in a thick Australian accent.

"You speak English?" I said, even more stunned.

"Yes, of course." Then she repeated her question. "Did you find your way?"

I misunderstood her. "I'm here, aren't I?"

She just shook her head. "Did you find your way here and here?" She reached over and placed one hand on my head and one hand on my heart.

It took me just a second to realize what she meant, and then a strong realization came to me like a dam breaking. I thought about the nameless earth-tone card and then I looked up at her, my eyes wide.

"The unsigned card—you sent it."

"Yes." She smiled.

"What does it mean?" I asked, confused.

"What do you think it means?"

I concentrated on remembering the words that were written across the page.

"One may find themselves where they do not look," I recited out loud.

I looked up at her as she continued to smile at me, waiting for my answer.

"I guess it means you can find yourself in the one place you never thought to look." I caught on to the meaning and then lowered my head as though I was ashamed I didn't realize this conclusion before. "Yourself," I whispered.

The elderly woman placed one of her wrinkled fingers under my chin and lifted my head so I could look at her. She didn't say anything, she just nodded and smiled. Just then an old pickup truck pulled up and a young aboriginal man jump out.

"Grandma, are you done here?" he asked.

"Yes, I believe I am." She turned and winked at me.

The young man opened the passenger door to help her into the truck. As he closed it and went around the back I noticed something move in the truck bed. He reached over and stroked something white and furry.

"Good boy," he said as he passed and a familiar white dingo stood up and looked at me.

I jumped in surprise. "Is that your dog?" I asked, thinking I might be wrong about my assumption.

"Dingo actually, and he's my grandmother's. He's name is I'wai."

"What does that mean?" I asked curious.

"Cultural hero." He smiled and then got into the cab of his truck.

"It was you," I whispered softy. "All of it."

She turned as if she heard my soft whisper and smiled. As they drove away she waved out her window and called out. "Djutjutj." I wasn't sure what she said but my instincts made me think it was good-bye. I was just about to wave back but when the truck moved the sun got into my eyes and I automatically closed my eyes for just a moment, and when I looked back the truck was gone.

"What, where, how…" I sputtered.

I looked at my watch and realized I better get back into the airport. My flight was getting closer and I didn't want to be on this side of security when it got here.

When I got back to Darci I could see the concern on her face. Stress lines creased her brow and her eyes looked worried.

"Are you okay?" she asked.

"Yeah, I'm sorry about that, I don't mean to be a pain, there's just some things I don't want to talk about. Can we just leave it at that?"

She looked at me, the lines from her concern gone as she finally seemed to understood what I'd been trying to convey to her.

We didn't talk much about the trip after that—just some idle chitchat. We were both engrossed in our own thoughts.

As I watched the Sydney skyline get smaller and smaller I took a deep breath and leaned back into my seat. When we flew over the outback I couldn't help but notice the beautiful canopy of colors below us. Then there it was Uluru (Ayers Rock), the place where my life seemed to have changed.

I thought about those few short minutes I spent out front at the airport with the little aboriginal women and her dingo, Hero, my Hero. What was it that she said to me that first day at Uluru? Did she know what was coming or did she cause everything that happened to happen?

I started thinking back on the strange things that occurred, clear down to the strange whispers I would hear as if the wind were actually speaking to me. Did she create all that herself? Did she have help? Was it all just to pull me and Jack together? Or was it to help me truly look inside myself and rediscover who I am and that I can live life? That no matter what challenges I ever have to face, I can survive? Because I had survived, not just this trip but life and the dangers that I had faced earlier in my childhood, and I was going to be okay.

I took a deep breath and filled my lungs completely, then exhaled a little too loudly.

Darci rubbed my arm softly. "Are you okay? Don't worry, we're not going to crash."

I looked at her confused, wondering what she was talking about, and then it hit me. I had been so preoccupied with my thoughts I didn't even think about my fear of flying. For some reason it didn't seem to bother me at all.

"Yeah," I answered, "I'm better then okay, I'm a survivor."

I turned in my small space to face her and decided it was time to open up.

"Do you believe in magic? Not the showy tricks and illusions you see on TV, but the kind that has to do with myths and legends."

She sat their thinking and I could tell she knew my question was filled with real sincerity, because she didn't joke or tease about what I just said.

"I didn't use to but I'm starting to think that there is. Why?"

"Some things happened while I was out there that I know weren't normal."

"Well, we believe in God, and I'm sure he had a hand in your survival."

"Oh, that I have no doubt, but I think he used some help along the way."

"What do you mean?" she questioned.

"Did anyone ever explain any aboriginal legends to you?" I asked.

"Tom did a little, something about a Dreamtime and spirits that created the land."

"Yeah, something like that. Well I think I had help from one of those spirits," I whispered.

"What?" she scoffed.

"No, I'm serious, listen…"

I began to tell her of all the strange things that happened down to my short visit with the aboriginal woman at Ayers Rock and then in front of the airport.

With each incident I could see in her face logic trying to make sense of it all but knew that there was no logic behind everything that happened. The fact that we survived was magic or a miracle in itself.

Our conversation didn't end with the topic of the magic in the outback. After a long pause I looked up at Darci and began to tell her the horror of my childhood drama. I never before told anyone about that night. It never seemed real enough and what I did remember was too frightening, but knowing I survived what I just went through made me more courageous.

We talked for hours about everything, everything but Jack—I was still able to leave him out of the conversation.

As the landing gear touched down Darci turned and Smiled at me.

"Welcome home."

I smiled back, but even though this was my home I knew that there would always be a part of me that would be home back in Australia.

The airline had arranged a wheelchair for me when we got off the plane. As they wheeled me down to the baggage claim I was expecting to see my family and a few friends, but what I wasn't expecting to see was hordes of people cheering and holding up welcome home signs along with news camera crews.

"What's this all about?" I murmured.

"I guess your story made the news back here as well?" Darci answered.

Just before we got to the baggage carousel we were met by my mom, Megan, Gina, and Darci's three kids.

My mom, hardly being able to wait any longer for us to get to them, rushed over and threw her arms around my neck and then grabbed my face and kissed each cheek over and over as tears flowed down her face.

"Don't you ever do that to me again, this old heart can't take it," she warned as she hugged and kissed me again. After my mom had her moment Megan and Gina joined in as Ryan, Miles, and Amy surrounded Darci.

I had to chuckle to myself as I overheard the boys start to interrogate Darci about souvenirs she might have brought them.

When I finally got home and was able to get into my own bed I was so exhausted. After hours of flight time and then what seemed like hours at the airport as I answered one question after another about my incident to different new crews, I laid in my bed happy to be home and ready for a long, restful sleep.

Sometime through the night my mind started to dream again, but it wasn't the uncomfortable, terrifying dreams I had in the outback. They were sweet, peaceful dreams of Jack. His cheeky grin when he gave me a hard time, and his laugh when I told my stupid jokes. I could see the warmth in his eyes when he looked at me and feel the touch of his lips when they pressed against mine.

I woke abruptly and stared at the clock next to my bed—four a.m. My room was quiet and still so dark that the glowing blue numbers on the clock were the only light around. I rolled over on to my back and mentally figured out the time difference between here and there. It was around six p.m. his tomorrow.

I closed my eyes and imagined Jack getting his plane fixed and then going back to his regular life. The image of Jack was a sweet but painful thought. I imagined him going back to dating the tall, slender beauties that he seemed to be perfectly matched for. I could never be one of his beauties and that was one of the realities I had to face. I was just me, a short curly top and still a little too round along the edges, wearing my jeans and T-shirts, but I was okay with that, because I was me and I was finally realizing that I was good enough for me.

I got up and walked over to the window and looked into the darkness. I could see the faint image of myself reflecting back at me. The woman I saw seemed so much older and stronger. She was someone that could look out into the unknown and not be afraid.

I got back into bed and glanced at the clock again, then closed my eyes. I let out a long exultant sigh knowing tomorrow the sun would rise again and a new chapter of my life was about to start.

25
A New Begining
❇✦❇

I looked at the date on my calendar at my desk. Five months had past since I flew to Australia and had the greatest adventure of my life and met Jack McQuewen.

"Man, time has really past." I thought out loud.

"Are you ready to go?" a cheerful baritone asked.

Dark chocolate eyes stared at me around the corner of my cubical. Andrew, the hottest guy in the office and my constant companion, was waiting for me to leave work for the day.

"I'll be there in a second, let me get my stuff together."

"Okay, I'll wait for you by the elevator."

I smiled at him as he turned to leave. As I waited to make sure my computer was off I thought about the last five months and how everything had changed.

After resting a few days till my ankle was healed I decided to start going to a therapist to work out my issues as well as my memories. But I knew it would take some time to get things completely worked out and to finally have a better understanding of why my life went spiraling downward.

Going back to a job that I didn't necessarily love wasn't my first choice, but since I needed insurance I needed a job, so I decided to take Mr. Bryant up on his offer about coming back while I got thing worked out. And true to his word—the good man that he was—he hired me back with no problem.

"I'm glad to see that you made it back safe," Mr. Bryant said. "We were all worried about you. It's nice to have you back."

"Thank you," I responded, a little amazed.

As I left his office and we headed back to my old desk, it felt as though I was suddenly visible to everyone around me, not that I wasn't visible before, but my insecurities seemed to put a barriers between me and the friends I could have made.

"Welcome back, Ally," Silvia an elderly women in accounting, said as she passed.

"Ally, good to see you weren't trampled by a herd of kangaroos out there," John, the obnoxious jokester remarked as I past his desk.

Then the sweet Spanish woman who always gave me a smile stopped me as I past her. She hugged me quick and then pulled away, speaking something in Spanish. Not knowing what she said I just smiled and nodded. She must have scene my confusion because she squeezed my hand and smiled.

"Ally, you are such a sweet spirit, I'm so glad you're back," she said in her thick accent.

"Thank you." I smiled again.

When we turned the corner a familiar face was coming up from behind the computer. Martin, our very helpful and most-of-the-time cheery IT guy, was getting everything set up. He turned and smiled at me.

"I knew you'd be back," he said. "We even have a new computer for you."

"Thanks, you didn't have to do that," I responded.

"Don't worry, you're not the only one," he grinned.

"Oh," I said, a little embarrassed.

All day that first day, everyone welcomed me back and offered me such well wishes that even though I was ready for more to my new life, ready to take on more challenges than what this job held, I was glad to be back for however long it was.

My memories of my first day back made me smile as I watched my computer go dark. I grabbed my purse and some college brochures I had acquired and headed out to the elevator. Andrew and a few others were waiting for me. We all planned to go get some dinner together when we got off.

As the elevator doors closed I couldn't help the smirk that crept up on my face. I looked over at Andrew and thought about the last day of my old life, not even being able to look him in the eye.

"What?" he asked, trying to read my expression.

"Nothing," I answered back casually.

When we walked out of the building I noticed a nicely dressed, clean-cut man with dark, wavy hair leaning against a car. I inhaled a short, quick gasp as I realized it was Jack.

His hair wasn't its usual ruffled look and his face was freshly shaved, which went nicely with the dress slacks and button-down shirt he wore under a black leather jacket.

"Are you okay?" Andrew asked anxiously.

"Yeah, I'm fine. I'll meet you at the restaurant."

"Are you sure you're okay? You look a little pale." I could hear the concern in his voice.

I nodded and then squeezed his hand, trying to look reassuring. He walked away and caught up with the rest of the group. I could hear them telling jokes and laughing with one another.

I walked slowly over to the car, my mind cautious, but my heart reckless as it started to beat faster the closer I got.

"Jack?" My voice was a little unsteady.

His amazing sapphire eyes seemed to beam when he saw me. He pushed himself away from the car and with just a few steps he was standing in front of me.

"What are you doing here?" I asked, amazed.

"Well, since Tom and Darci are getting married I figured i' was a good excuse ta come ta the states and visit." His voice was as charming and casual as usual.

"But why are you here, in my work parking lot?"

"Darci told me where ta find ya."

I closed my eyes and shook my head, trying to figure out if I was dreaming or if this was real.

"I had ta see ya, Ally. I had ta tell ya somethin'."

"What?" My voice caught in my throat as I asked in confusion.

"After ya left I started thinkin abou' whit ya said. Ya were righ', somethin' did happen ou' there. Somethin' happened ta me."

He took a step closer, standing just a few inches away as he gazed more intently into my eyes.

"I wanted ta jus' go back ta me old life, forget abou' ya, forget everything tha' happened bu' I couldn't, all I could do is think of ya."

He reached out and gently stroked my cheek with the backside of his fingers all the way to my chin as he spoke.

"Yer face, yer eyes, everything abou' ya was everywhere," he continued.

My heart felt like it was going to beat right out of my chest and I had to concentrate on breathing in and out as my stomach fluttered, but I couldn't help but lean into his touch slightly as each word drew me closer to him like a magnet.

"All I could see in every woman around me was yer beautiful face."

My skin started to burn under his touch and I had to turn away from his gaze.

"Ya said a lot of things ta me tha' hit a nerve when we were ou' there. I was angry at firs' bu' ya were righ'. I do use certain things ta avoid connectin' with people."

He gently placed his finger under my chin and lifted my head slightly so I had to look at him.

"Bu' I do want ta connect with someone; I want ta connect with ya."

I grabbed his wrist and gently pulled his hand away trying to avoid his eyes, I stared downward.

"Jack, it's too late; it won't work. It never could, we're still so different, our lives are still so different."

"Ally, I know yer life, I know who ya are. I want ta be part of i'."

"It's no use," I murmured. "I have to go."

I turned and started to hurry away, but before I could get two steps he was right behind me. He caught my arm and turned me back around to face him.

"Maybe i' won't work ou', maybe i' will, bu' I know one thing tha' there are no boundaries tha' we can't overcome if we try. Ally, I've changed, trust me. I've even go"en rid of that old friend of mine. Give me a chance."

Before I had a chance to dispute his remarks his lips were pressed firm against mine and his arms wrapped tight around my waist. I could feel his determination in his kiss and like before I couldn't resist him. My lips melted against his, surrendering to his touch. He pulled away from me just a few inches and looked straight at me.

"I love you, Alison Pierson, and I want ta be with ya."

He kissed me again, determined but not as fierce, passionate but slow and romantic. Once he sensed my defeat he pulled me closer as our lips continued to move eagerly with each other.

We pulled away at the same time, and I caught my breath as I got my senses back. I looked away, wondering if things could work. He seemed to sense my slight hesitation and hugged me close to him.

I wanted to break away from his grip and run, but with each second he held me in his arms it was if the walls I spent years building were crumbling to the ground and I suddenly had full confirmation of my tomorrow. I pulled away to look at him.

"You're right, we have no boundaries that we can't overcome, except ourselves."

I reached back and took his hand from around my waist and placed it over my heart.

"Whit are ya doin'?" He asked, his eyes bewildered.

"I told you I could only give my heart to one man. I'm giving it to you. I love you, too."

I looked into his face as he smiled and it was like a million beams of sunlight that lit up my darkness. He turned his hand that was over my heart and intertwined his fingers with mine. Then he tenderly pressed his lips to mine and I kissed him back as they danced perfectly once again.

I pulled away abruptly as I remembered Andrew was waiting for me at dinner.

"I have to go. I have to meet someone," I said a little anxious.

"Is tha' someone the guy tha' ya walked ou' with?" he muttered.

I heard something in his voice that I hadn't heard in him before—jealousy? I couldn't help but smirk.

"Yeah, why?"

"He's a good lookin' guy."

I chuckled to myself. "Yeah, he is. He's one of the best-looking men around, inside and out." I sighed. "Too bad he's gay."

I looked up at Jack and couldn't help the big smile that was on my face. He laughed with me and then pulled me tightly into his arms and kissed me with so much joy and enthusiasm I could never doubt that he loved me as much as I loved him.

Epilogue
※❖※

My fingertips moved slowly off the keyboard of my computer. I sat there quietly looking at the screen with a pleased smile on my face as my heart settled into a relaxed and comfortable rhythm.

I could feel the warmth of the sun streaming through the open window and feel the breeze of the mid-spring afternoon air flowing across my face. I closed my eyes and inhaled deeply threw my nose. I could smell the honeysuckle just outside as well as the freshly mowed grass. As I exhaled a slight sigh came out, not from stress or frustration. It was contentment.

My life was never quite what I originally thought it would be, but I was content, no more than that, much more. I was happy, truly, utterly happy. My life took longer to get to this point than most—but what a ride.

"Ally," a gruff but happy voice called.

I turned and looked toward the kitchen, toward my future. Jack was sitting at the table looking at me—a smile spread across his face.

I couldn't help but admire everything about him. His broad, muscular build, his dark wavy hair—ruffled like the first day I met him. His breathtaking smile and his expressive deep-blue eyes that always complemented his smile.

"Are ya done?" he asked.

"Yeah, finally." I answered back, reflective.

I got up and walked over to where he sat. Sitting across from him was the carbon copy of his eyes, and his smile, looking up at me with all the excitement and love a mother's child could give.

"How's my sweet little guy?" I cooed.

I picked up my beautiful baby boy from his high chair and held him close to me, caressing his sweet little cheeks to mine, and then kissed him gently.

"I love you," I whispered in his ear.

Even though he was just an infant I knew he knew.

Jack stood up from the table, a glint of light shooting off the gold band around his finger, and in just two steps had his arm around my waist. His arms were always one place where I always felt safe and happy.

"I love ya both," Jack said.

He sweetly kissed the top of our baby's head, and then leaned down and softly pressed his lips to mine, lingering for just a moment. I sighed happily as he pulled away.

"I bought ya somethin'." His voice sounded very excited.

He reached in his pants pocket and pulled out a small, dark-blue velvet box. I couldn't help but smile as he slowly open it and turned it toward me.

"It's… beautiful," I gasped.

"I's a rock," he answered, a slight smirk on his face.

He pulled the dime-sized opal cased in silver that hung on a beautiful silver chain out of the box. I turned so he could place it around my neck. As he finished hooking the clasp his warm lips gently caressed my neck. I turned and smiled at him.

"I know i's not much, bu' I couldn't git ya a piece of Uluru." He chuckled. "Opals are native ta Australia and I wanted ya ta have a little reminder."

"I do," I answered, "I have you."

He leaned down and kissed me again, "Happy anniversary." Then he wrapped his arms around me and our son.

So here I was standing with the two loves of my life, my sweet angelic baby and my strong, handsome husband, and my thoughts floated back to the last words I typed on my computer.

"And they lived happily together forever."

THE END.

About the Author

※❂※

E lyce Peterson is a processor for an aircraft insurance company who has a nomad-
ic spirit and lifestyle. A current resident of Dallas, Texas, she has lived in Utah,
Virginia, California, Nevada, and Idaho and spent eighteen months in Australia serv-
ing a mission for The Church of Jesus Christ of Latter-Day Saints.

Peterson brings her passion for Australia and her love for the landscape to life in
her debut novel, *Magic in the Outback*, which carries readers through the land down
under on an adventure full of action, mystery, and unlikely romance.

Inspired by the sentimental, wholesome beauty she saw in everything from the
books she enjoyed as a child to her favorite "feel-good" movies and family-friendly
televisions programs, Peterson's work is clean, crisp, and sensible—a charming alter-
native to most modern romance novels on the mainstream market.

Made in the USA
Charleston, SC
12 March 2014